D0881334

THE WOMAN IN RED

By Paula Gosling

THE WOMAN IN RED
SOLO BLUES (published in England as LOSER'S BLUES)
THE ZERO TRAP
FAIR GAME (published in England as A RUNNING DUCK)

THE
WOMAN IN RED

PAULA GOSLING

PUBLISHED FOR THE CRIME CLUB BY
DOUBLEDAY & COMPANY, INC.
GARDEN CITY, NEW YORK
1984

All of the characters in this book
are fictitious, and any resemblance
to actual persons, living or dead,
is purely coincidental.

The lines from the poem "Salutation" are reprinted from Ezra Pound, *Personae*, by permission of New Directions Publishing Corporation. Copyright 1926 by Ezra Pound.

Library of Congress Cataloging in Publication Data
Gosling, Paula.
The woman in red.
I. Title.
PR6O57.075W6   1984   823'.914
ISBN 0-385-19105-7
Library of Congress Catalog Card Number 83–11606

For John Anthony Hare—
my rock in the midst of chaos

THE WOMAN IN RED

7:53 P.M., September 28.
Puerto Rio, Spain

The wide, dark skirts of the sky were filled with enough stars to enter a ballroom-dancing competition and win on twinkle alone. Below, the olive trees bent together in the soft evening breeze, conferring about the prospect of rain. A few cars moved along the highway that edged the beach, headlamps scimitaring the shadows.

Behind nearly every lighted window in the modern apartment block at 400 Avenida de la Playa, someone moved or spoke. But no one looked out.

As the man fell past the first window below the parapet, Mrs. Kemmer stopped stirring the rice and turned to answer her husband's question from the other room.

As the man fell past the second window, the Nicholson baby seemed to wave from its cot. He did not wave back.

As the man fell past the third window, Holly Partridge was measuring out two long strands of crimson and ochre wool, squinting against the light as she compared them.

As the man fell past the fourth window, the García children were jumping up and down in front of the television set and refusing to change the channel. Their father was starting to rise from his chair.

As the man fell past the fifth window, he was no more than a blur to old Mr. Vousden, who glimpsed him from the corner of his eye and assumed it was a diving gull.

As the man continued to fall, his body twisted and turned. His jacket billowed out like a white balloon and his hair stood on end, blown upward by the wind. His staring eyes reflected the lights of the windows. The teeth in his wide-open mouth gleamed. His cuff-links and watchband were gold. His tie was a discreet dark blue, and matched his socks perfectly.

As he dropped through the night, he made no sound. No sound at all. Until he hit the ground.

CHAPTER 1

After a moment he realized it wasn't the alarm clock.

Flailing in the general direction of the bedside table, Charles Llewellyn's arm hit, in turn, the lamp (which switched on as it fell), the ashtray (which spilled ash all over the edge of the bed, causing him to sneeze), an empty glass (which dropped to the floor and shattered), the alarm clock (which promptly began to ring), and, finally, the telephone.

He tried to turn the alarm clock off while holding the telephone receiver against his ear with his shoulder. The alarm clock would not stop ringing, so he shoved it under his pillow where it continued to whir sullenly, in a gradually diminishing way. Retrieving the phone from where it had slipped off his shoulder and under his arm, he found the cord was cutting off his circulation and had to unwind it.

All the while a tiny voice could be heard shouting, "Hello? Hello? Hello?" with increasing impatience, as if an irritable wasp had been trapped in the receiver.

"Momentito!" Charles shouted in the general direction of his navel as he unwound himself from the coils of the phone cord. He brushed away a cigarette end that had become stuck to his arm. As he lay down again, he struck his ear on the now silent alarm clock, which had worked its way out from under the pillow during his struggles with the cord.

"Quién es?" he snarled, squinting at the alarm clock, which said he should still be asleep.

"Baker, here, Charles." It would be. "Hope I didn't interrupt anything *special.*" Smart ass.

"Very special."

"Oh. *Awfully* sorry . . ." Baker apologized warily.

Charles sighed and relented. "It was just a dream." It usually was, these days. "What the hell do you want at three in the morning? Has the bloody consulate burned down, I hope?"

"No. Something rather special here . . ."

"Oh?" He brushed ash off himself as Baker stammered on.

"Rather delicate matter. *He* thought you should go . . ."

"He," pronounced with that pseudo-reverent air that Baker did so well, could only mean the consul himself. So he's been awakened, too? Charles rolled onto one elbow, frowning. "Go where?"

"Little place up the coast called Puerto Rio. Know it?"

"Oh—you mean Surbiton-on-Heat," Charles said sourly. Puerto Rio was one of the many coastal towns that had become infested in recent years by hoards of retirees from England, Holland, Germany and other countries rich in huddled masses yearning to be free.

"Well, been a spot of bother there, I'm afraid. Chap found dead in front of one of these newish apartment blocks. Thought it was suicide at first, now they've changed their minds and are calling it murder. Just arrested one of our nationals by the name of Partridge. No sooner had the Guardia informed us than his wife rang through in hysterics, wanting help. You know the drill, Charles, thought you might straighten it out."

"I see," Charles said drily.

"Well, it will be light soon. You could be up there by breakfast-time, you know, less traffic on the road and all that. The Partridge woman was very upset, Charles."

"I can imagine. Who is this Partridge—a tourist?"

"No, a *residente.* Retired Civil Servant, actually, Customs and Excise."

"Ah." That explained a lot. Baker waited on the other end. He even breathed differently from other people. "What did the Guardia say?"

"Oh, just official notification. You know how they can stick to the letter when they . . ."

When they didn't want any questions asked. He knew only too well. With a sigh, Charles threw back the covers and swung his legs down onto the floor. His left foot landed on a piece of broken glass. Cursing, he upturned the foot onto his right knee and inspected the damage. No more than usual.

"Hang on a minute, I'll get a pencil and you can give me the details." He hopped across to the bureau, grabbed his notebook and a stub of pencil, hopped back, and in the light of the fallen lamp scribbled down what details Baker could supply. "Anybody could handle this," he muttered when Baker had finished.

"Well, but . . . you've been here so *long,* Charles."

"No need to rub it in."

"I can tell him you'll be handling it, then?"

"Yes. Tell him to rest easy, old Llewellyn is on the job."

There was a brief silence. "Actually I'm not sure that *will* make him rest easy, Charles. Actually."

"Thanks very much."

"Tread carefully, Charles."

"Uh-huh." He hung up the phone and regarded his bleeding foot balefully. So his first impression had been right. It was one of *those* jobs. If you did it right, everyone else took the credit. And if you did it badly, nobody else took the blame.

The kind they managed to stick *him* with, every damn time.

Charles had once believed he could make a difference. Fresh from Cambridge, armed with a good degree, ambition, and high hopes, he'd waded into the Foreign Office as if it were an Olympic pool. He soon learned that individual competitors were frowned on, that "procedure" was all, and that the elegant days of inspired diplomacy were gone forever. In their place was hard bargaining, long waits, petty detail and insults.

He'd been an only child, accustomed to manipulating adults from an early age. This, he discovered, was poor preparation for dealing with his more childish colleagues, to whom the ascendant order and its symbols were all-important. (*He's* got a carpet, *I* want a carpet. Right now!) They didn't exactly stamp their little feet and howl, but they might as well have.

His profound shock at learning everyone in the FO was *not* reasonable, fair-minded and intelligent lasted for some time. It was not that he was naive, but he'd had his illusions. What young man of twenty-two does not? By the time he'd become an old man of twenty-seven, and was posted to a minor assignment in the Canaries, he'd learned to keep a copy of Machiavelli by him at all times. Not for dealing with the foreigners—who were usually pretty straightforward—but for dealing with his own side.

A minor negotiation, routinely assigned to him, blew up one afternoon into a moderately dicey situation. By keeping his head and his temper, he settled everything amicably almost before anyone had realized there was a serious problem. Fortunately for Charles, however, someone *had* made a note of his performance. When an opening came in the Madrid embassy, he was given a posting. Because he'd found sweet reason worked once, he kept on using it. Because he'd found that keeping his temper had worked once, he kept doing it. He put Machiavelli aside and stopped looking behind him. He was on his way.

One well-aimed poisoned dagger was all it took to bring him down.

From being a rather up-and-coming young career diplomat in Madrid, omnipresent at embassy functions, popular, ready to play a little jazz piano at late-night parties with Madrid's more sophisticated socialites, ready to flirt lightly, and charm effortlessly, he suddenly found himself flat on his face. And lay there for all to ignore.

Fools have few friends, Charles learned, but, fortunately, they sometimes have one or two.

So instead of being asked to resign (which would have been an admission of sin his superiors found awkward in the extreme), or sent home ("Dammit, the man's useful"), he was promoted sideways and banished to the newly established consulate in Alicante, where younger men on their way up drew their own conclusions. His, after all, was a cautionary tale.

Born to solid, sensible people, however, Charles discovered banishment was not punishment. He discovered the Work Ethic in himself. Time wore away the gilt and the guilt (and most of the illusions), and now, here he was. Sound, reliable, careful old Charles.

He did well, especially when he worked directly with the ordinary Spanish people, whom he admired. More and more things were left to him: the awkward jobs, the difficult negotiations for petty points, the everyday tasks of commerce. In summer he pitched in and helped on the tourist side—for the Alicante consulate was in the thick of it all summer, and had been established largely because of it.

But although Charles worked hard, his position remained nebulous. He was primarily a floating trouble-shooter, and, as such, he was valued by the senior staff—and kept in that very valuable place by those who had come to depend on him. He was aware that others sometimes took the final credit for his efforts, or had their passage forward facilitated by his work. He didn't care. He often said it. One day, he was certain, he'd come to believe it.

He had a busy career in a beautiful setting, his pay was adequate, his free time his own, and life was good. Did it matter that he was now forty, alone, and had few prospects left for achieving the spectacular success dreamed of at Cambridge?

Only sometimes. Say, late at night, or early in the morning. When he'd lie in the dark staring at the ceiling and wonder what the hell he'd done with himself and his life. Times like now, for instance.

He sighed. Right. After he cleared up this little "spot of bother" that Baker had so kindly dropped in his lap, he would do something about it. He'd get off his backside and start pushing for promotion. He'd get organized. He really would.

By the time Charles had showered, dressed, made himself a cup of coffee, spilled it, and made another, it was nearly five-thirty. He tiptoed down the stairs, trying not to wake anyone, and stepped out into the dawn. The coolness was, he knew, deceptive. Summer wasn't through with the Costa

Blanca yet—although the vast majority of the tourists were. Far below, the city was stirring and the ships in the harbour showed a moving sailor here and there. In a few hours the heat would come—already the sun was glaring a little from the bonnet of his car. It was an old Seat, once white and now rust-stained. Its appearance matched that of the old hacienda perfectly. Parked in the right place, one could hardly make it out against the walls that looked as if they had been gnawed by something large and random in appetite. Once the graceful house had been a rich man's pride—now it was converted to apartments and the garden was a gravelled car-park, pitted with holes.

Charles reckoned it the perfect setting for a career diplomat who'd started high on the romance of Spain and was now thigh-deep in the petty details of hauling package-tour drunks out of the jail and acting as liaison between plastic tycoons and cardboard-box manufacturers in England and Spain. The old Spain was beautiful, graceful, haughty and fascinating. The new Spain was hustle, bustle, and full of ex-civil servants from Acton who wore thick white socks under their sandals and complained constantly because they couldn't get *The Times* delivered daily without paying a fortune. They had fallen for the sales talks about perpetual summer and cheap gin and had purchased retirement homes and flats in many of the smaller dormitory towns springing up all along the coast around Alicante and Benidorm. Puerto Rio was one such. No doubt Partridge was just like all the rest.

With a heavy sigh, he got into the car and started it, rolling down the hill and joining the main road a few minutes later. Charles Llewellyn was a torn man. He loved Spain. Moreover, he loved the Spanish. Their pride—which to many less sympathetic people seemed like arrogance—was simply a reflection of their self-containment. Carried to extreme, of course, it could be very obstructive. Each Spaniard was the centre of the world—*his* world, and everyone else's point of view was quite foreign. And a Spaniard's decision was always final. "If you have made a mistake, defend it, and don't correct it." No Spaniard would ever admit he'd made a mistake. Nor would he appreciate being told that he had. In fact, no Spaniard appreciated being told *anything*. He liked to be asked instead.

It always amazed Charles how long it took each new arrival from the FO to learn that simple fact. Of course, it took effort. In fact, sometimes it took a great *deal* of effort not to take a Spaniard by the throat and hurl him across the room.

But Charles was British. As hard as he tried, as much as he studied and absorbed about Spain, he would always be British. And, as a member of the consulate, he represented the British.

They always seemed to be the worst ones, too. He knew there were thousands of nice Britons who came to Spain for a holiday and behaved well and appreciated what they saw. He just never seemed to meet any of them. He wanted to tell them all how wonderful the country was, how rich in culture and beauty and excitement. But by the time he got there, they were usually too drunk or too angry to notice. And the Spaniards involved were usually too eager to be rid of them to waste time talking to Charles about the insight of Lorca or the Moorish influence on Andalusian architecture.

So he was torn between the two sides of himself, and the two sides of all the problems he was expected to solve.

And he was forty. And perhaps getting a little bald, not that it showed, yet, but he knew it was coming. And tired. But mostly, bored.

And being got out of bed at 3 A.M. to deal with some stupid clod who'd killed someone on foreign soil was not the role he'd envisaged for himself when he'd graduated from university.

He pulled into the main square of Puerto Rio at just after seven-thirty. The metal shutters were still over most of the shops, although the café across the way was open to early morning customers such as lorry drivers and delivery men. A white-shirted shape moved within, like a fish in a dark aquarium, and the smell of coffee and fresh churros filled the air. Later motor cars would fill the square; now the open space was still. Later it would shimmer with exhaust fumes. It would echo with laughter and arguments, and the hot pavements would bake under the sun. Now only an occasional pigeon walked there, gravely circling the fountain.

Charles entered the Guardia station and saw immediately that the sergeant on duty at the reception desk was not one he knew. This one, heavy-set and thin-lipped, regarded him suspiciously as he advanced.

"*Buenos días,* Sergeant. I wonder if you could help me?"

The sergeant's face changed, marginally, for the better. He'd known immediately that Charles was a foreigner, but he spoke excellent Spanish. (Touched with a regrettable Valencian accent, it was true.) He, the sergeant, was therefore prepared to listen. There was, after all, another half hour before he went off-duty, was there not? And a dull time, too.

Charles produced his credentials and explained that someone from the consulate had rousted him out of a perfectly good bed and informed him that a British national was being held here on a charge of murder. Was this true, and if so, could the sergeant tell him what to do?

Placed in the position of adviser, the sergeant took his responsibility seriously. Sententiously, he outlined the book procedure (which Charles knew by heart), and produced the appropriate forms.

Charles filled them in meticulously under the sergeant's eye, having to ask for help only once, which was quite graciously given. The sergeant had decided that he wasn't too bad, this foreigner, he knew his place.

Having accepted the forms and inspected them carefully for any irregularity, the sergeant deposited them in the proper tray and excused himself. He would, he said, see what was passing concerning this particular case.

Only after the sergeant had left did Charles permit himself a glance at the clock on the wall. Eight-fifteen. Not bad, considering.

At eight twenty-three another Guardia sergeant appeared, removed his patent-leather hat, said good morning, and came to stand behind the desk. He was a tall, thin, horse-faced man whose eyes were not awake yet.

Charles said good morning.

There was a pause.

Was there something? the sergeant asked.

Charles explained that the other sergeant was attending to him.

The horse-faced man shook his head. Sergeant Buiges was off-duty, now. *He,* Sergeant Cholbi, was in charge.

Without batting an eye, Charles went through the entire thing again, indicating the forms in the tray. These the new sergeant inspected.

Since the forms were in order, he said he would find out the present position concerning the British national, Partrijes. And *he* disappeared.

Charles lit a cigarette and went over to stand in the open doorway, watching with little interest as a shopkeeper struggled with the steel shutters over the window of what, eventually, proved to be a jeweller's. There was a sound of throat-clearing from behind the desk and Charles turned. Yet another sergeant stood there. Charles's heart sank. He flicked the cigarette out into the dusty gutter and returned to the desk. This time, however, he got a smile. As he got it, Sergeant Cholbi reappeared, and also smiled.

That should have warned him.

"Good morning, señor," the third sergeant said. "I am afraid we cannot help you."

Charles forced himself to look forlorn, rather than furious. "And why is that?"

"The officer in charge of the case is not here at present, and you must see him first, before interviewing the prisoner, Partrijes."

"Then he is here?"

"No, he is not here, but comes on duty . . ."

"No, I meant Señor Partridge. He *is* here?"

"You will have to speak to the officer in charge," was the reply.

Charles considered. This one's eyes are very sharp. Partridge *was* there, that much was obvious—but he'd have to do it their way. As usual.

"I see. And when will the officer in charge be available?"

"Later this morning, señor. About ten o'clock."

So it was a fairly senior officer, then. They were taking it all very seriously. That was bad. "And whom shall I ask for when I return?"

"For Capitán Moreno, señor."

Charles kept his face neutral, but inwardly he groaned. That was not only bad—that was bloody awful.

"I will return at ten. Many thanks."

"De nada, señor."

Charles went out, and crossed the square to the café. A few pigeons fluttered up, then resettled near the fountain after he'd passed. He ordered coffee and rolls, and chose a table near the window looking out at the open door across the square. Through it he could see Sergeant Cholbi had settled down behind the desk and was yawning.

And only nine o'clock.

Capitán Moreno was a man with cold eyes in a fat face, who did not like foreigners of any kind, particularly English. Charles had had to deal with him before, on several occasions, and had found him consistently obstructive and unhelpful. He seemed to delight in balking everyone he encountered at each and every turn. Perhaps his sex life was not all that it should be, Charles thought, without the least trace of sympathy, for Moreno was behaving true to form again.

"The prisoner Partrijes must go to Espina this morning."

"I wish to see him before he goes."

"And from there he will be taken to Alicante."

"I drove here from Alicante this morning . . ."

"A wasted journey."

". . . and I intend to see him. I also wish to see full details of all charges being preferred against him, as is my legal right."

Moreno shrugged. "The case notes are being processed now. It is a very complicated case, there is much detail . . ."

"A simple outline will be sufficient."

Moreno looked out of the window, bored already. "I will see what I can do."

"You could tell me, yourself," Charles pointed out.

"It would be better if you could read it."

"All right, then, I'll read it. Where is it?"

"If you will wait, I will see if an extra copy can be found." Moreno, with a last glance out of the window, left the small interrogation room where he had deigned to see Charles. He moved slowly and deliberately. Annoyed, Charles lit a cigarette and stood up to stretch his legs. Moreno had kept him waiting in the little room for twenty minutes before even granting him an audience, and the chair was hard. He went over to the window and stiffened as he saw what it was that had so fascinated the capitán.

A Guardia van was parked in the courtyard, and even now a prisoner was being taken out to it. Not a Spaniard, but obviously an Englishman.

Partridge.

"Godammit." Charles exploded, throwing his cigarette into the tin ash-tray in the centre of the table and flinging open the door to the hall.

The first uniform he encountered in the hallway was filled by none other than the horse-faced Sergeant Cholbi, who looked only slightly more awake now.

"I must see the prisoner Partridge before he leaves; how do I get down to the courtyard?"

"But Capitán Moreno . . ."

"I have already seen Capitán Moreno," Charles said, implying by his tone that permission had been given for his interview.

"Oh, I see. Then you must go through that door at the end of the hall and down the stairs. The second door on your right will lead you to . . ."

"Muchas gracias, amigo," Charles said over his shoulder, making for the door. Out of the corner of his eye he saw Moreno returning. He didn't wait to hear what poor Cholbi would have to do to expiate the sin of helping a foreigner. He clattered down the iron stairs and burst out into the heat and whiteness of the courtyard. The van's engine had been started, but the GC officer in charge was still closing the rear doors.

"Teniente!" Charles shouted. *"Espera, por favor!"*

The uniformed officer turned slightly, one hand on the doors and the other going towards his holstered revolver, but when he saw his caller was only a harassed-looking Englishman, he relaxed. The sun glinted off his patent-leather hat and the mirrored lenses of his sunglasses.

"Señor?"

In rapid Spanish Charles explained, holding out his rather impressive-looking credentials. "I am Charles Llewellyn of the British Consulate, and I must have a chance to interview your prisoner before he goes to Espina. I have already spoken to Capitán Moreno."

A glimmer of something like sympathy flashed at the corners of the GC lieutenant's mouth. Moreno was not typical of the GC, as Charles knew from long experience. They could be tough as hell when the situation called for it, but for the most part they were polite and helpful to foreigners. The lieutenant glanced at his watch, then up at the windows overhead. "We have a few minutes' grace, señor. But only a few minutes, if you please."

"I am very grateful," Charles said, meaning it.

The lieutenant waved this aside gracefully. "As the prisoner is now in *my* charge, it is no trouble. But, please . . . be brief." With a slight bow, the lieutenant went round to speak to the driver. Charles glanced up at the windows of the room he had recently left, saw Moreno glaring down at him, and realized that the lieutenant must be attached to the garrison at Espina, and thus was not worried about Moreno. Perhaps that hint of a smile had had a further hint of satisfaction in it, too. Moreno was probably as much a pain in the ass to fellow-officers as he was to the public at large. The lieutenant was lounging against the front wing, now, lighting a cigarette. Obviously he wasn't very worried about his prisoner escaping. When Charles mounted the steps into the van, he could see why. Reg Partridge would play the game fairly, whatever it was. It was written all over him.

He also didn't look very well.

Reginald Thomas Partridge was a hawk-faced man with a prominent nose and chin. If he lived into great old age, he would probably come to resemble Mr. Punch. But there was none of Punch's malevolence in the brown eyes that regarded Charles with lively interest as he settled himself on the hard bench opposite. Just great intelligence, good humour and considerable relief. As for the rest, he was of medium build, but with a pronounced paunch that his loose jacket did its best to hide. His hair was beige and thinning, his skin was tanned, but pale underneath, and Charles liked him immediately. He started to introduce himself, but Partridge interrupted.

"I heard you speaking to the lieutenant. Thank heavens you're here, Mr. Llewellyn—now can we get this all straightened out?"

"I'm afraid it isn't that simple, sir. You'll have to go over to Espina, there's nothing I can do about that at this stage. I haven't even had a chance to go over the charges yet. The thing is, the case must pass into the hands of the court before anything can be done about bail and so on. The GC have only made the initial arrest—after that it goes to the judge and the Judicial Police, which are the equivalent of our CID. I'm sorry for the delay, but . . ."

Partridge put his hands on his knees and looked down at his feet in their laceless shoes, crossed at the ankle. "Something damned humiliating about having your shoelaces taken away," he observed distantly. "Makes you feel like a child, shuffling about." He kept staring downwards.

"I realize how you must feel, sir," Charles said, sympathetically. "Please bear with me until I can get everything in hand. At any rate, you'll find the quarters at Espina considerably more pleasant than you've had here."

"They'd have to be," Partridge said wryly. "This must be the oldest building in Puerto Rio."

Charles smiled encouragingly. It was hot in the van. Beyond the wall he could hear traffic beginning to clog the square. People called and laughed and there was a general sensation of the town waking up and coming to life. Inside the courtyard the bare packed earth reflected the rays of the sun and reminded Charles of the bullring, as did the blank white walls.

"Would you like to tell me what happened, sir?"

Partridge looked up. "Llewellyn—that's Welsh, of course."

"Yes, a long way back."

Partridge nodded. "Born in Scotland myself. Accent rubbed away over the years, I suppose. They tell me I sound quite the Englishman now. I didn't kill him. I'm damned glad he's dead, but I didn't kill him." He spoke all of this in the same tone, and it took Charles a moment to catch up.

"I gather he was some kind of criminal . . ."

"Not some kind. The worst kind. Someone who lets other people take the blame for his crimes. It's his fault my son is dead." He said it tiredly, as if mouthing something he'd said a hundred times before, lying in the dark, walking in the street, facing himself in the shaving mirror. "I said I'd kill him, but that was over two years ago. I think I would probably have skipped making the effort now. Pointless, really. I was half out of my mind at the time. One . . . says things."

"Yes, sir. Did he threaten you or—"

"I never saw him, Mr. Llewellyn. I haven't the least idea what he was doing at my flat—he'd made no contact with me whatsoever. I didn't even know he was out of jail. We left the flat at around seven-thirty to go to a bridge evening, as we do every Tuesday. About half-way there, Mary realized she'd forgotten her spectacles, so I turned around and went back. I left her in the car, went up, found the glasses, turned around and came down, locking the door behind me as I'd locked it when we originally left. They say he went over about the same time I was there, but I swear to you I saw or heard nothing. We went on to the bridge. It was duplicate and we came top. Do you think a man who's just murdered someone could win a bridge competition immediately after? I ask you."

Charles looked at him. "Some men could."

Partridge raised a bushy eyebrow, then smiled. "I might take that as a very great compliment under different circumstances. As it is, I can only say, not I. To have taken a human life, however evil that life might have been, would render me useless for common activity. I would, in short, tend to gibber. I would attempt to explain myself to the first person I could find, I would lead them back, I would command them to look and forgive. To coolly trounce friends at bridge would be quite beyond my poor powers of concentration. I would be wondering all the while, you see. Wondering what the hell I'd come down to, with all my strict Presbyterian upbringing. And wondering if I'd left any clues." The smile widened to a grin. "One couldn't help wondering that."

Charles found himself grinning back.

Suddenly, Partridge's smile twisted into a grimace, and his face went white beneath the tan as he bent forward, slightly, breathing in with a catch at the end. "Damn," he muttered, his hand going to his stomach beneath the jacket.

"Are you all right, sir?"

After a moment, Partridge straightened slightly, and smiled again—a wan copy of his earlier effort. "Indigestion—martyr to it. Told to stay on a bland diet, which isn't exactly a description of the food in a Spanish jail."

"Have you anything you can take?"

Partridge shook his head. "Came away from the flat in rather a rush, yesterday, you know. Will you be going to see my wife at all?"

"Yes, of course, directly after I see you."

"Be a good chap and ask her to send my medicine over to Espina, will you?" The spasm seemed to be easing, slightly, and Partridge no longer had that queer catch in his breath.

"I'm sure she'll be glad to bring it along when she . . ."

"No!" Partridge interrupted him. "Don't let her come to see me, whatever you do. She couldn't take it . . . I wouldn't want her to have to go through that. Have someone else bring it over, please. Nigel can bring it, or Alastair. Anyone will do, but don't let Mary come, please."

"I'll do my best, Mr. Partridge."

"Reg. For heaven's sake, call me Reg. Will you get me a lawyer?"

"You don't have one of your own?"

"He's an old man, no use in this kind of situation. Find me a young one—with stamina. I have a feeling he's going to have to work hard."

"But if . . ."

Partridge sat up. His colour was a little better now. "How long have you been in Spain, Charles?"

"Just over fourteen years, sir."

"Then you must know what I'm getting at. I know the evidence is damning and so on . . . I guess you have yet to find that out—but they've made a mistake in arresting me, you'll see. The trouble is, they'll never admit it. They have to have proof . . . and proof is something I am very short of, apparently. They don't seem to think my word is sufficient." His mouth twisted wryly. "And . . . you see . . . I have a bridge tournament coming up. I must defend my title to that, you know, and I can't do it from jail, can I?" He was only half-joking.

"I'll do all I can, sir."

Partridge nodded and sighed. "Thank you."

They were easy words to say, one often said them automatically, but Charles had the feeling that Partridge had brought them from the depths of his heart. He accepted them as such, knowing that, once again, he was hooked into working himself witless for someone he hardly knew.

Two minutes later, he watched the van pull out of the courtyard and then turned to walk slowly back up the iron stairs. When he got to the top and stepped into the hall, Moreno was waiting for him in the door of his office. He smiled cynically as Charles came up to him.

"I see the lieutenant was no more willing to let him go than I was."

"You weren't even willing to let me see him," Charles snapped.

Moreno raised his hands. "I thought he had gone already," he lied blandly. "Unfortunately, the reports of the case went with him. Everything must be forwarded to the Policía Judicial, of course, as you know."

"Tell me what you have."

Moreno glanced up at the clock on his wall. "I have an appointment in five minutes . . ."

"Then do it in five minutes," Charles said, pushing past him and sitting down in the chair by Moreno's desk. "Or I'll ask to see someone here who will. Or perhaps the consul himself will ask . . ."

Moreno came back into the office and stood behind his desk. "What do you wish to know?" he said, his jaw tight. He knew Charles meant what he said, and although it pleased him to be difficult, it did not please him to have such things noted above.

"About the victim first."

"He was a Swiss named Horst Graebner. Suspected of criminal activity but never arrested. Until two years ago, when he and Partridge's son were charged with fraud."

"Bank fraud?"

"Art fraud. Forgery. But before we could bring them to trial, there was an accident. The vehicle carrying them to custody was in collision with another car and the son, David Partridge, was killed. Also a GC officer. The second officer and Graebner himself went to hospital, both badly injured."

"And only Graebner was tried?"

"That's it. But by then it wasn't much of a trial, because while he was in hospital he had time to think. He pleaded guilty as an accessory, claimed the whole thing was the boy's idea. His word against a dead man's—never could be proved one way or another. They were glad to get a guilty plea, and the whole thing was over before it began. I suppose that's why Partridge threatened him at the time. His sentence was reduced because of the time spent in the hospital on remand. He was released two weeks ago."

"And went straight to a man who'd threatened to kill him?"

Moreno shrugged. "He was after the money, of course."

"What money?"

"The son's share. It was never recovered. Forty-five million pesetas."

Charles almost whistled, but stopped himself in time. Even reduced to pounds, it was two hundred and fifty thousand. Worth going after, undoubtedly. Yet Partridge said he'd never seen Graebner. Charles said as much to Moreno, who laughed derisively.

"Oh yes, he says he is innocent, of course he does. But we know he was there at the relevant time and he admitted it. When we still thought it was suicide and told him a neighbour had seen his lights go on at a quarter to eight, he 'remembered' going back for his wife's glasses."

"He'd hardly admit that if he'd killed the man, would he?"

"He had to, since he assumed somebody had seen him," Moreno said calmly. "He didn't know we suspected him then, you see." He glanced at the clock. He would have liked to draw this out, but there was no time. "There was a notebook in Graebner's pocket with the address, the date, and a notation of seven-thirty. He had made an appointment with Partridge, clearly, and kept it. An appointment with death." The melodramatic phrase seemed to please him, for he repeated it. "An appointment with death."

"Did anyone see Graebner go over?"

"No. The body was discovered later."

"That's odd, surely?"

"It is a fact."

"And the time of death—you're certain it was . . ."

"Graebner's wristwatch was smashed in the fall, showing seven forty-five."

"Did anyone hear him? He must have screamed . . ." Charles insisted. Moreno shook his head.

"No one heard him. But then, that is hardly surprising, seeing that he was already dead when he was pushed over the parapet."

Charles gaped at him, much to Moreno's satisfaction.

"He was already dead?"

"That is correct. He was stabbed. Through the chest. Twice. The post-mortem described the weapon as a long, thin blade. We found the weapon hanging on Partridge's wall—one of those *espada y muleta* decorations you foreigners are so fond of displaying. Traces of the victim's blood were on the sword, although it had been hastily wiped, and also Partridge's fingerprints. As soon as we knew that, we arrested him. That is all."

"But . . ." Charles was dumbfounded.

"You have made me late," Moreno said impatiently. "You will have to get any more questions answered by someone else. I must leave." Without further comment, he picked up his hat and gloves and went out, leaving Charles still rooted to the chair.

With a cold feeling in the pit of his stomach, Charles stared blindly at the window.

They had the motive. They had the opportunity. They had the weapon. And they had Partridge.

They had it all.

CHAPTER 2

Four hundred Avenida de la Playa was an apartment block made up of three separate towers, each stepped back from the other, and joined at ground level by a common lobby. This was long and narrow and totally impersonal, save for the bright tiles that were so typical of modern Spanish decor. Almost all the names on the mailboxes between the three lifts that served the towers were foreign, and the Partridge name was shown twice in the rank by the centre one. He remembered it was the penthouse, and pushed the top button in the lift.

As it laboriously rose, he thought about Reg Partridge—not the man in the van, but the man who lived here. He must have many friends among the two thousand or so English people who lived in the area, he was that kind of man. How many of them knew what had happened? For all of them, life here was almost like life had always been, except that it was hotter, and you had to know a few words of Spanish to get by in the supermarket. Partridge had apparently made an effort to learn the language, which was more than most of them did. He gave the man full marks for that. But there he was, charged with murder—and all he could think about was his damned bridge tournament. Oh, he knew Partridge had been trying to lighten the situation, but his remark had been partly serious. It hadn't sunk in, yet. He didn't really *believe* what was happening to him, because things like that didn't happen to ex-civil servants who'd done well in Customs and Excise, raised two children, led a good and honest life and then retired.

He supposed it was a defence mechanism.

Partridge was in a terrible position. The background to the killing was obviously complicated, but the case itself was horribly simple. That was the beauty of it from the police point of view.

The whole business about the stabbing had been a shock, and he wasn't even certain Partridge knew about that (unless, of course, he *had* done it). He hadn't mentioned it, but he must have realized they'd taken the sword away, he must have let them do it. What could he have thought they wanted with it, if not to examine it for evidence? He must have thought they were crazy. Unless, of course, he *had* done it.

And they must have questioned him about the sword and about Graebner, and about his coming back, and he must not have had ready answers for all of that. Unless, of course, he *had* done it.

The lift doors slid back, and Charles stood there, unmoving, until they started to close again. He stepped forward, got caught between them, and pushed his way into the lobby of the penthouse. There were only two doors opening off it. One was marked *Escalera* (stairs), and the other said nothing at all. He pushed the bell beside the blank door and tried to brush the dusty marks left by the lift door off the sleeves of his jacket.

There was so much he didn't know about the case, so much to learn of the background, and yet he already found it hard to believe that Partridge was a murderer, no matter what the evidence said or would say. The man was so reasonable, so gentle, so intelligent, and he'd retained his sense of humour as well. Of course, all that could be a highly polished act, covering up the calculating mind of a cold-blooded murderer.

He pressed the bell again. Still nothing happened. Then, as suddenly as a slap in the face, it was opened by a young woman with a mass of blazing red curls over a pair of turquoise eyes. She was very pretty.

Charles was puzzled. Nobody had said anything about Partridge's having a young wife. Was she his first or his second? Had he been divorced? Widowed?

Sudden, unbidden images of mass murder and mayhem flashed through his mind, unsettling him almost as much as the defiant and unwelcoming stare of the girl herself.

"I'm sorry, I'm looking for Mrs. Partridge."

"Yes?"

The old dog—it wasn't fair. "My name is Charles Llewellyn. I'm from the British Consulate in Alicante."

"My God, it's about time," she said, standing back. "Come in."

As he stepped across the threshold his heel caught in the edge of the rug and he lurched, slightly, before continuing down the narrow hall. He glanced back at her questioningly.

"All the way to the end—on the left," she directed, coming along behind him on a wave of fragrance that engulfed him as she passed. Surely that had been an American accent? That could complicate things, with the people from the American Embassy . . .

As he stepped through the door into the sitting room, he was struck by three things: the view, which was spectacular; the pictures on the walls, which were profuse; and the woman huddled in a chair, her eyes reddened by crying and her mouth held still only by great effort. The red-haired girl crossed to her and bent down, slightly, resting her hand on the older woman's shoulder.

"It's a man from the consulate—at last." She glanced at him coolly. "His name is Llewellyn."

"Oh." That seemed to be all the older woman could manage.

"I'm sorry if you've been concerned," Charles apologized. "I was held up at the jail."

The girl straightened, her expression altered. "Oh—then you've *seen* Reg."

"Yes. I have yet to get a solicitor—because I really wanted to talk to you first." He smiled. "I'm afraid I need more facts about the background and so on before I can properly brief a lawyer. My time with Mr. Partridge was . . . limited."

"How is Reg?" The older woman's question was such a small whisper, Charles almost missed it. Obviously this was Mrs. Partridge.

"He seems in good spirits," Charles answered, trying to sound reassuring. "He said you weren't to worry or to visit him. They've moved him to Espina anyway. Oh, he did ask if you'd send along his medicine. Something for his indigestion, I gather."

"It's not indigestion, it's an ulcer," the younger woman commented.

"Oh?" Charles frowned. "He didn't tell me that."

"He wouldn't," she said. "He doesn't like fuss. Sit down—I'll get some coffee. Don't start until I get back." With an affectionate, but worried, glance at the older woman she went out.

Charles sat down and smiled. Mrs. Partridge tried to smile back. "It was kind of you to come so quickly," she murmured, then pressed a handkerchief to her mouth with a shaking hand. "I'm sorry . . . I'm not usually so . . ."

"It's all right. We'll get this all straightened out as soon as we can. That's what I'm here for, to make some sense of it. And we will." He was horrified to see tears rolling down the woman's cheeks. All he'd done was try and reassure her.

"Ah—I see you've started without me, after all" was the girl's sarcastic observation as she returned with a tray of steaming coffee cups and a plate of biscuits. "Nice work." She deposited the tray on a low table between the chairs and then went over to kneel down by the older woman. "Now look, Mary—this has got to stop. We have to give this man all the help we can, and we have to be careful and clear about everything. You won't do Reg any good like this, you know."

"I know—I'm sorry." Mrs. Partridge apologized to both of them. "I don't suppose I'd be such a liability if we were back in England, but I feel so . . . isolated here. I don't understand what they say, I don't understand what's happening, or why . . ." She took a deep breath and put on a brave smile that nearly broke their hearts. "Anyway, I can't have all that many tears left in me, can I?"

She was an attractive woman in her early sixties, Charles judged, who'd kept her figure as well as her spirit. Only the backs of her hands belied the youth in her face. Her hair was tinted a soft blond, and her jumper and skirt were simple but elegant. Like the room in which they sat, in fact. The furniture was modern and good—and there wasn't too much of it. Sensibly the room was given (or perhaps surrendered) to the view and to the pictures. Prints, paintings, abstracts, landscapes and portraits—they were everywhere, grouped here, isolated there—with an eye for colour and pattern. Whoever had hung them had obviously been the source of the son's artistic ability. It was a welcoming room.

"I think I would have gone right out of my mind when they took Reg away last evening—if it hadn't been for Holly," Mrs. Partridge said, smiling gratefully at the girl as she handed her a cup of coffee.

When she handed him his cup, Charles looked at her with a wry apologetic smile. "When I asked at the door, I thought *you* were Mrs. Partridge . . ."

"I am," she said, offering him the sugar. When he refused it she replaced it on the tray and took up her own cup. "And then again, I'm not." She sipped at her coffee. "I suppose you could call me Mary's ex-daughter-in-law. Or a late daughter-in-law, maybe."

Light dawned. "You were married to David Partridge," he said.

"My, my, he's a quick one," she said wryly.

"Holly, don't be sarcastic," Mary reproved automatically.

Charles sipped at his coffee, which was very strong and very hot. The girl had gone on drinking hers and seemed not to notice. She was still considering the question of her identity. "Actually, I kept the name because it had started to get known, and I didn't want to confuse everyone by changing it in midstream, so to speak. It's an easy name to remember."

"Are you an actress?"

"No way," she said, munching a biscuit.

"Holly's an embroiderer," Mrs. Partridge explained.

"Oh. You mean petit point, that sort of thing?" Charles asked, politely. His mother had done petit point. "You mean—that's how you earn a living?"

"That's right." She brushed at the front of her robe, impatiently, and then proceeded to replace the crumbs by starting on another biscuit immediately.

"Oh," Charles said. He didn't really give a damn what she was, but he did wish she'd stop regarding him so balefully from behind those turquoise eyes of hers. "Well, what I need to know first is the background on all this, if you wouldn't mind." He got out his notebook.

"Okay, like what?" Holly asked briskly, settling down in her chair. The sooner they got this over with, the better, she thought. Look at him, with his gold pen and his little leather notebook. Our man in Alicante, all narrow tie and polished shoes. She glanced down. Well, not so polished, at that. And his socks didn't match. For some reason that cheered her immensely. Despite his square shoulders and stubborn chin, he'd looked at the door like a classic example of the genus *Clericus britannicus*, a common or garden-variety fuss-pot. Which was probably what he was at that. Even upside-down she could see the writing in his notebook already was small and precise.

"Where would you like us to start?"

Charles, in his turn, regarded her with dismay. His limited experience with American women caused him to have dark premonitions. He felt a burning sensation on his knee and jerked his coffee cup level just a moment too late. As she lit a cigarette with one hand, Holly Partridge leaned over and mopped up the spill on his trousers with a napkin, making Charles feel about four years old. Premonitions confirmed. "I think it had better start with this fraud thing your late husband was involved in with the victim, Graebner. Was Graebner an art dealer or something?"

"Graebner was a crook," Holly said flatly. "He conned David."

"I see," Charles said, making a note.

Holly blew smoke, rather like a little engine by a station platform, signalling the journey was about to start. Mary Partridge sipped her coffee, her eyes down, apparently content to have Holly tell the tale. Charles waited.

"David was a lousy artist," Holly said. "He had only a little talent for original work. His real skill was as a copyist, and when we were first married he made a very good living at it."

"You mean . . . he was a forger?" Charles asked, startled.

"Of course not!" Holly said indignantly.

Mary Partridge spoke up in her soft voice. "There are a great many museums in the world, Mr. Llewellyn, and not all that many great masterpieces. A really skilled copyist can do very well, and David was quite extraordinary. He had imagination, you see. He somehow *became* the artist he was copying, so that the work he reproduced had true life in it. It's hard to explain, but sometimes his copies seemed more real than the real thing—and that's why museums were eager to commission him."

"I apologize," Charles said, embarrassed. "I really know nothing about the art business."

"He was no crook," Holly said, glaring at him.

"Holly . . . it did come to that in the end, you know," Mary murmured.

"No, it didn't," Holly said firmly. "He never signed those pictures."

"Which pictures?" Charles asked.

"The ones Graebner sold as originals," Holly said. "David would never have signed them. Graebner saw he was on to a good thing and got someone else to sign them before they were sold. It was a frame-up. David would never have done that, *never.* I can't believe he would have changed that much."

"He had," Mary said, shaking her head sadly. "You didn't see him, you weren't *here.*"

"Please . . ." Charles said, helplessly, looking from one to the other. "Could we go back to the beginning?"

"All right . . . where was I?" Holly asked irritably.

"When you first were married . . ." Charles prompted.

"Oh. Yes. Well . . . that's what David was doing then. And we had a nice life and everything was fine. But he got restless, really . . . in fact, he got impossible, to tell the truth. He began to hate what he was doing. He kept going on about 'doing his own thing,' which—as far as I could tell by the stuff he tried doing—meant falling flat on his backside between the Impressionists and the Abstract Expressionists. It really was crap."

Charles looked at her curiously. One minute she was defending her late husband and the next attacking him. She really was an odd girl.

"We had a lot of arguments, I just couldn't understand why he was so . . . intractable. It got pretty unbearable. And when Reg and Mary moved over here, that did it. He followed them—for the 'light,' he said. It was really just an excuse to opt out . . . the gin was cheap here, and he could mooch off his parents whenever he wanted to." Her voice was quite matter-of-fact and a little weary, as if she'd lost patience with her husband long before he'd left her. She caught the look on his face and flushed, then glanced at her mother-in-law. "I'm sorry if that . . ."

Her mother-in-law smiled understandingly. "You must understand, Mr. Llewellyn, that we all loved David very much. Too much, perhaps. He'd always been a brilliant boy, far too clever for his own good, really. Everything had come easily to him at school, and perhaps we indulged him. He had a quality . . ."

"He could charm the socks off an Eskimo in a blizzard," Holly said abruptly, and jabbed her cigarette out in an ashtray, as if angry with herself for admitting it.

"That's why it was such a tragedy when the marriage broke up," Mary went on, watching her daughter-in-law. "Our sympathies were with Holly, to tell you the truth, but, well . . . he *was* our son. We wanted what was best for him, and when he came out here, Reg bought him a studio flat in Espina in the hopes that he'd settle down and get all this rebellion out of his system. But it only seemed to get worse."

"And did he meet this Graebner here?" Charles asked, wanting to cut short these obviously painful recollections before they degenerated into what-might-have-beens.

"No—I think he knew him already from somewhere," Mary said vaguely.

"He conned David," Holly said, coming back to life with a vengeance, and sitting up in her chair with her red curls bobbing indignantly. "He said he was an art dealer, told David he had galleries in Geneva and The Hague, and promised David a one-man show. And David fell for it. He wrote me all about it, about his 'big chance.' People are conned because they want to be conned, Mr. Llewellyn—David wanted so much to believe that Graebner was right about his work that he went ahead, even though something inside him *must* have told him it was a lie. I think he wanted me to believe it, too, wanted to force me to admit I'd been wrong. And because he wanted to prove it, he agreed to do Graebner a little 'favour' in return."

"Paint a forgery, I suppose?" Charles asked.

"Twelve forgeries, as a matter of fact," Mary said.

"He *thought* they were going to be sold as copies," Holly said stubbornly.

"Oh, Holly, why can't you accept that David *knew?*" Mary said. "You're as bad as Reg. The canvases he used were *old,* not new. How could he think otherwise? He knew they were going to a private client, not a museum."

Holly explained, or tried to. "Look, it was like this. Graebner had an American client, who gave him a 'shopping list' of artists he was interested in collecting, all right?"

"Yes," Charles said. "I guess so."

"A lot of dealers work like that," Holly said hurriedly. "Anyway, all the artists were Spanish. David asked for and received, quite legitimately, permission from the Prado to copy twelve of their paintings. They knew him, he'd worked there before. He'd worked at most of the top museums and he had a good reputation. He reproduced four paintings by Velázquez, three by Murillo, two by Morales, two by Ribalta, one by Carnicero, and one by Bosch." She counted off the names on her fingers.

"Bosch isn't a Spanish painter," Charles said immediately.

"No, but the Prado has the world's greatest collection of Bosch works."

"And anyway," Charles went on doggedly, "that makes thirteen—and you said he'd done twelve forgeries."

"Mary said he'd done twelve forgeries, *I* say he did twelve copies. And anyway, the Bosch wasn't sold with the rest, and it wasn't exactly a copy, either . . ."

"Oh." He ground his teeth. "Can I just get this straight in my mind? Did David do copies or fakes?"

Holly sighed. "He did thirteen pictures. Twelve of them were sold to this American client of Graebner's, and shipped to the States as 'copies'—it said 'copies' on the customs declaration. Reg checked."

"It said 'originals' on the bill of sale," Mary said, softly but insistently. "And the price was five hundred thousand dollars."

Holly clung to her position stubbornly. "The paintings left David unsigned, he never signed copies. He had a thing about forgeries, he *hated* forgeries. Graebner had someone else sign them. The Bosch was still in David's studio when he was arrested—it was already varnished and framed and it was *unsigned.*" She looked at Charles's rather confused expression. "You can only be sued for fraud if a picture is signed," she explained impatiently.

"Ah . . . I *see,*" Charles said, understanding at last. "And the client sued, is that it?"

"The widow of the client," Holly said bitterly. "The client, the old fool, had the bad manners to die while the pictures were in transit. When they arrived, the court had them appraised as a matter of routine, because of estate taxes, you see. And they were declared fakes, of course. She screamed 'fraud,' and the police came for David and Graebner. Reg was there at the time, he'd just arrived as the police drove them away. David shouted to his father that it was a lie, that he was to look at the Bosch if he didn't believe him. But he never had a chance to say anything else—on the way to the jail some drunken tourist rammed the Guardia Jeep and killed him."

"As well as a Guardia officer," Charles said.

"What's that got to do with it?" Holly demanded.

"Did Mr. Partridge look at the Bosch?" Charles went on quickly, before she attacked him bodily.

"Of course he did; he brought it back with him, in fact. Would you like to see it?"

"You mean you still have it?"

"I'm afraid so," Mary Partridge said, as if embarrassed by it.

Holly got up and went out. There was a sound of thumping and banging from another room, but eventually she reappeared with a cloth-wrapped bundle that she opened to reveal a gilt-framed picture about two feet square, which she propped against the table. It was a landscape with God and his angels floating in the clouds. The colours were rich, the touch delicate, and it could have been painted by any early Flemish master—except for what lay below the clouds.

Charles had seen the Bosch works in the Prado. He was aware that experts claimed the overtly obscene content of his paintings were in fact mystical rather than pornographic, supposedly resulting from his membership in a strange religious sect. But he'd never stood before the triptych of "The Garden of Earthly Delights" without feeling an adolescent sexual itch, a combination of avid curiosity and embarrassment lest it show. One wanted to look more closely, but one wished heartily to do it in private.

This picture gave him the same sensation.

All across the landscape, grotesque groups of tiny humans were busy committing every conceivable debauchery, while around them, unnoticed or ignored, the earth was splitting and giving up its dead. Obviously it was intended as a Last Judgement.

He was awed by the technical expertise—and unnerved by the content. This painting screamed "Bosch" from every writhing inch, but it was more detailed and specific than any he'd seen. He shifted in his chair. "Very impressive."

"I think it's hideous." Mary Partridge shuddered. "I've made Reg keep it hidden ever since. We've often argued about it—*he* says it's a masterpiece."

"Well, it isn't," Holly said flatly. "It's a fake." She went over to a desk and came back with a magnifying glass. She handed it to Charles. "Upper left-hand corner. The angel in blue."

Charles picked up the picture. It wasn't as heavy as he'd expected. He tilted it on his lap to catch the light from the window and after a moment he spotted what she meant. It was very minute, almost invisible, but it was there. "Well, I'll be damned," he said.

The angel was wearing a digital watch.

CHAPTER 3

Charles asked to see the patio, and Holly took him out through the sliding glass doors. The sea was sparkling under the bright sun, which was warm on their shoulders. If it hadn't been for the steady breeze from the sea, the patio would already have been very hot. Mary Partridge had gone to "rest," exhausted finally by the discussion of the past and the prospect of the future.

"Reg was very bitter when he found that watch," Holly said, lifting her red tumbled hair briefly from the back of her neck to catch the coolness of the breeze. "He was sure it would have cleared David's name, because it indicated that David had never intended to fool anyone. He was certain there would be similar anomalies in the other paintings. It seemed to him— and to me—proof that David had suspected Graebner's intentions from the beginning, and had done that to protect himself. But, of course, Reg never had a chance to mention the watch in court, because he wasn't called to testify. Graebner went on trial, not David. He blamed the whole thing on David, framed him, really, and they accepted that as a basis for his plea. I suppose they were grateful not to have to try a long, costly case. What did it matter? David was dead and couldn't deny it. Reg never even knew about the trial until it was all over—and by then nobody wanted to waste time or money to clear a dead man's name. The case was closed. They were sympathetic, but . . ."

"I can see why he would be upset," Charles murmured. "But would he have carried the grudge for over two years? It seems rather unlikely."

"Oh, Reg can be stubborn, almost as stubborn as David used to be. But those threats were uttered in anger—and Reg never stays angry for long. He's too good-natured, it just isn't in him."

Charles looked around. "I see there are three penthouses. Why are the police so certain Graebner went off this one?"

"The penthouse patio goes around three sides of the tower," Holly explained, waving an arm gracefully. "If he'd landed below the front of the patio, then there might have been some question, because all the flats below have balconies on that side, facing the sea. But the body was found directly below the one side of the tower in which there are no balconies, and no windows that open. Awkward, isn't it?"

She went over and looked down. "This was the place. He was found straight below on the concrete forecourt. The body wasn't discovered for some time because it was hidden by those troughs down there." She leaned over at an alarming angle, and Charles instinctively reached for her, becoming entangled in one of the prickly green plants that grew in the troughed top of the parapet all the way around. By the time he'd gotten his sleeve free, she'd straightened up and was looking at him impatiently. "See?"

Dutifully, he managed a timid lean and glanced downwards over the edge.

"As you can see," Holly continued as he straightened up rather quickly, "there's a good ten-foot gap between the towers at the closest point, and they only overlap slightly. He couldn't have landed in precisely that place unless he'd been thrown."

"He was."

"What?" She raised a hand to shield her eyes from the sun and stared at him. "What do you mean?"

"According to the police post-mortem report, Graebner was dead *before* he went over the parapet. He was stabbed first."

"Stabbed?"

"I'm afraid so."

She went on staring at him, but not seeing him. *"That's* why they took it."

"The sword off the wall?" Charles asked.

She nodded. "We thought it must be illegal or something, but . . ." She stopped. "How did you know about the sword?"

"The captain of the Guardia in charge of the preliminary investigation took great pleasure in telling me that the weapon used to kill Graebner was that sword," Charles said quietly. "It had been carelessly wiped and it had both Graebner's blood and your father-in-law's fingerprints on it. I'm sorry." He reached for her again, then let his hand drop. She didn't look as if she would welcome sympathy, for she was standing there rigid with anger.

He went on awkwardly. "You see . . . they reason . . . the blood and the fingerprints . . ."

"He was bullfighting," Holly said tightly.

"I beg your pardon?"

"Last Sunday week, here, on the patio. He and Nigel were playing about, working out a scene for the Christmas pantomime. Reg belongs to a local amateur theatrical group that put on a traditional English pantomime every year. He was going to produce it this year, and he wanted to put a bullfighting scene in it. That's how his fingerprints got on it."

"That still doesn't explain the blood, I'm afraid," Charles said, apologetically, feeling that it was somehow his fault the police had found the thing.

"He didn't do it."

"I think I agree with you, but I'm only trying to tell you what the case is against him. The evidence is pretty conclusive, and I think you should prepare yourself to help your mother-in-law through what's going to be a very nasty time. He's been taken to Espina, as I said. The Guardia Civil only do the preliminary investigation in murder cases. After that the case is taken on by the Judicial Police, which are an arm of the court. They're more like our own CID. From Espina he'll be taken to Alicante, and the trial will take place there."

"Trial? You think it will get to trial?" she demanded.

"I'm afraid, with the evidence as it stands, it seems very likely," Charles said, regretfully. "Of course, if new evidence comes along . . ." He shrugged. "Tell me, is your mother-in-law all right for money?"

She glared at him. "Why? Is there a charge for your services?"

He kept his tone even with difficulty. "There will be a charge for the lawyer. The Spanish do have an equivalent of Legal Aid, but if you can afford to retain a private *abogado*, I would strongly recommend you to do so. As it happens, *I* come free with the passport. I only asked about money because men taken to jail without notice rarely have time to make sure they've left their wives enough cash for the housekeeping. If your parents-in-law have a joint banking arrangement, then there's no problem. But if that isn't the case, I would see what I could do about arranging something for her."

She was quiet for a while, then turned away and looked at the sea. "I'm sorry," she finally said. "I've always been told I get aggressive when I'm frightened. I guess it's true . . . and, God knows, I'm frightened."

"That's all right," he said, relieved. "After all, you don't know me from Adam. I could be the tea-boy they sent because no one else was available, I could make things worse instead of better through sheer incompetence, right?"

"Well . . ." She turned and smiled suddenly—and for a moment the sun seemed a shade dimmer by comparison.

He leaned against the parapet and folded his arms. "I've been in Spain for over fourteen years. I've been stationed in Madrid, the Canary Islands and Alicante. I've spent most of my time in those places getting people out of difficulties. In fact, people don't usually see me *unless* they're in trouble. Now, I can't guarantee to get your father-in-law out of his predicament, but I can at least see that he's treated well, represented fairly, and has every possible advantage the law permits. I'm also here to see that your mother-in-law is neither distressed nor harassed, and that she is comfortable both physically and financially. Anything I can do to help, I will do."

She looked at him with an odd, assessing air. "Are you a Virgo?"

"Not since I was sixteen."

"I meant . . . oh, *very* funny," she said impatiently. "God, I'm sick of that joke."

"Sorry," he said rather stiffly. He'd felt quite witty there for a moment. "I believe I'm a Capricorn, as a matter of fact."

"Oh." She thought about that, quite seriously to all appearances. "Maybe that's a good thing. Capricorns are good at detail work, very determined, very hard-working."

"That doesn't sound like me," he said doubtfully. "I'm lazy as hell."

"Am I supposed to find that reassuring?"

"I haven't the least idea what you would find reassuring, Ms. Partridge," he said, and turned away to scowl at the penthouse on the right-hand side.

She chuckled suddenly. "What do they call you, anyway?"

He grinned, realizing she meant his job title. He could hardly tell her he didn't really have one. "They call me Charles, mostly. Occasionally Tonto."

"Tonto?"

"Spanish for stupid," he explained. "Gives you a whole new insight on the Lone Ranger, doesn't it?"

She looked at him as if she expected him to break out in purple spots and yellow balloons any minute. She opened her mouth to respond, then jumped as if someone had poked her with a sharp stick. Charles, too, was startled, as a cracked voice assailed them, seemingly out of thin air.

"What the devil have they done with Reg? Alastair went down to see him, and the Guardia told him he wasn't there!"

Charles turned around like a lighthouse until he located the source of the noise. Across the gap, on the patio of the penthouse on the left, stood a small elderly man in British Army fatigues, with a spraying apparatus in his hand. Behind him, a long line of geraniums dipped and nodded in the breeze. Some were in the troughs along the top of the parapet, more were in huge stoneware pots ranged on platforms just inside the parapet wall.

"Haven't shot him, have they?" the old man went on jauntily, obviously intending the question as a joke. Holly sucked her breath in suddenly, and Charles spoke quickly and quietly.

"There's no death penalty in Spain anymore. Who the devil is that?"

"Our one friendly neighbour," she said back under her breath, then smiled and raised her voice. "Good morning, Colonel Jackson. I think they've taken him to Espina."

"Espina, hey? What for? Who's that chap with you?" the old man went on, peering quizzically at Charles.

"This is Mr. Llewellyn, from the British Consulate in Alicante," Holly said.

"Ah, that's good. Fine. Whole thing's a ghastly mistake, typical of the Guardia, though I say it myself, being a military man and all. Go for the obvious, bound to, way they're trained. Damned nonsense. Reg wouldn't harm a flea, charmin' man, everybody thinks so. Might have to get up a crowd and storm the place if they don't let him go."

"I don't think that will be necessary, sir," Charles said with a smile. "We should be able to convince a judge to grant bail, pending investigation."

"Whole thing is crazy—said so all along. Man came to rob the place, perfectly obvious, heard Reg come back, ran out here, lost his footing in the dark and . . . whoops, over he went." He waved his watering spray enthusiastically as he expounded this theory, leaving a trail of dark water spots on his trousers and the tiles beneath his sandalled feet. "Damn near gone over myself a couple of times, until I got the pots there. Makes a good inner perimeter, you know, keeps the kiddiewinks safe."

"Colonel Jackson has six grandchildren," Holly explained.

"None here at the moment, though. School holidays over." He seemed to consider this sad truth for a moment, as if looking for a loophole, then nodded. "That's it. They'll be back, soon enough, I dare say. Well, if there's anything we can do, my dear, just say the word, won't you?" He started to turn away.

"Did you hear anything on that night, Colonel?" Charles asked. The old man swung around again, causing another overflow from the watering can.

"Damn," the colonel muttered, shaking his wet foot. "Hear anything the night the chappie went over, you mean? Not a dicky-bird, I'm afraid."

"That's odd, surely?"

"Not really. Weren't here, were we?" Jackson laughed in glee, having successfully trapped Charles into his little joke. "Went to the pictures around seven, don't you know? Sorry now, of course. Perhaps . . ." He paused, then shook his head. "Damn silly film, as it happened. Would have been better off at home, but Queenie insisted. Always go to the pictures on a Tuesday, regular thing. She likes to go out, does Queenie. Can't blame her. Boring for her, only me and my geraniums, once the grandchildren go home. Still . . . she bears up. Good girl, Queenie, damn fine girl. Anything else, young man?"

"I guess not."

"It was the colonel who discovered the body," Holly said softly.

"Oh . . . I didn't realize . . ."

"Wasn't *me* that found the feller," the colonel protested. "Wish it had been. It was Queenie. Always goes around that way . . . started making a terrible fuss, poor old girl. Upset her dreadfully."

"I can imagine," Charles said, feeling sorry for the old woman. Injuries incurred by a 150-foot drop are seldom superficial and usually involve a considerable splashing of blood and bone. He could well imagine she'd been "upset."

"Not over it yet, really," the colonel went on, leaning forward confidently, with a glance over his shoulder towards the open doors of his penthouse. "Won't go near the spot now. Walks all around to avoid it, won't even *look* that way. High-strung, you know. And the Guardia were a bit rough with her."

"You surprise me," Charles said. In male Spanish eyes women were vulnerable and must be protected. "You should have complained . . . we would have been glad to make a protest."

A small grey poodle had trotted out onto the colonel's patio and sat down beside him, regarding them all with bright black eyes.

"Oh, we didn't like to make a fuss," the colonel said modestly. "We're getting over it, aren't we, Queenie?" The poodle looked up at him with patient, intelligent eyes, and yipped once. "Anyway," the colonel went on, "all water under the bridge now as far as we're concerned. It's Reg one has to worry about. Queenie misses him. And Bimla, of course."

"Bimla?" Charles asked Holly, in a strangled voice.

"Reg and Mary have a little dog named Bimla. She's at the vet's at the moment, recovering from an operation on her gall bladder."

"I see."

"The two dogs play together all the time."

"Oh."

"They're great friends," she went on, rubbing it in.

"How nice for them," Charles said, wondering if other people had the occasional impulse to strangle Holly Partridge, or if it was just some genetic weakness in himself.

"Well, give 'em hell, young man," Colonel Jackson advised. "Don't let them walk all over you."

"I'll try not to, sir."

The colonel nodded, then, with a sweet smile at Holly, wandered back to his geraniums. Queenie put her front paws up on the parapet, looked across at them with her unnervingly intelligent black eyes, and yipped a question.

"Not today, Queenie," Holly said, avoiding Charles's eye.

The dog cocked her head on one side, in a gesture strangely reminiscent of her owner, seemed almost to shrug her shoulders, then trotted off after the colonel.

"You might have warned me," Charles said through his teeth.

"Warned you about what?" Holly asked innocently.

"That the old twit was crazy. What about the penthouse on the other side?"

She turned and looked. "That's owned by a German couple, the Neufelds. He's an invalid in a wheelchair, she's younger. And there's a male nurse."

"Old or young?"

She smiled wryly. "You're quick. Mr. Neufeld himself could be any age—he's usually so wrapped up when they wheel him out, you can hardly see anything of him. I think he's pretty well totally paralysed, I've never heard him speak or seen him move much, other than a hand now and again. She's *probably* around thirty-five."

"And beautiful."

"How did you know?" She looked up at him, pushing her hair back as the wind caught it and tugged at her curls.

"Because of your tone. How old is the manservant?"

"Oh, younger. In his twenties. Quite handsome, in fact. He's asked me out once or twice, but . . ."

"Not your type?"

"Let's just say I wouldn't like to have her as an enemy."

"Ah."

"And, anyway, it was one of *them* who told the police about the lights going on in our penthouse at seven forty-five, that night. I'm not exactly feeling friendly towards them at the moment."

Charles regarded the heavy draperies drawn across the windows. "Do you know anything else about them?"

"Well, he's rich, that I *do* know. Sometimes they put the lights on before drawing the curtains, and from what you can see through the windows, they've spent plenty on the furnishings. And these places don't come cheaply, you know."

"Then how come your parents-in-law could afford to buy one? From what I hear of the Old Country, retired civil servants aren't in the super-tax bracket yet."

"They were lucky. When these were first put up, penthouses were a novelty. They knew the builder involved, and got in on the ground floor." She grinned. "In a manner of speaking. Also they got a good price for the house they had in Montana Sol, and Mary came into a small inheritance from an aunt. Reg said at the time they must be fated to have it, everything fell into place so neatly. I don't suppose he'd say that now." Her face clouded momentarily. "Anyway, they've held on to the penthouse, but the other two have changed hands a couple of times, each time nearly doubling the price. The Neufelds bought theirs about eighteen months ago, I guess. I remember the deal was going through when I came over . . . for the funeral."

"Then the possibility that Graebner was a thief isn't as far-fetched as it might be," Charles mused. "You say they have a lot of expensive things over there?"

"Yes, from what we've glimpsed."

"This whole area is becoming more like the Riviera every day—all we lack is a casino," Charles said. "And where the rich are, there the vultures gather. The number of robberies has risen a lot over the past year."

"Well, then he certainly came to the wrong flat," Holly said firmly. "Mary has her rings and a string of pearls and that's about it. No furs. Nothing worth risking his neck for . . . not even a colour television set. They're still making do with an old black and white, although Reg keeps talking about getting a video so they can see some things in English once in a while. Anyway, Reg has two good locks on the door, and it's the only way into the penthouse. One of the drawbacks of living up here is the fact that the guests come in and the garbage goes out through just the one door."

"So he does take precautions?"

"Well, of course. Nobody likes being robbed. My flat in London was ripped off twice, and *I* don't have much worth stealing. It's becoming pretty common back there. It was me who suggested he get the second lock."

"I wonder if I'd like London now," Charles said. "It's beginning to sound more and more like New York or Hong Kong."

"Oh, it's still London," Holly said with deep affection.

"Is that why you stayed after your marriage broke up? Because you like London?"

"I suppose so. All my career contacts are there—I'd have to start up cold if I went back to New York or San Francisco. Anyway, I have a twenty-year lease on the flat, so why should I leave?"

Charles wondered how much of a "career" there could be in embroidering pussy-cats or roses on things. Maybe she had a contract with Ye Olde Gifte Shoppes or something. He brought his thoughts back to the problem at hand. "So on one side you have a crazy old retired colonel and his dog, and on the other a man in a wheelchair, his wife and his male nurse. Is that it?"

"That's it."

"The colonel was out and the Neufelds were in, presumably, since they noticed the lights going on and off. Didn't they notice anything else?"

"They said they were watching a film on their video—a rather noisy war film, apparently. The police seemed to believe them."

It was becoming more and more apparent why the police had seized on Reg Partridge as the only likely suspect, although Charles thought he'd like to know more about this male nurse of the Neufelds.

"Well, I suppose that's all I can do here at the moment. I just wanted to get a better idea of the background and make sure Mrs. Partridge was all right. Will she want to come to Espina to talk to the lawyer?"

"I don't think so . . . and I think I'd better stay with her. Do you mind?"

"Not if I have her authority to choose the best lawyer I can find, and if she'll trust me to do so."

"I'm certain she will."

Charles took a last look around the windswept patio. It would have been hot there, had it not been for the wind off the sea. In the height of summer it would be very nearly intolerable except mornings and evenings. Ah, but the evenings would be wonderful. The velvet darkness closing in, the glitter of the sunset on the water, the lights of the surrounding plains, and the massive mountain-pyramid of Montgo breaking the horizon. He could almost have envied Reg Partridge his rooftop domain.

If a man hadn't been murdered there.

CHAPTER 4

When she had seen Charles out, Holly went along to the darkened master bedroom and looked in. Mary was watching the door and smiled from the pillows. "Has he gone?"

"Yes." Holly came in and sat on the end of the bed.

"What does he think Reg's chances are?"

Holly shrugged. "He didn't say, exactly."

"You were out on the patio for a long time, he must have said *something.*"

"We just talked about the murder and the neighbours and so on. He doesn't really know enough yet, he says. The colonel was out there."

"Oh, dear," Mary said.

"Oh, he was all right, for once." Holly smiled. "At least he didn't go into his usual long song and dance about how just the same thing happened to a friend of his in the regiment, or how they dealt with such things in Darjeeling or Nairobi or wherever it was."

"Hong Kong," Mary said absently. "Do you think he'll help?"

"The colonel?"

"No, dear . . . Mr. Llewellyn. He seemed a nice, reliable sort of man. I feel better now I've seen him, I must say."

"I suppose he'll do. We're stuck with him, anyway, aren't we? I mean, we can hardly ring up and say, 'Look, we don't like the sample you sent us; please send several more so we can make a choice,' can we?"

"Oh, Holly."

"Can't you just see them, lined up in a row, with their umbrellas furled and their Old School Ties carefully . . ."

"Stop it," Mary said. "You're getting carried away."

Holly was pleased to see something like a smile on her mother-in-law's face. "As usual, you mean? He's a Capricorn, you know. They're *very* Old School Tie."

"You asked him his birth sign? Really, Holly, sometimes I despair of you, I really do. For an intelligent girl . . ."

"Oh, I know, you think I'm cracked. It's just a habit, an easy way to work out what people are like. I don't take it *seriously.*" Holly sighed and stood up restlessly. She knew she'd been less than kind to Charles Llewellyn at first, but it had been the situation ruling her. She was so fond of both her parents-in-law, it was agony to see them upset and suffering unjustly. She'd expected the consulate to send someone brisk and efficient. Instead they'd sent him, and although he *looked* all right, and probably spoke excellent Spanish, there had been that fussy little notebook. It worried her. People who took notes were watchers, not doers. And something needed to be *done*.

"Can I get you anything?"

Mary shook her head. "No, thanks. I think I *will* be able to sleep, now that I know Mr. Llewellyn's doing something."

Holly nodded vaguely, but went out without commenting.

Washing up the coffee things, Holly stared out at the baking-hot beige and green vista of fields and olive groves, with the brooding hulk of Montgo looming on the horizon on the right. What a strange outlook, so different to the woodsy view from the Partridge's flat outside Reading or her own London flat. This land was so bleak, so dry, so glaring in every sense. How odd that Mary and Reg, quintessentially British, should come here.

How odd that *she* should be here, for that matter.

Always out of place, that's me, she thought ruefully. Always a stranger in a strange land. American-born, English resident, now washing dishes in Spain.

And all because of David.

Dark, intense, sophisticated, sarcastic, even demonic. And yet he'd had kindness in him (much to his own embarrassment), and goodness (vigorously denied), and fun (how mundane).

Then one day the public David, all rebellion and intellectual derision, had taken over the private David, too. And the fun had stopped.

She still didn't understand why. Of course, he'd always maintained that she was basically naive. Out of all the recriminations and accusations he'd hurled at her, one still remained to pierce her carefully built-up armour of confidence.

"You only see the surface, never the substance," he'd said. It was why she'd taken up embroidery, which was all to do with surface, and "said" nothing, "explored" nothing. He was probably right, she conceded, ready even now to bow to his superior insight. What lurked beneath the skin of other people had always frightened her. Her volatile temperament, attributed glibly to her red hair, had always had more to do with defence than aggression. She went at things simply to prevent them getting at her.

Her delightfully impractical mother had evolved a philosophy to deal with torn hems and missing buttons: "Walk fast and no one will notice." Holly had extended it to cover her entire life. Lately, however, she'd begun to wonder if by walking fast she was missing some things along the way.

She put the last cup on the rack and dried her hands. Then, with her work calling her but feeling disinclined to leave Mary alone, she went out onto the patio and dragged a deck chair over to the white table that stood in the corner, putting up its umbrella to shade her fair skin. After sitting down for two minutes she was up again, to find a book and make herself a cold drink, before going back outside. After another two minutes she let the book drop and stared at the sea, the unwatered plants, the battered table. The latter could really do with some attention—there was paint scraped off the legs all the way around. She wondered where Reg kept his paints and then decided it was too much like hard work. The plants . . . Mary usually watered the plants every day. All of them were drooping in the relentless heat and some of them were quite flattened, poor things. She went back into the house yet again and returned with a jug of water. She poured life into the trough all around the patio wall, then stood back. There. The colonel would approve, she thought, glancing over at his precious geraniums. They were all healthy and blooming, nodding in the breeze from the sea, their colours bright in the sun. Mary's more modest display seemed slightly pathetic by comparison. Oh well, Holly thought in her defence, that's all the colonel has to do with his time, look after his damned geraniums.

Holly had always been amazed and slightly exhausted by Reg and Mary's constant social round, never understanding how they kept going, or why. She preferred quieter pleasures. Dinner with Mel Tinker, a swim at the club with drinks after a film. He was trying to teach her chess (David had tried, too, but usually had ended up throwing the pieces across the room in exasperation). She liked Mel. He'd become a little insistent and possessive lately—in fact, he'd been pretty insistent from the day they'd met. He was rather like David in that respect. They overwhelmed you. She was rather tired of being overwhelmed.

Although she'd only known him for a short time, he'd tried to monopolize her every moment, and she'd been glad at times to be able to plead her work as an excuse not to see him. Nobody seemed to understand that she preferred to be alone. That she'd discovered the pleasures of solitude and was loath to relinquish them. No one accused you of anything. No one demanded anything. No one made decisions for you. No one had to be considered except yourself. Selfish, yes, but decidedly and luxuriously satisfying. Some people found the word "alone" terrifying. David had. She rather thought Mary and Reg did, too. She didn't.

At least, she never had until now.

She forced her eyes back to the book, but it gradually dropped into her lap, and she found herself gazing out to sea again. The man from the consulate was going to take care of everything. Soon she could stop feeling helpless and guilty about being able to do nothing for Reg and Mary except make coffee and bad jokes to lighten the tension. The man from the consulate would find a lawyer, and things would be cleared up and Reg would come home and everything would be fine. The man from the consulate knew the ropes. He'd take care of everything. He'd handle it.

Wouldn't he?

Charles had never felt quite so inadequate before.

The case against Reg Partridge didn't seem to have much to offer a lawyer. Of course, the Guardia had only done a preliminary investigation, but their conclusions were round and hard and smooth—weapon, motive, and opportunity, all accounted for, with only Partridge's insistence on his innocence to counter it. Charles wanted nothing more than to go back to Alicante and put his head under the covers for about a month. He'd been looking forward to taking some time off just about now, after the hectic rush of the summer season.

Driving along the road across the little peninsula to Espina, he pondered the best course to take on this one. If he found a good *abogado* in Espina, there might be a chance he'd find a way to get Partridge out on bail. On the other hand, if he waited until Partridge was transferred to Alicante, he could get a better lawyer than whatever he might find in Espina. But could Partridge take those extra days? That was the question.

He parked outside the Provisional Detention Prison in Espina and went in, producing his credentials yet again. This time he got a better reception, for he'd been here fairly often in the past few years. It was only some twenty minutes or so before he was taken to Partridge's retention room, a new record. When he got there, he saw why things had been expedited. Partridge was not alone.

The man who stood up when the *carcelero* let Charles into the room was slim and elegantly dressed in a midnight-blue suit, white shirt and dark-crimson tie. His shoes were polished to a mirror shine, and across his waistcoat there was draped a gold chain. His face was high-boned and aristocratic, his hair black save for an almost theatrical streak of white that ran just beside the widow's peak that made his face into an elongated heart-shape.

"My God, what the hell are *you* doing here?" Charles burst out before he could stop himself.

The man smiled. "It's been a long time, Carlos. How is your life in exile proceeding?"

Charles hesitated a moment, then took the outstretched hand and shook it enthusiastically, grinning all over his face. "Never mind that, why are *you* here? You haven't been exiled too, have you?"

Don Esteban López of the Policía Judicial shook his head. "No, my friend, nothing like that. I am on a temporary transfer, that is all. Supposedly to aid in a provincial training programme, but actually for my health."

"You're not ill, are you? You look fine."

A faint smile lifted the corners of Don Esteban's mobile mouth. "Not my health in that sense, Carlos. 'Continued health,' let us say. A matter of threats, you understand. Some of these terrorist organizations don't seem to understand one is only doing one's job. They take it so personally if you arrest one of their precious kind."

"Ah, I see." It wasn't the first time, Charles recalled, that López had been on a hit-list. He was honest and he was fair, but he was also ruthless.

"And this is my new assistant, Paco Bas," López said, turning.

In the corner stood a singularly ugly young man, short and stocky, with black close-cropped hair and the face of a resentful bull-calf. He seemed wedged into, rather than dressed in, a brown suit and shoes, and he held his short arms stiffly at his sides.

"Paco," said Don Esteban, "this is Señor Charles Llewellyn of the British Consulate. He and I knew one another in Madrid some years ago. He is a very stubborn man."

"Señor Llewellyn," Bas grated, as if unused to speaking, and gave an awkward little bow. "I am happy to make your acquaintance."

"And I, yours, Señor Bas," Charles said. Paco Bas would have been a frightening item to meet in a dark alley, but in a well-lit alley one could see his eyes, and therefore would have felt no fear. They were the eyes of a child in a bull's face. Candid, mild, and patient, they showed—at the moment—both humour and unease. Charles knew instinctively that Paco Bas was from a small village in this or a nearby province, that he had probably done well at school but been shy and possibly much teased by his fellows, had recently joined the Judicial Police, and was both terrified by and in awe of López, who was probably his first "mentor." The boy was lucky.

And so, perhaps, was Partridge.

"Mr. Partridge, your wife sent your medicine," Charles said, handing over the large brown glass bottle. "And her love. Your daughter-in-law is with her, and they're both doing just fine."

"Thank God for that," Partridge said. Charles wasn't sure if his relief stemmed from the sight of his medicine or the report on his nearest and dearest. What concerned him most was Partridge's appearance, which had definitely deteriorated. "If you'll excuse me . . ." Partridge said apologetically and, opening the bottle, he put it to his lips and took down several gulps of the liquid inside. Wiping his lips with a paper towel, he sighed. "Usually one isn't so . . . lacking in grace," he said. "But I lack a spoon, and quite a bit of the dignity I seemed to have only yesterday." With a faint smile, he carefully placed the bottle on the small shelf over the basin and reseated himself on the edge of the bunk with a little shudder.

"Well, Señor Partridge," López said, "I hope I have answered your questions, and I thank you for answering mine. The transfer to Alicante will take place in the next day or so, and I suggest you rest as much as possible until then. I regret there is no separate accommodation there for foreigners, but I am sure you will be treated well."

"Thank you," Partridge said, without looking up. He seemed, since Charles had seen him a few hours ago, to have aged about ten years.

"I shall stay in Espina until you're transferred, Mr. Partridge," Charles said, which was news to him as well as to everyone else. López raised an eyebrow, but said nothing. "I'll give my phone number to the *carcelero* so that you can get in touch with me at any time—and I'll make certain your wife has all she needs. I'll be getting you an *abogado* sometime today, and I expect he'll be along either this evening or tomorrow morning." He realized that he was speaking slowly and at a slightly higher volume than normal, as if Partridge were a senile old man. He lowered his tone and tried to speak more naturally, but wasn't sure if Partridge was listening to him or to something going on inside himself. "I have several men in mind . . . it's a matter of finding out who's free to take the case . . ."

Partridge looked up, and Charles saw a glint of laughter in his eyes. "And who's prepared to take a chance," he said. "According to Señor López, I should plead guilty."

Charles looked at López in surprise, but López shook his head. "I only told you it was an alternative to consider, Señor Partridge. The court might well be lenient in your case, considering Graebner's background, your age and your previous record . . ."

"I'd prefer it to take into account the fact that I didn't kill the man," Partridge said mildly.

"I understand, señor," López said. "And now, if you'll excuse us . . ."

"I'd like a word with you before you go," Charles said.

López glanced from Charles to the hunched figure of Partridge and nodded toward the door. When the *carcelero* had let them out, they walked a little way down the corridor, speaking quietly. Paco Bas came behind, saying nothing.

"Esteban, he is a very sick man," Charles said. "He has an ulcer."

"He said nothing to me about it."

"Stiff upper lip and all that," Charles said with a wry smile.

"Ah, of course. You are so Spanish, you English." López grinned. Then the grin faded. "I will speak to the *carcelero* and ask that he be given a special diet. Perhaps it would also be a good idea to have a doctor visit before we move him to Alicante."

"It would be an even better idea to let him out on bail," Charles said.

López pursed his lips briefly. "We are talking about murder, Carlos, not a traffic offence."

"We are talking about a sixty-eight-year-old ulcer-sufferer who is supposed to have stabbed a younger, stronger and bigger man, picked his body up and hurled him off a roof, and then driven to a bridge tournament where he came in top," Charles said pointedly.

"I have not had an opportunity as yet to review the evidence gathered by the Guardia," López said carefully. "You go too fast . . ."

"Well, I leave the evidence to your logical brain," Charles said. "Your heart would be a better bet, perhaps. That's a sick man, Esteban. Being in jail isn't making him any better, I promise you. His son died before getting to court; I'd hate to see his father go the same way."

"Indeed, so would I."

"Then you'll do what you can about getting him released on bail?" Charles asked eagerly.

"I did not say that. I will make sure he has good medical care while he is in my charge, obviously. But bail is not *my* decision, Carlos, you know that. It is up to the judge—"

"Who listens to your recommendations," Charles interrupted.

López smiled. "That is so. I will examine the evidence, Carlos. I will consider your suggestion. I can say no more."

"I ask no more," Charles said. "But what I do ask, I ask for his sake."

"Still the bleeding heart, then?" López laughed. "You are always the romantic, Carlos, even in your exile." He glanced at his watch, then turned to Bas. "Tell them we will require a room to work in, Paco."

"*Sí.*" Bas thumped off.

López watched him go, and shook his head. "Why they gave me this one I have yet to discover," he said mournfully, then glanced at Charles. "I had dinner with Doña María before I left Madrid last month, Carlos. And with her husband, of course."

"Oh?" Charles said in a flat voice.

"She is as beautiful and as wicked as ever. There are rumours of another

. . . protégé . . . but she has learned discretion, at last. Enrique is as blind and as powerful as ever, and so on she goes."

"Nothing changes," Charles said, looking out of a barred window at the gulls flapping above the harbour.

"On the contrary, many things change, Carlos. Would you come back to Madrid if the opportunity offered itself?"

"Is it likely to?"

"One hears things. I gather you've done well here."

"I haven't been a naughty boy, if that's what you mean," Charles said bitterly. "I, too, have learned discretion. At last."

"And would you go back?"

"I . . . don't know," Charles admitted. "There's something rather attractive about the thought of frittering away the rest of my working life on the beach."

López snorted. "And how often do you get to the beach, my friend? You're as pale as a fish's belly below the collar, I'll wager."

"You'd lose." Charles smiled. "Let's just say I'm not all that keen to rejoin what passes for society in Madrid these days. Perhaps I'm too old. I've lost my taste for competition. I shall grow old gracefully instead."

"It sounds to me as if you've already begun to do just that." López scowled. He turned as Bas reappeared. "Well, Paco? What news on the Rialto?"

"Sir?"

López sighed. "Is there a room we can use?"

"Sí. The papers are waiting there now."

"Very good." López turned to Charles. "I will review the position, Carlos. I promise nothing, you understand."

"I understand. Thank you."

López shrugged. "And where are you staying, that I might reach you?"

"I don't know—I'll have to find somewhere. I'll be in touch."

CHAPTER 5

Charles found a local *fonda* and got a room. He'd learned always to keep a packed suitcase in the boot of the Seat, and he carried it up the stairs to the room, which was sparingly furnished and immaculately clean. As it was off-season, he could have afforded to stay at one of the larger modern hotels, but he preferred a *fonda* where he was able to speak and polish his Spanish. As always, the proprietor was delighted to have an Englishman who spoke his own language so well. The Spaniards were justly resentful of the many foreigners who flooded the area, lived there, but made no effort to learn even the rudiments of Spanish. And, as Charles had learned, it was a graceful, lyrical language that fell gently on the ear when spoken slowly. One of the problems was that the Spaniards themselves delivered the words as if from a machine-gun, at top speed and volume, daunting beginners and often stumping even those with an ear for linguistics. As a result, every Spanish conversation sounds like an argument.

Charles opened the case and took out the shirts, unspeakably crumpled from their long incarceration. Running some water into the small basin in the corner of the room, he soaked them, put them on hangers, and hung them in front of the open window. In a few hours they would be completely dry and fresh. That taken care of, he stood in the middle of the room and tried to decide whether to get something to eat or to rest. He'd been up since three that morning, and decided that food on top of all that driving and talking would be a mistake. And his mid-section could certainly stand to miss a meal.

As he lay down on the bed with his hands behind his head and stared at the ceiling, López's question about going back to Madrid immediately surfaced and obliterated everything else. Did he want that? The work would be more varied and more important, and instead of hovering impotently, his career might begin to ascend again.

To what?

Did he really want to work his butt off merely to end his life eagerly hoping the next Honours List would have something for him? And would Madrid be fun? He'd discovered, down here, that fun *was* all it was cracked up to be. Oh, not the mannered, sophisticated entertainments of society, but natural, open pleasure. What was that poem by Ezra Pound? He'd memorized it, because it summed up the attitude he'd developed in his "exile."

> O generation of the thoroughly smug
>   and thoroughly uncomfortable,
> I have seen fishermen picnicking in the sun,
> I have seen them with untidy families,
> I have seen their smiles full of teeth
>   and heard ungainly laughter.
> And I am happier than you are,
> And they were happier than I am;

And the fish swim in the lake
and do not even own clothing.

Madrid was full of tidy, gainly laughter. And the prospect bored him suddenly. How he had ached at first to be there, and how cruel his exile had seemed. Then gradually he'd realized that he loved Spain, and Madrid wasn't Spain at all. It was a capital city and therefore international. He'd had enough of capital cities. And yet . . . he'd made few friends down here. In Madrid he'd been part of the free-wheeling society of the rich, the famous, and the relatively idle, only by virtue of his position at the embassy, which was an *entrada* to even the most exclusive circles. He'd known everyone it was right to know. And, of course, he'd been attractive and single and light-hearted there. He glanced over at the mirror above the small pine bureau.

Now you're paunchy, balding and tired. You've spent all your time here looking and learning, just an observer. Solitary most of the days and most of the nights, you've immersed yourself in Spain as in some warm, solacing bath. And you're afraid to go back to Madrid.

It's a different country, and you're a different man.

He fell into a restless, unsatisfactory sleep, with the warm air from the window flowing over him, the shirts on their hangers clinking gently and flapping like sails in the breeze, the sounds of the street below distant and random; he woke with a dry mouth and an aching head.

After a wash he felt better, and changed into one of the fresh shirts, hanging the rest on the pegs behind the curtain that served as a wardrobe. Then he went out to find a telephone.

Lining up his coins on the ledge, he dialled the consulate in Alicante, and got through to Baker. Gritting his teeth, he explained the position.

"Look, it's a bit hairy down here. He's been moved to Espina and the Judicial Police have taken over already. The evidence against him is pretty strong."

"Did he do it?" Baker wanted to know. Very basic, old Baker.

"I can't see him killing anyone, but then I'm no expert."

"Not a bad judge, though, old man. You must do what you can to get him off," Baker came back enthusiastically. But then Baker would be enthusiastic about anything that kept Charles away from the consulate for a few days. So much could be done to consolidate his growing influence there, without the dry sarcasm and unarguable experience of one Charles Llewellyn. Charles scowled. Baker was a gung-ho type who believed a firm stand was the answer to everything. Organization and rules, that was the way to deal with these Spanish boys, he was convinced. He seemed totally unable to comprehend that the only men whom the Spanish allowed the luxury of direct confrontation were the bullfighters and the footballers, who took on that responsibility for the nation. Even there, it was not their strength that was admired, but their skill and guile at outwitting the adversary. Guile, style, and an airy refusal to see anyone's point of view but their own—that was the Spanish. They would forgive you for besting them if you did it in style—but they wouldn't forget it.

"It might take some time," Charles said.

"Never mind, we'll stagger along without you somehow," Baker said in a tone meant to be reassuring. Suddenly Charles had a moment of beautiful realization. Left to his own devices, Baker would probably alienate every Spaniard the consulate had business with in days. Then, when Charles came back and smoothed it all out, who would look good? Not Baker. Charles wouldn't have had such a Machiavellian and thoroughly nasty thought if it hadn't been for the note of absolute delight in Baker's nasal voice.

"Well . . ." Charles said slowly. "If you don't mind . . . I'd like to see it through."

"Splendid," Baker said. "You do your best for him, and let me know if you need anything."

"Thanks very much," Charles said. "I'd like the list of English-speaking *abogados* in Espina, please."

"What—right now?"

"Right now. I'll hang on." He watched the telephone devour another couple of fifty-peseta coins, and Baker eventually grumbled his way to give him two names, Ribes and Henriquez.

"That's all?" Charles asked, scribbling them down.

"That's all on our list," Baker said.

"Any comments?"

"Someone says Ribes is 'aggressive,' whatever that means."

"It means I'll try him first," Charles said.

"Enjoy yourself," Baker said expansively. "Soak up the sun, old son." He chortled.

"I'll try." Charles hung up the phone, only just remembering in time to snatch up the last coin before the telephone made a final grab. When automation becomes animation, one had to be quick, even in Spain.

Two hours later he parked in front of the wall that surrounded the gardens of 400 Avenida de la Playa. He walked in through the "gate," and wandered between the palm trees spurting up from their small patches of sandy earth and the massive tubs of flowers that crouched in the shadows of early evening like crested toads. He went over to where Graebner had been found, judging it by looking up and aligning himself with the central tower. It was pretty obvious that the body had to have come from there and not from either of the others. The angle and distance were too great, and dead bodies are not noted for their ability to glide. Glancing around, he could also see how the body might have lain there for some time unnoticed. The path into the building was straight from the gate, and the area was shielded by the plants and trees. Indeed, had it not been for the natural instincts of a poodle, Graebner might well have lain there until morning.

Had somebody counted on that?

He took the lift up to the penthouse. As he raised his hand to ring the bell, he made a discovery. There seemed to be a party going on.

He could hear many voices and the clink of glasses.

He rang again, and eventually the door opened. He found himself staring at yet another stranger. A man in an open-necked shirt and tan trousers looked questioningly at him, a glass of what seemed to be gin and tonic in one hand, and the traces of several others in his brown eyes.

"I've come to see Mrs. Partridge. I'm from the British Consulate."

"Oh." The man backed away and motioned him in. "She's in the lounge with the others."

Charles came in. "Others?"

"Friends. Came to do what we could. Terrible thing for her, their arresting Reg like that. Good mind to go down there myself, and tell them a thing or two about handling suspects."

"And who are you?"

"Nigel Bland. Glad to meet you."

Charles shook the proffered hand. "Charles Llewellyn. What do you know about handling suspects?"

"Plenty. Scotland Yard, retired." Bland led the way proprietarily down the narrow hall.

The lounge was full of people. It took Charles a moment to locate Mary Partridge who, in fact, was in the same chair she'd been in when he left that morning. She had changed into a dark-blue dress in the interim. Her face was even paler, and she had a slightly hunted look that reached out to him across the room. He went over, and as he did so the conversation in the room slowly dwindled.

"How is he?" Mary demanded.

He bent down slightly, keeping his voice low. "They've moved him to quite comfortable quarters in Espina, and the Judicial Police have taken over the case. I know the man in charge, whose name is López. He's honest and fair-minded. He's making sure your husband is treated well, and is arranging a special diet and a doctor to look in on him before they move him to Alicante. Please don't worry."

"Don't worry?" came a voice from behind him. "My God, how can she not worry when her man is in jail for murdering?"

Charles glanced over his shoulder. A tall, florid woman in a tight dress was glaring at him. He started to say something to her, then thought better of it, and turned back to Mary Partridge. "I've managed to get an excellent lawyer for him, who may be able to establish bail. I've also spoken to López myself about bail, on compassionate grounds—your husband's age and health. He has a good record, of course, and that helps."

"But . . . if they don't . . . then he'll have to go to Alicante?"

"I'm afraid so."

"Can't you bribe someone?" This from the woman behind him again.

Charles straightened up and faced her. "I'm afraid that's out of the question."

"Not 'done' by the so-nice British, is that it?" she sneered.

He detected, now, a faint accent. German, perhaps, or Dutch. She'd have to say more for him to be certain, but he didn't look forward to it. Like the man who'd admitted him, she seemed to have had a fair quantity to drink. *He'd* been friendly—she was not.

"On the contrary, I'm quite prepared to bribe people if I thought it would work. It won't."

"Why not?" she demanded.

"Have you lived in Spain for very long?" he asked quietly.

"A year or so. But everyone appreciates money, even the Spanish."

"Oh, especially the Spanish—they have so little of it. But they don't appreciate an insult, and I assure you, offering someone a bribe would be construed as an insult, and would only ensure that Mr. Partridge stayed in custody even longer."

"I don't believe you," she said flatly, her eyes and mouth sullen.

"Have you had any dealings with the Spanish police, madam?"

"No."

"Then . . ."

"He's quite right, Maddie," a man said, coming up. He was tall and fair and didn't seem to have been drinking at all. "The Spaniards are *not* like other people, and especially not like the people *you're* used to dealing with." He glanced at Charles and smiled. "Maddie used to live in Lebanon."

"Ah," Charles said, and nodded.

"What do Reg's chances look like?" the fair-haired man asked. "My name's Morland, by the way. Alastair Morland."

"Charles Llewellyn," Charles said automatically. "If you mean his chances of getting off, I couldn't say. His chances for being treated fairly are excellent. I know the man in charge now. His name is López and—"

"Not El Águila?"

Charles looked at him in surprise. "I believe that's a nickname he has," he admitted. "Do you know him?"

"Dear God," Morland murmured.

"Why? What's wrong with this López man?" came Mary Partridge's anxious voice from the chair beside him. Both men turned.

"Nothing's *wrong* with him, Mary dear," Morland said quickly. "By all accounts, he's an honest and excellent policeman, as Mr. Llewellyn said."

"Then why did you say 'Dear God' like that?" she wanted to know, her voice quavering. Charles wondered, too.

"Because, my little love, it's said that once he catches his prey, they stay in the nest. If he refuses Reg bail, it will be because he's very sure of his case." He turned again to Charles, apparently unaware of the effect his words were having on Mary Partridge, who was looking paler by the minute. *"Does* he have a good case?" Morland asked Charles.

"There seems to be a certain amount of physical evidence," Charles said cautiously. "I'll know more after the lawyer has looked at it. They aren't inclined to tell a mere consular representative very much." He looked down at Mary Partridge. "I really think you ought to be getting some rest. Your daughter-in-law said she was going to call your doctor this morning. Did he come?"

"Oh yes, he came," Mary Partridge said, her knuckles white where she clutched the arm of the chair. "He gave me some tablets and said to sleep— but I can't."

"Not with all this din, you can't," Charles agreed. "Who the devil are they all, anyway?"

"Friends," Mary said wearily. "They only came because they were worried and wanted to help."

"We want to do all we can for poor Reggie," said Maddie, who was still standing there, listening avidly. "And for dear Mary—she has only to ask and I will do all for her. Shopping, cleaning . . . whatever."

"That's not necessary," Mary protested.

"Well, you have only to ask . . ." Maddie said reproachfully.

"Oh, I am grateful, Maddie, it's very kind of you to offer."

Charles could see that what was really wearing Mary Partridge out at the moment was having to be grateful to everyone. The people in the room seemed to be mostly English, with a few other nationalities thrown in, but no Spaniards. He had no doubt that the motivations of everyone in the room were kind, and that they were truly concerned about Mary and Reg. But the English instinct to "rally round" was exhausting Mary, and in any case had become rather like a wake. As the gathering had grown, people had begun carrying on their own conversations. Nigel Bland, no doubt at Mary's request, had taken over duties as a barman and everyone had a drink. Another woman (Mrs. Bland?) was passing and clearing ashtrays, but the whole thing was getting a little out of hand. Morland seemed to sense this, too.

"Have to tread carefully," he said sotto voce. "Don't want to offend anyone."

"I'll leave it to you then," Charles said.

"Righto." Morland accepted the assignment of bouncer cheerfully enough, and began moving through the room slowly, pausing to have a word here and there. Charles turned back to Mary.

"I think they'll be gone soon. Then you can get some sleep. Why don't you slip away now?"

She seemed shocked by the suggestion. "Oh, no . . . I have to say goodbye, they've all been so kind to come . . ."

Charles felt like shaking her. She was obviously the kind of woman in whom social obligation died slowly. Indeed, it seemed to require killing. "Your only concern should be for yourself," he said brusquely. "You won't do your husband any good if you're worn out. He needs your strength and support now . . . not airs and graces."

"Yes, well, of course," she murmured. "But it will only take a moment . . ." She glanced up at him and smiled. He realized, abruptly, that she would have her own way. In fact, now that he looked at her more closely, he thought she probably had her own way most of the time, but it rarely showed. Spain was no doubt a natural home for her. Like the Spanish, she adroitly avoided direct confrontation. They slipped away like melon seeds, these women, whenever you tried to exert any pressure on them. A will of iron? Most certainly. And so charmingly, so delicately expressed that you never realized you were being manipulated until it was over, and there you stood in the corner with no way out. Nevertheless, he knew she had no malice in her, and took no pleasure in power. She simply saw it as doing what was necessary, if she thought about it at all. He guessed she had a very high IQ, and at present a very limited outlet for it. When he learned later that she had been a mathematics teacher, he was not in the least surprised.

"Where is your daughter-in-law?" Charles asked, looking around.

"Oh, she went down to her flat a little while ago to change her clothes," Mary said.

"She does not approve of us," put in Maddie scornfully.

"That's not true," Mary said, defending her adopted cub with a sudden show of spirit. "She had some work to do."

"Hah . . . work!" Maddie snorted. What she meant Charles couldn't have said, but the look on her face offered several alternative explanations, none of them particularly flattering to Holly Partridge.

"Can we ring her to come back up?" Charles asked, feeling the need of an ally. Certainly, on the evidence of that morning, Holly's concern for her parents-in-law ran deep and warm.

"No, she had the phone cut off. It distracted her," Mary said. The first of her guests were approaching for their take-away portion of thanks. "It's flat 804."

"Right," Charles said. He was glad, in a way, for he wanted to discuss with Holly what he had done about the lawyer. It could have been brilliant, or it could have been a total disaster.

Either way, someone should be told, and Mary Partridge was in neither the position nor the condition to deal with it.

As he knocked at the door of 804, he could hear music coming from within. Another party? No—the music was classical, and there were no voices. When the door opened with that abruptness that seemed characteristic of Holly, he discovered she wore glasses, which she snatched off quickly.

"Oh, it's you." She gave a kind of stretch and shake, and Charles was reminded of a swimmer coming up for air. Her hair was dishevelled and little bits of thread haphazardly decorated her faded sweatshirt and jeans. "Come in," she said. "Sorry to be so dopey—I was working."

He followed her in. The entrance hall of this apartment was no more than a tiny square, unlike the penthouse above. She went through an archway and he followed, quite unprepared for the sight he encountered. He was so stunned he stopped dead, literally gaping. It was a very undignified attitude for a consular official, but it took him several minutes to realize it.

Almost every stick of furniture in the room had been removed. All that remained was one easy chair and one floor lamp, smack in the middle of the floor. Before them, a large low table that looked rather like an old-fashioned chemist's shelving laid on its back and given legs. Its entire surface was made up of small compartments, each of which overflowed with skeins and balls of wool, cotton and silk in varying textures. The entire thing was laid out neatly in the spectrum, beginning with white and palest yellow in the upper left-hand corner and progressing through all the colours in turn, to end in brown and black at the lower right. Charles only noticed it belatedly, for what had held his eye initially held it for a very long time.

He felt visually deafened.

Three of the four walls were invisible, for in front of them, on tall structures of metal tubing, were stretched three tapestries. He realized instantly that they were meant to show Winter, Spring, and Summer, although how he knew it was purely instinctive, for they were not pictorial but abstract. The third tapestry was incomplete, and in front of it a ladder-like structure stood. It was obviously meant to represent Summer, and the hot reds and oranges blazed at him. He could practically feel heat pouring from the surface. He also saw why Holly had been so off-hand when he'd made his inane comment about petit point. This might be embroidery, but it bore no resemblance to those prickly little cushion-covers his mother used to turn out.

His eyes informed him it was embroidery, and also collage, and some other techniques he didn't know. The result was stunning.

The Winter tapestry was in icy blues and greys, with metallic threads and crystalline beads overlaid in lacy cobwebbed patterns. The tapestries were apparently meant to go around a room, as they did here, for the leading edge of the Winter tapestry seemed to be starting to thaw—under the cold colours ran a suggestion of the young willowy greens and pale yellows that predominated in the Spring pattern, along with traces of all the other pastels found in those burgeoning months. The leading edge of Spring seemed to wither and dry into the hot glaring colours of the incomplete Summer. Each of the tapestries was easily three by four yards in area, massive efforts. And yet, as Charles noted from the one closest to him, Winter, the work was detailed and meticulous. The whole effect was richly satisfying. He wanted to go on looking and discovering for hours.

"Thank you," said Holly quietly beside him.

He gave a start and focused on her. "I didn't say anything."

She smiled. "Not out loud, no. But you said something."

"I had no idea . . . I mean . . . when you said *embroidery* . . . I just assumed . . ." He suddenly felt foolish, and cleared his throat of its confusion. "It *is* a bit overwhelming."

"Oh, sure," Holly agreed in a practical tone. "They're intended for the four walls of a Borough Council chamber, maybe three or four times bigger than this one. When I got the commission I knew I'd be in trouble eventually. My studio in Hampstead was just too small. Doing *two* panels there was all right . . . but I need them all out like this to get the relationships right. No matter how carefully you plan something on paper, when you grade it up, it changes a lot. I thought I was going to have to break the bank and rent a loft somewhere, but then Reg suggested I come here. The flat belongs to a friend of theirs who's spending a year in the States. I have to be out by May, though, because . . ."

"Because of the summer lets." Charles nodded. It was the usual pattern for residents like the Partridges to spend the winter months in Spain, away from the ice and cold, and then finance that stay by the colossal rents their flats or villas could command in the summer. He looked round. "What are you going to do when you get to the Autumn one?" he asked curiously. "If you put it in front of the window you'll cut off your light."

"I know," she said mournfully. "I think I'll put them diagonally then, and let them overlap. It should be all right. Would you like a drink?"

"No thanks. I've just been upstairs."

"Oh." She scowled. "I know what you mean. It's the old blitz spirit, you know. All hands to the pump to put out the fire."

"Yes. I think it might be a good idea if you came back up."

She brought her glasses down from her forehead, peered at him for a moment through the big round lenses, then pushed them up again with a sigh. "I knew it the minute I saw your face. That's really why you've come down here, isn't it? Whatever it is, you can't tell Mary."

"Sort of. Maybe I will have that drink, after all."

The faint sprinkling of freckles across the bridge of her nose stood out more prominently. "Is it that bad? Maybe I'd better have one, too. Sit down." She indicated the chair. He hesitated, and she smiled. "I'll just go on working while you talk, if you don't mind. It . . . helps me."

"Oh . . . fine," he said, relieved, and sat down. He didn't think it would be easy to face those turquoise eyes when he explained what he'd done. When she'd brought him a glass of wine and a plate of cheese and biscuits (why did Americans always feed you when they watered you? he wondered), she carried her own glass up the ladder-like platform and resumed work. She sat about six feet up, the wineglass beside her on the rubber-faced top step, her bare feet dangling like a child's, and dropped her glasses back down onto her nose. "Shoot," she said over her shoulder.

"I've retained an *abogado* named Ribes," he said abruptly.

Her needle, about to plunge once more into the heavy canvas, froze. She turned around and glared at him. "Ribes? *Pedro* Ribes?"

"Yes."

"But . . . but . . . he was *Graebner's* lawyer . . ."

"Yes," Charles said. "I know."

CHAPTER 6

"You must be joking," Holly said.

"No." Charles put his drink down on the floor. "Look, it makes a lot of sense, when you think about it."

"Oh?" Her tone was as icy as the images in the tapestry behind him.

"I mean, he said the same thing you did immediately—that he'd been Graebner's lawyer, I mean. He was very open about it. But that's an advantage, because he knows all the background without having to have it explained to him." An advantage he wished he'd had himself. "And when I questioned him, it turns out that he was assigned to Graebner by the Court. He only visited him once, in the hospital; he was covered in bandages then and barely conscious."

"Ribes or Graebner?" she asked sarcastically.

He ignored that. "The point is, he simply advised Graebner that, in his view, considering the state he was in, his best bet would be to plead guilty and get the whole thing over with. Otherwise he'd have had all his time in hospital plus the trial afterwards, plus any sentence that might come if he was found guilty."

"Well, I suppose that makes sense," Holly conceded. "From Graebner's point of view, anyway."

"Exactly. As far as Ribes is concerned, it was just another case assigned to him, in which he advised a client in that client's best interest, without any personal involvement. Once Graebner agreed, it was really just a matter of paper-pushing."

"How did he agree, if he was so ill?"

"He was conscious, his brain was clear, Ribes said. There was no question of any coercion or influence being exerted. The man knew what he was doing." Charles considered for a moment. "He was taking the easy way out. Can you blame him?"

"Yes." Her needle jabbed into the canvas.

"Oh yes, I forgot. You and Mr. Partridge blame him for . . ."

The needle darted in and out as she filled in an area of clear yellow. "I'd like to meet him."

"Why?"

"I just want to be sure, that's all. It's not that I don't trust you, but—"

"He's a Leo," Charles said abruptly.

"How do you know that?" She turned on the ladder, amazed.

"I asked him."

"And he told you, just like that?"

"I told him you were crazy. He didn't seem bothered."

"Didn't you feel like a fool, asking him that?"

"Yes. But I knew you'd want to know."

She regarded him from her perch. She just didn't know what to make of Charles Llewellyn. He wasn't much above five ten, and fairly compactly built, with light-brown hair and grey eyes, and seemed so . . . so . . . well, a bit vague really. He dropped things. There, he'd dropped another biscuit onto the floor. The man was an amiable idiot, he must be. Pleasant enough, yes. And obviously fluent in Spanish, so he couldn't be totally stupid. But he didn't seem to understand what was going on here. He seemed defeated before he even started. No wonder England is going down the drain, she thought. You'd think the Foreign Office would have more sense. They couldn't *really* believe a neat appearance and a nice smile were all a diplomat needed, could they? Well, she wasn't going to allow him to let Reg down. She really wasn't. "We're going to have to do this ourselves."

"Do what?" He was still retrieving bits of cheese from the floor.

"Get Reg off. Find the real killer."

He looked up at her, appalled.

Oh, God, he thought. Oh, God, God, God. I *knew* she was going to say that.

The next morning, Charles collected Holly and they drove over to Espina to visit Reg. When they walked into the cell-like room, Reg looked angrily at Charles.

"I told you not to let her come."

"You told him not to let Mary come," Holly said firmly, but her face was slightly paler than it had been a moment before. "I am going to meet this lawyer Charles has found, but first I want to know what you think of him."

"He came to see me last night. I think he's fine." Charles noted the weariness in the voice. More of Partridge's strength had deserted him. He looked as if he were in pain, and moved restlessly on the edge of the bed, smoothing his trousers repeatedly over his knees.

"He was Graebner's lawyer when—"

"He explained that," Reg said. "I think it's all right."

"Oh. Well." Holly glanced at Charles worriedly. "Then that's fine."

"Yes."

"Has the doctor been to see you?" Charles inquired, still worried.

Reg sighed. "Oh yes. He said the usual, gave me some more stuff to take. And they've started giving me the usual milk puddings and toast. At least Mary could make them taste like something . . ." He sighed again. "They're making an effort. I appreciate it. They're not too bad. Did you bring me anything to read?"

"Yes, of course." Charles put down the paper carrier full of paperbacks they'd purchased in one of the larger bookshops. It was virtually their entire English-language stock. "I'm afraid they're rather a mixed selection, designed mostly for holiday reading, I'd say."

"That's fine. I'll read anything," Reg said, with an effort at a smile. "Thanks very much."

They talked for a few minutes longer, but they could see that he was really not up to prolonged conversation, and finally left. Holly had a few moments of tears outside, and then they went over to the main street and Ribes's office, on the second floor of a two-storey modern office block. His secretary, a young man, showed them in and shut the door quietly behind them. Ribes looked up.

From Charles's point of view, the interview with Ribes started badly and went downhill from there. The minute the young lawyer's eyes lit on his client's daughter-in-law, sweet reason went out of the window. Ribes was around thirty, had lived in England for two years while attending university, and was considered an up-and-coming chap with a promising future. But that didn't, apparently, diminish a lifetime steeped in the male traditions of Spain. Before Charles had even introduced them, Ribes had launched on an impassioned recitation concerning the allure of Holly's eyes, mouth, throat, hair, figure, and their effect upon him, which was profound and deep. Even Charles was hard-pressed to keep up with Ribes's rapid-fire recitation, for the whole speech was, of course, in Spanish. This highly suspect panegyric actually had a name—the *piropo*. It was considered to be a social requirement, a hangover from the days when relationships between the sexes in Spain were so circumscribed that some release was needed for the Spanish males' unquestioned virility. Caught between the devil of their passionate emotions and the deep blue sea of a rigid social structure, they had evolved this verbal assault to replace the physical. Ribes obviously enjoyed the challenge. Holly was a white gazelle come to drink at his pool, a dove in flight, an arrow of beauty in his heart, a dagger of desire in his loins.

"What's he saying?" Holly asked Charles.

"He thinks you're attractive," Charles said.

"But . . . he doesn't even know me."

"That couldn't matter less." He stepped in a breach in the flow when Ribes had to pause for breath, raising his voice a little. "Pedro, this is Holly Partridge, Señor Partridge's daughter-in-law."

"Ah, Señora Partridge, I am honoured to meet you," Ribes said in English. "*Habla usted español?*"

"No . . . I'm sorry."

Ribes immediately launched into the traditional second half of the *piropo,* which consisted of a description of the more earthy things he would like to demonstrate to her and the physical passion she aroused in him. Knowing now that he was safe in her ignorance of Spanish, he became quite scatological. Even then, the beauty of the language made it seem as if he were still reciting poetry. A glance at Charles finally told him enough was enough. He bowed, kissed Holly's hand, and was immediately all business.

Holly, aware of the change, looked at Charles in puzzlement. "What happened?"

Ribes had gone around to sit behind his desk and was shuffling papers, but Charles could see he was listening, the corners of his mouth turned up. Charles could have hit him. Holly had probably never been subjected to this ritual, which Spanish girls took in their stride.

"Oh, nothing. Spanish men often introduce themselves . . . that is . . . it's an old tradition to . . . make a speech."

"Oh."

"It relieves the tension."

"What tension?"

"Here, sit down," Charles said in desperation. He drew out a chair for her, then one for himself. Ribes closed the file on his desk, clasped his hands in front of him, and smiled.

"I am afraid your friend Teniente López is unwilling to recommend bail in this case," he told Charles. "I did all I could to persuade him, but . . ."

"Why?" Charles demanded.

"I don't know." The young lawyer's face was puzzled. "It seems obvious to me that Señor Partridge is no threat to society, but . . . they insist on treating him as such. It is very odd."

"You were Graebner's lawyer," Holly said abruptly.

Ribes's black eyes went to her. "His *abogado* of record," he agreed gravely. "I was assigned to him by the Court, and witnessed his deposition in the hospital. He was very ill, and his injuries made it difficult for him to communicate. He spoke little Spanish, I little French, but somehow we managed—in English, mostly. I grant you it was I who suggested the plea of guilt by association, but that is my job, to get the best possible result for my client. It seemed to me that the case against him was strong, and that the alternative would have been a long-drawn-out trial, which he was in no condition to withstand. A plea of guilty to a lesser charge, a reduced sentence, seemed the most expedient course. He eventually agreed. Behind the bandages I had the impression of a highly intelligent but weak man who was willing to cut his losses. By the time of the trial he was still horribly scarred and faced more treatment. A prison hospital or a civilian one seemed to make little difference, and so it came to pass. I did the best I could for him. Does this trouble you?"

"It did at first," Holly admitted, disarmed by his open manner and the logic of his explanation.

"Well, that is all I was to this man Graebner. I do not feel it in any way affects my representation of Señor Partridge, but if you have . . ."

"No, Reg says it's all right," Holly said. "We've just been to see him. But I want to talk to you about something."

"Oh?" He beamed at her. Delight me, the smile said. Reward me with jewels from your lips, pearls from your heart, diamonds from your eyes, rubies from your soul.

"We've got to find the bastard who really did it," Holly announced. "If the police won't get off their backsides to do it, then I figure it's up to us. Do you know any private detectives?"

"Dios mío," Ribes said, giving Charles a glance of horror as his illusions about her feminine delicacy tinkled to the floor.

Charles cleared his throat. "I've tried to explain to Ms. Partridge that there is no such thing as a private detective around here. She thinks I'm lying."

"But no, this is perfectly true, señora. If anything, we are overrun by police in Spain. We have much crime, but very few mysteries. We are a passionate people, we make our hatreds known to one and all. When a man is killed, it is usually quite obvious who has done it. I do not refer to the organized criminals or the terrorists, you understand, but to what one might refer to as private crime. In your father-in-law's case, as in all others of this nature, investigations are carried out by the Judicial Police, who are extremely competent. Divorce is rare. In the large cities you might find one or two private inquiry agents, but not here . . ."

"But this López that Charles seems to think so much of won't be doing anything to clear Reg, he's on the prosecution side. They're happy with their case, and that's it. All neat, all cut and dried, all nice and sewn up tight

. . . and all wrong. To them he's just an old man with an ulcer who lost his temper . . . they won't admit the possibility of anyone else. But there *had* to be someone else, because *Reg is innocent!*"

For the first time, Charles realized just how angry Holly Partridge had become. He felt a sinking sensation in the pit of his stomach, rather the way he might have felt if, on going through the zoo, he'd noticed the lock was undone on the tiger's cage. Should he shut it himself, or shout for a keeper? He opened his mouth, but Ribes got there first.

"Señora, that goes without saying." He smiled. "The minute one speaks with him, his innocence is clear."

"Not to the police," Holly said.

"Yes, well, they have no one else," Ribes said, as if that were sufficient explanation. "In the course of time, justice will—"

"Justice can get stuffed. If *they* won't do anything, and *you* won't, then Charles and I will just have to take a hand," Holly announced flatly.

"Oh, señora, please . . ." Ribes said, with a sympathetic glance at Charles, who had closed his eyes. "Surely not . . ."

"Where would we begin?" Charles asked in an awful voice, hoping her determination was unfocused. It was not.

"We begin with who killed David," she said.

Both men stared at her.

"But your husband died in an accident . . ." Ribes began.

"Rubbish," Holly retorted. She could have said worse, and wanted to, but she didn't think either of them could have handled it. Really, they were a pathetic pair. Charles all defeatism and twitches, Ribes all smiles and snake-oil. She didn't *have* to understand Spanish to figure out some of the things he'd said earlier. He obviously thought she was just another passive female who'd accepted his words from on high and felt lucky he'd bothered to explain anything at all to her, which he hadn't. She felt so exasperated she could have screamed. Didn't anyone see it? Didn't they have brains in their heads? "It was no accident."

Ribes raised his hands and eyes to heaven, and Charles leaned forward in his chair. "Holly, David was not the only one killed. A Guardia officer died also. Don't you think that if there was any doubt, they'd have pursued the matter? The Guardia is as ruthless about chasing cop killers as any other police force, I assure you."

"Who was the driver of the other car?" Holly demanded of Ribes.

Ribes shrugged. "A tourist, señora, just a tourist. A very drunken tourist who also spent time in hospital as a result of his stupidity."

"What time did the accident happen?" Charles asked.

"In the middle of the morning . . . around ten o'clock," Holly said, very carefully.

"Seems an odd time for anyone to be drunk," Charles observed.

"Exactly." She pounced, as if she'd been waiting for one of them to say just that. "I didn't sleep at all last night trying to make some sense out of all this. What if someone *else* had been in on that forgery thing?"

"Graebner insisted always that he had acted alone, save for your late husband's services . . ."

"That's as may be," Holly said. "What if there *was* someone else? And this someone else decided to help Graebner and David escape?"

"Why?" Charles wanted to know.

"So they couldn't testify in court," Holly said triumphantly. "That's why. Only it went a bit wrong, and David was killed. Maybe they even meant to kill him. Both of them. But Graebner was only injured, so they went to him in the hospital and bribed him to plead guilty and keep his mouth shut."

"And when he got out?" Charles asked.

"They paid him off."

"By killing him?"

"Yes."

"But, señora." Ribes's voice was soft. "They could have killed him anytime and saved themselves a risk. In the hospital, in jail. Why did they not kill him before? Why now?"

She thought about that, but only for a moment. "Because they believed he'd do as they asked. And he did. But then he came to them and demanded something—more money, maybe. Or to get back into the action. And . . ."

"This nebulous 'they' you speak of, señora. It could be said that instead of 'they' it was 'he'—your father-in-law. After all, he knows a good deal about Customs, does he not? All that you have said could be true, I agree, but it could be true of Señor Partridge."

"Except that it *isn't.*" Holly exploded. "For goodness' sake, I thought you were on *our* side."

"I am, señora, believe me," Ribes said in a placating voice. "I was just indicating what the police would say in answer to your theories. Only *they* might be more harsh. *I* don't believe it to be true, but they might. I would humbly suggest you don't mention it to them. They hardly need further fuel for their fire."

"It might make them investigate further," Charles said. "If I speak to López . . ."

"I strongly recommend that you don't," Ribes said. "You say you know him well, but have you ever known him as an adversary? I know him, too, by reputation, and I am sure he would have no difficulty in separating his duty from his friendship for you. Nor would you be wise to attempt to trade on it."

"Right," Holly said. "That's why the best thing to do is to present them with a fait accompli. If we find out who these other people are . . ."

"Then they might kill us," Charles said bleakly. "I don't think that would be much of a help."

"Well, at least it would prove Reg didn't do it," Holly said with spirit.

"Somehow I never visualized myself in the role of sacrificial lamb," Charles murmured.

"Look, it has to be done and that's all there is to it!" Holly said, standing up suddenly. "I'm sick of sitting around wringing my hands and listening to you all tell me to be good and hope for the best. Dammit, I have work to do, if nothing else. Do you think I can concentrate on that with all this going on? I've spent a year on this commission already, and I'm in debt up to my ears. Even if that weren't the case, I can't just sit around and watch Mary fall apart and Reg get sicker and not *do* anything, can I? If you won't help me, then I'll have to find someone who will."

With a final glare at both of them, she marched out of the office and clattered down the stairs. Ribes was the first to speak.

"Are many American women like that?" he asked thinly.

"I believe so," Charles said tiredly. "I haven't met very many, but they all seem very . . . energetic."

"Dios mío," Ribes said again. "If she were ugly, I could understand it better."

"And I could ignore it more easily," Charles agreed, standing up. He stood there for a moment looking at Ribes. "Can you get hold of the police files and so on concerning the fraud case?"

"I will have to get permission from the Court," Ribes said.

"Then please do so," Charles said. He scribbled down the number of the *fonda* where he was staying. "You can reach me there—if I'm not in, I'm sure they'll take a message."

He thanked Ribes for his time, apologized with his eyes and shoulders, and followed Holly down the stairs.

When his footsteps had died away, Ribes reached for the telephone and dialled quickly. The voice that answered was one he hadn't spoken to for a long time.

Not for two years at least.

Charles found Holly at a table in front of a *merendero* a little way up the street from where he'd parked the car. A waiter was hovering, but she hadn't noticed him, still being too caught up in her anger.

"*Dos cafés, por favor,*" Charles said quietly, and sat down across from her. The waiter nodded and left them. Charles leaned back in his chair, lit a cigarette, and regarded her. Her eyes were blazing, and there was a red flush across her cheekbones. He offered her a cigarette. She took it without looking at him, and puffed at it in angry jerks once it was lit. He, too, smoked in silence until the coffee arrived.

"Spaniards don't like being made to look foolish, especially by women," he finally said mildly. "If it weren't for the fact that Ribes spent some time in England as a student, we'd have just lost ourselves a very good lawyer."

"Oh, nonsense," she said, her tone peevish with guilt. After a few minutes she glanced at him and away quickly. "You think I'm terrible, I suppose, loud bossy American female and so on."

"You *were* a little strident," he agreed. "Still . . ."

She turned in her chair to face him. "What are you afraid of?"

"Hard work?" Charles suggested.

She looked slightly puzzled. "I don't think so."

"What then?"

"Making a fuss, I think. They've trained you too well. Sometimes, you know, you have to *cause* trouble to end trouble."

"An interesting point of view—means and ends, that sort of thing?"

"You know what I'm saying."

"I know the difficulties. You don't."

"Fair enough," she conceded. "But if you know them, it seems to me you're the ideal man to overcome them."

"Knowing Everest is big doesn't make it any easier to climb," he pointed out.

"Ha, ha." She swallowed. "It was just . . . seeing Reg. He looked so *old*. If you only knew what he was like, normally, you'd *want* to do something."

Charles sighed. "I don't think you quite understand my position here. I represent Her Majesty's Government. I have to tread very carefully with the Spanish, especially López. If we start ferreting around in his territory, he's going to get rather annoyed, to say the least. It's *his* job to investigate the case, not ours."

"But he isn't doing his job. He thinks his job is done."

"I think you're misjudging him," Charles said. "He's a very good police officer and a very fair-minded man. If there are unsettled aspects of the case, he'll probably go to a great deal of trouble to clarify them."

"*Probably.*" Her voice dripped sarcasm. "Can't you force him to look at all the facts? Haven't you got any authority over him?"

"No," Charles said simply.

"Oh." That stopped her temporarily. She stirred her coffee and drank some, then stood up suddenly. "Show me this López character."

Charles peered up at her, his eyes watering slightly in the sun's glare. "I don't think that's a very good idea."

She looked at him in disgust. How could any man as dependable-looking as this one be so mealy-mouthed and feeble? "Does he speak English?" she asked.

"Oh, yes, he's very . . ."

"Then I'll go myself. I know the way back."

She turned and started up the street, slinging her jacket over one shoulder resolutely. Charles would have been terrified if she'd walked into *his* office looking like that, but he was certain López could have quite a different reaction.

He put some money beside the coffee cups and caught up with her. It was like acting as convoy to a comet. "Ummmm . . . what do you plan to say to him?" he ventured to ask finally.

"That depends on what he says to me."

"Yes, but . . ."

"And if he tries to palm off on me the same kind of crap you have, I'll let him know what I think of lazy, stupid, opinionated petty despots like him."

"Oh, God . . ."

"Well . . ." She glanced at him out of the corner of her eye. "Maybe not *quite* that. But I want him to know I'm in a snit."

"A snit?" Charles asked, in a choked voice.

"Miffed," she amplified. *"Cross."*

"Ah."

"And that he'd better try looking at other things." She snapped her fingers. "David's things, for instance."

"What things?"

She waved a hand. "Oh . . . his effects. You know. The things that were left behind when he died. We went through them after the funeral . . ." She slowed, then came to a full stop in the middle of the pavement, staring towards the end of the street where, between the converging line of buildings, a sliver of the sea could be seen. A gull screamed overhead, and two car horns exchanged insults somewhere behind them. When she looked at him, her eyes were dull. "Have you even been to a funeral here?" she asked. Her voice was suddenly dull, too.

"Yes."

"Aren't they . . . awful?" The memory clogged her throat momentarily. That hot, throbbing day. Her London clothes itchy and suffocating. The dusty *cementerio* with its stone ranks of mausoleums, tall flat structures where the dead were pigeon-holed like letters. The coffin had been slotted into place by a labourer in shirt-sleeves driving a fork-lift truck, right in the middle of the ceremony. Then the opening had been boarded up and sealed over by a little scruffy man who'd slapped the plaster on with a trowel, a cigarette dangling from the corner of his mouth. Gulls shrieking overhead and cicadas humming all around. People shuffling their feet and averting their eyes while the grinning funeral directors had overseen the casual proceedings like bandits newly arrived from Sardinia. David. David in that place, inserted like a parcel in a lost-letter office, waiting to be collected. David, with his fire and his zest for argument, silenced and encapsulated forever next to an empty pigeon-hole where a dirty milk bottle had stood discarded by some anonymous worker, its sour curds drying in garlands on the inside of the thick, greenish glass.

"The Spanish are ambivalent about death," Charles said. "They celebrate its mysteries in their festivals, their bullfights ritualize it, they view it with metaphysical awe—in the abstract. But when faced with its reality, they're very practical." He paused and cleared his throat. "It's a hot country," he added bleakly.

There was a bench nearby, and Holly went over and sat down on it. For some reason her feelings and distress at the time of David's death and funeral had swept over her again, leaving her weak and disoriented, as she had been then. The phone call at midnight, the headlong rush to catch a flight filled with cheery holiday-makers laughing and talking all around her, the dreadful shocked face of Reg at the airport, Mary trying not to weep in public, the awful, *awful* funeral.

"Reg and I had to clear the studio afterwards. We kept bursting into tears, both of us. I can't bear to see a man cry—not because they shouldn't, but because it seems like the end of the world when they do. He took the things he wanted, mostly painting gear and a few pictures. There wasn't much there." She faltered, took a breath, went on. "I told him to go home, that I'd deal with the rest myself . . . but I couldn't. I couldn't face it, touching his things . . . not then. I'd said I would ship it back to London, but I chickened out and shoved it all into the garage and locked it away. I let the studio without the garage . . . and it's all still there. I'd planned to go through it all before I went back to London in May. It might as well be now as then."

"You think there might be some kind of clue there?"

A Spanish family, laden with bundles and chattering happily, passed by. Slowly, and with some trepidation, he saw the present problems resurrect themselves and drive out the shadows of the past with the glare of their urgency. She sat up a little straighter and faced him. Despite Ribes's flowery effusions, she was not beautiful in the conventional sense. But there was a gamin quality about her, rather like the jaunty recklessness of an adolescent boy, that sat well on her face with its long nose and wide mouth. She had gone pale, and her freckles stood out clearly. Her chin lifted.

"Well, dammit, why not?" she asked. Her defiance had returned, perhaps intensified by her recollections of David's death. Having things taken away from you is not the same as giving them away.

He sympathized with her. But stamping her foot at López wasn't the way to go about relieving her frustration or her outrage. It *was* possible they might find something in David Partridge's personal effects that would prove helpful in the light of hindsight. More important to him at the moment, it would give her something to do as an alternative to throwing down the gauntlet to the Policía Judicial. It would give them *both* something to do. He found Esteban's attitude inexplicable. He'd never before thought him the kind of man to accept injustice, and yet keeping Reg Partridge locked up was unjust. When, exactly, he'd begun to care about Reg's plight more than his own comfort Charles couldn't say. Something *should* be done. But carefully.

"Right," Charles said. "Do you have the keys with you?"

Her eyes clouded. "No, they're back in Puerto Rio, on my dressing table." Her face brightened again. "But we could just break in, couldn't we? It's only a little lock . . ."

"Fine," he agreed enthusiastically. He stood up and looked down at her, then himself. "Mind you . . ."

"What?"

"It's going to be a pretty messy job. And hot, with the sun overhead as it is now. The heat, plus two years' dust and spiders . . . won't do much for that white dress."

She looked down. "Oh dear," she murmured.

He waited. She sighed.

"I guess it *would* make more sense to go back and get the keys and change and maybe get a few boxes . . ."

"We're less apt to miss anything if we're organized," he said, letting regret tinge his voice very, very slightly.

"Oh, I doubt *you'd* miss much," she said lightly. She stood up. "I'm beginning to realize that much about you, Mr. Llewellyn."

"I beg your pardon?"

"Trying to cool me off, distract me, aren't you?" She looked up at him, sparks once more in her eyes. "It won't work. I concede going through the garage later makes sense, but that's *all* I concede. If you think I'm going to give up or back off . . . think again."

"Fine."

"Fine?" She glared up at him suspiciously.

"Yes. Press on. Full steam ahead and all that. I'm right behind you all the way. Absolutely." He beamed at her.

She raised a doubtful eyebrow, but turned and started back towards the car without speaking. Charles followed, thanking the patron saint of minor officialdom, whoever he or she might be, for the small mercy of temporary respite. What would Machiavelli have done, he wondered, faced with Holly Partridge on one side and Esteban López on the other?

Drunk the hemlock the Borgias offered, no doubt. And gratefully.

Across the street, from the window of his office, Ribes watched them until they got into the car and had driven out of sight. Then he spoke into the telephone again.

"I think they're on their way now," he said.

CHAPTER 7

Charles pulled up in the parking lot behind 400 Avenida de la Playa and turned off the engine. They'd been silent for most of the journey back from Espina, each of them caught up in their own thoughts. Charles, appalled at what he'd got himself into so far, decided to make his position more clear before they went on.

"I think we ought to talk a bit before we go up."

"Why?"

"Because you have to be careful."

"About what? I'm not afraid of any—"

"I didn't mean that, I meant . . . your attitude."

"What's wrong with my attitude?"

"Well, you have to understand that you aren't going to change the attitudes of an entire nation overnight with your outrage. If anything, you consolidate them. In Spain, women are still to be seen and enjoyed, not heard."

"But Spain is modern . . . look . . ." she gestured at the bright angularities of the new buildings around them.

Charles's lip curled. *"This* isn't Spain."

"You just said it was."

"I meant the attitudes, not the . . ." He sighed in exasperation. "Look, don't you see? They *tolerate* us here. They need our money, but they don't have to put up with abuse of their hospitality. Why should they? You can put up all the fancy apartment blocks you like, but you're only putting up doll's houses in some other kid's garden. The land and the rules of the land are theirs, and always will be. But the people who retire here or live here part-time may go to the end of their lives without noticing that or being inconvenienced by it. They stay with their own kind, patronize shops run by their own kind or supermarkets that are impersonal. They live in a little bubble warmed by the Spanish sun but sealed off from Spain itself. Until real trouble strikes—like this—and then they're totally unprepared for it. The Spaniards are treating this very, very seriously because they have no other way of reminding you all that this is still *their* country." He took a breath. "To put it crudely, they don't intend to put up with our rubbish on their carpet."

"I bet they wouldn't treat a Spaniard the way they're treating Reg."

"You're right, they wouldn't. They'd treat him a hell of a lot worse, believe me. Look at it from their point of view—a compliment, I might warn you, they are unlikely to return. Don't think about Mr. Partridge as your father-in-law or a nice man or anything else. Just think about the case objectively on the evidence alone. Please."

He could see she didn't like it, but she did her best. After a moment, she spoke very softly. "He could have done it."

"Good girl. Now, please, stop flying off the handle every time anyone else expresses that point of view, will you? Nobody appreciates being told they're idiots, particularly a Spaniard. They did the obvious thing under the circumstances."

"Does this mean you're not going to help me?" she asked warily.

"No. But if I'm to go ahead with your hare-brained schemes, I want you to understand that this is a country *I* understand—well, nearly understand —and that you don't understand at all. You'll just have to accept it when I tell you not to do or say a certain thing. Despite appearances to the contrary in matters of dress and so on, Spaniards are *not* Europeans. They are

Spaniards. Any attempt to treat them like anyone else is odds-on for disaster. Okay?"

"You make them sound like Outer Mongolians or something."

"Then think of them as Outer Mongolians," he suggested. "It might help."

There seemed to be another party going on.

Well, Charles conceded, not quite. But when he'd picked Holly up that morning, Mary had been alone. Now Helen and Nigel Bland, the colonel (and, of course, Queenie), Alastair Morland, a couple called Beam who hadn't been there the night before, and another man were also there. The last was named Mel Tinker, and he was one of those handsome, athletic-looking American men with beautifully cut greying hair and a deep tan. His face lit up when he saw Holly.

"Well, there you are!" he said, his deep voice registering warm approval and relief. "I was beginning to worry, sweetheart."

"I don't see why," Holly said offhandedly. "I was with Charles, who knows everything there is to know about Outer Mongolia."

"Pardon?"

"Private joke," Charles murmured uncomfortably. "Charles Llewellyn, British Consulate."

"Ah . . ." Tinker nodded, extending his hand. "Mel Tinker, late of Tinker Electronics, presently bumming around Europe. Decided I'd had enough of the rat race, you know?"

"I know." Charles nodded. "As one of the rats still racing, I envy you."

Mary Partridge introduced him to the Beams, who lived up to their name by grinning at him enthusiastically, and the colonel bellowed a greeting.

"Got the lay of the land yet, Llewellyn?"

"Sorry?"

"We're planning how to spring Reg from the calaboose," the colonel crowed. "Need an inside man, though. Any ideas?"

"You're not serious," Charles said.

The colonel smiled ruefully and shook his head. "Sorry to say, no. Too old for heroics. Besides, it would be pointless."

"Not really," Morland said. "Properly planned, we could get Reg away pretty cleanly, I'd say."

Charles glanced at him as Mary handed him a drink he hadn't asked for —gin and tonic, of course. He preferred Scotch but he sipped it, trying not to grimace. "It wouldn't be a very good idea," he said mildly.

"Oh, we know that," Morland said good-naturedly. "Only a guilty man runs and so on. I just meant logistically—it *is* quite feasible."

"It's also quite feasible you'd get somebody hurt or killed," growled Nigel Bland from the depths of the sofa. Charles could see anger in his eyes and remembered he was ex–Scotland Yard. Bland is stuck, he thought. As a former cop his conditioning and training put him on the side of López. But his heart was loyal to Reg, an old friend. The result was, at the very least, moral indigestion.

Charles described their interview with Ribes and relayed messages from Reg.

"Poor Reg," Helen Bland said. She was a plumpish, vivacious woman with a beautiful way of moving that intimated that she might have been a model or a dancer in her younger days. He had the feeling that under normal circumstances she would have been the one who kept the party lively. At the moment, however, she was more concerned with Mary. He was pleased to see that, with a good night's sleep behind her, Mary was looking more relaxed and stronger. She'd taken the news of Ribes's lack of progress in the matter of bail quite calmly. She was also relieved to hear the doctor had been to see him. All in all, the gathering was a considerable improvement on that of the previous evening.

"Now, you all understand that we'll expect you about six," Mrs. Beam said to the room in general. "You, too, Mr. Llewellyn, of course."

"I'm sorry . . . I don't . . ." Charles was lost.

Helen Bland grinned at him. "Dick and Dot have invited us all over to dinner this evening," she said quietly. "Sort of a spiritual uplift and a change of scene for Mary."

"Oh. Well, there's no need to include me . . . I mean . . . it's very kind . . ."

"And very sensible," Nigel Bland said, heaving himself out of the sofa with some difficulty and coming over to stand beside him. "You're in an hotel, aren't you?"

"Yes, but—"

"Then don't be silly and come along. La Casa de los Pavos is well worth a visit, even without the food."

"Oh." Charles, startled, took another look at the unremarkable but cheery-looking Beams. Of course. He'd look happy, too, if he happened to have a couple of million in the bank. He knew the name Beam—anyone who'd been long in the area knew the name—he just hadn't connected it with these very ordinary people. Dick and Dot Beam had moved to the Costa Blanca long before it had become popular. Well-to-do even then, Dick

Beam had apparently had the foresight to purchase large tracts of then fairly worthless coastal and near-coastal olive groves and smallholdings. When the boom hit (and some said he'd been instrumental in setting the fuse), he'd made a fortune. Rumour had it he still held a considerable quantity of land, to be sold as he felt the mood strike him. Rumour also had it that Dick and Dot Beam were recluses, who refused to mix with the new arrivals or indeed anybody else. Yet there they were, he in a pair of inexpensive gabardine pants and an open-necked cotton shirt, she in a simple cotton dress and sandals, smiling hugely at the assembled company.

"Juanito will be cooking paella outside tonight . . . probably the last time this year," Dot Beam said enthusiastically. "If it gets too chilly we can move inside, but I think we might be lucky. You will come, won't you, Mr. Llewellyn?"

"Thank you very much, I'll be delighted." He smiled.

"Grand," Dick Beam said. "That's grand. Well, come on, Mother . . . time we were gone. Sun's high." They started for the door and Mary Partridge followed them. *"Hasta la vista,* all." Dick Beam waved from the doorway, and their voices murmured with Mary's to the door. Holly came across the room and glared at Charles.

"What about the garage?" she asked in a fierce whisper.

"Well, we can do it tomorrow . . ." Charles said vaguely.

"I wanted to do it today."

"Look . . ." He took her by the arm and they went out onto the patio, wincing at the glare of the sun. "Your father-in-law is in a tough spot, and your mother-in-law could use some distraction. But the most important thing is that the Beams have a lot of clout in the area, believe me. If I'd realized they knew your family . . ."

"They're old friends," Holly murmured reluctantly, and glanced through the sliding doors sulkily. Out of the corner of his eye Charles could see Tinker glaring at them through the glass.

"Then believe me, they should be cultivated," Charles said. "If you ever needed a bridge to the Spanish, you need it now, and they're it. Their son married Justina Merolles, whose father is a rather important man in the Department of Justice. I wouldn't ask their help lightly, but . . . if it comes to the crunch . . . you could do worse. By coming here and asking your mother-in-law over for dinner, they're demonstrating in the strongest way possible their backing for Reg. That alone may make a difference."

"Yes, but—"

"I thought you agreed to do what I tell you."

"I have got a mind of my own, you know," she said irritably.

"Then *use* the bloody thing."

"Anything wrong, Holly, honey?" It was Tinker, strolling out casually, drink in hand. His cold eyes raked Charles up and down.

"No, of course not, Mel," Holly snapped. "Charles just remembered something he wanted me to do, that's all."

"Can I help?"

"No, we can handle it," Charles said shortly.

"No need to get huffy," Tinker said with specious ease. Charles noted his size, his reach, and his air of possession as he wrapped an arm around Holly's shoulders. "I happen to be very fond of Holly here, and I want to do all I can to help her daddy-in-law out of this mess."

"Very commendable," Charles said. "I'm sure she appreciates your concern."

"But you don't?"

"It's none of my business one way or the other, unless you happen to . . . make difficulties."

"Now, how could I make difficulties?" Tinker wanted to know. He smiled down at Holly. "A nice, inoffensive good old boy like me?"

"Oh, stop it, both of you," Holly snapped, and stalked back into the penthouse. Tinker looked after her in surprise, then returned his gaze to Charles. There was no friendliness in it whatsoever.

Charles raised his drink, and the sunlight winked on the rim of the glass.

"Cheers," he said.

López looked at Paco Bas with weary resignation. The boy was eager to learn, but lamentably lacking in either self-confidence or style. There was no subtlety in him whatsoever. He was a plodder and he would always be a plodder. That was well and good, if one realized one was a plodder. But the plodders always wanted to fly. What was worse, they were convinced they *would* fly.

He had a fond, fleeting thought for his usual partner in Madrid, the wily Boas, now stalking yet another nest of vipers in the northern mountains. He didn't envy him the task, but he did envy him the food he was getting. Here on the coast it was all fish, fish, and more fish. He knew he was being unfair, that in the heat of the coastal plains, light eating was not only the rule, it was the sensible rule. But he had a fancy for a good, rich *cocido* or *podrida,* with plenty of bread on the side. He knew he wouldn't get it. He also knew that if he *could* get it, he would not eat it, for he had a great regard both for his digestion and his figure.

It was just that when he was frustrated he became ravenous. And the fact that his own good sense prevented him from assuaging that hunger with unsuitable mixtures did not prevent him from resenting it, and becoming sulky and cross. Boas would laugh him out of it. But poor Paco Bas only assumed it was something *he* had done.

López poked a fork into the mixture on his plate and came up with a curling sardine. "The report from Interpol should be with us by this afternoon, Paco."

"Yes. I rang this morning, but it had not as yet arrived. They said not to call again, they would send it when it came."

"Then call again."

"But . . ."

"Tell them *I* said to call again, tell them I want it *now,* not tomorrow or next week."

"Very well." As long as he could quote the command as coming from López, he was happy. There had been a lot of resentment when he had been assigned to López. There were many who felt he was not of sufficient experience or stature to take on the task. They were right, he agreed with them totally, but he was not going to turn the chance away, was he? And what if it came because his uncle had pulled a few strings? A man would be a fool if he did not use what there was to hand in the way of influence. And he, Paco Bas, was no fool. True, he did not as yet understand what López was working on. He had understood it to be a simple case of murder. But no, it was so much more. And not to be able to talk about it to anyone, to be able to brag that he, Paco Bas, was working on a problem of *international* importance . . . it was almost too much to bear. When it was all solved, then, of course, they would know. *Then* they would see that . . .

"I do not like having to keep the Partridge man in jail," López said.

"No, sir. He is not well."

"He might become a good deal less well were he to go outside those thick walls, Paco."

"We don't *know* that would happen."

"No, but the risk is too great."

"But if his family were at least to be told, or Señor Llewellyn . . ."

"That, too, is a risk we cannot take. The wrong word at the wrong time . . . it does not bear thinking about. After all, had it not been for this stupid death coming so unexpectedly, we might well have closed the case entirely by now. As it is . . . it grows and grows like some monstrous cancer. And I do not relish the moment when the truth is revealed, Paco." He sighed and consumed another *tapa,* this time a circle of smoked sausage. "Ours is not a kind profession, Paco Bas."

"This is true." Paco nodded slowly, regretfully.

"We are not much loved, you know."

"This is true." He was used to that.

"On the other hand, we must not let the natural desire to be loved interfere with the objectivity we must maintain. Old friends cannot be given quarter, Paco. Nor old enemies, either."

Paco said nothing. Just sat there, wishing he knew what López meant.

"Paco, I want you to do something that will make you very unloved."

"Very well." Paco drew himself up.

"I wish you to go to the Guardia and get all the available information on these men." He handed Bas a paper from his breast pocket.

"But you said *you* were going to . . ." Bas was shrinking again.

"Yes, I know. But there is something else I must attend to." He leaned forward. "If it is any consolation, it will not make *me* many friends, either."

"No, sir." Bas put the bit of paper into his own pocket. They would be rude, the GC. They would make remarks. They would be slow and give him many excuses, and it would take hours. López could have done it in ten seconds, with no back-talk. And they would be suspicious. They would want to know why he wanted the background on two of their own men.

He also would have liked to know.

But López wouldn't say.

Charles checked the written instructions lying on the seat next to him, just to make certain. Yes, they very clearly stated the *third* turning on the left after the village. The road looked very uninviting, slinking as it did into one of the few forested areas on the flanks of Montgo, with grass poking up here and there in the gravel and a general air of not having been cared for by anyone, ever.

Shrugging, he turned the Seat off the highway and onto the gravel. Crunching slowly into the gloom, he flicked on his headlamps. The evening was still bright, but under this dense growth it was already twilight. The road twisted and turned abruptly and he wondered how the Rolls (for the Beams drove an ancient maroon Rolls) managed to make it around the curves. He was just about convinced he'd got the wrong road after all, when the trees broke away on either side, like curtains parting, and he looked down on paradise.

A very small paradise, it was true, and decidedly wedge-shaped at that. Nevertheless, after the dry coastal plains, it was a shock. Above rose Montgo, purplish-brown against the evening sky, its rocky shoulders curving around this area of its flank protectively. There, deep in a fold of rocky outcrop, had been thrown a carpet of deepest green around a white hacienda with a red-tiled roof and a formal rose garden and—dear heaven, who would have believed it?—a bloody maze. The entire area was not more than three-quarters of a mile square, but in it had been created, in miniature, an English country estate. True, the house itself was of Spanish design, and a beautiful example it was, too. Perfectly balanced, with deep-set windows and a patio running the full length of it, but beyond that and the loom of Montgo, he could have been home again. He let the clutch out and the car began to roll down the slight incline into the central well of the little valley. As he did so, a wild cry rent the air, eerie and raucous, making him jump.

La Casa de los Pavos. Peacock House.

There was one now, strolling across the lawn, its iridescent plumage shimmering in the evening light, its long, impossible tail folded and trailing behind.

"This is bloody ridiculous," Charles muttered, suppressing an impulse to laugh aloud. It was, he decided, the ultimate nonsense. Coming to Spain, and then not just pining for England, but recreating it on foreign soil. The Beams were part of that ancient tradition of British eccentrics who had left their mark all over England and, here and there, upon the world at large. He passed two more peacocks before gaining the gravel semicircle in front of the hacienda, where other cars had preceded him. There was no sign of the Rolls he'd seen in the car-park behind the flats earlier that day, but presumably the Beams were at home to greet their guests. My God, he thought, where else could they be? Where else could they survive?

The interior of the house was not, as Charles had expected, another attempt at replication. Instead, the Beams had kept it true to tradition, and the long cool rooms were furnished with that heavily carved dark furniture that wealthy Spaniards had always seemed to favour. There were bright rugs on the terrazzo floors, and some really fine paintings on the walls. He saw Holly looking at several of them during the course of the "cocktail hour" and raised an eyebrow. She nodded. They were genuine, apparently. Not the expected Goyas and Murillos, however, but Impressionists and even a Miró or two. Somehow they blended in very well with the old furniture.

"You have a beautiful home, sir," Charles said to Dick Beam, who was passing around with a bottle of champagne in each hand, topping up glasses. In addition to the two Partridge women, the Blands, the colonel (and Queenie, who spent the entire time with her nose pressed against a window yearning after the peacocks), Tinker and himself, there were several other guests present. Everyone was drinking champagne because nothing else had been offered.

Beam smiled, pouring. "You seem surprised, Mr. Llewellyn."

"Oh, not at all. The whole . . . setting . . ."

Beam laughed. "Perhaps it will explain things if I say that Dot is responsible for the garden, and I am responsible for the house. Our tastes . . . differ. I might warn you about the rear garden—there are gnomes there. You know, those awful plaster things? She has them shipped out especially. I believe, at the last count, there were more than fifty." His tone was wry. "I think the little buggers breed at night."

Charles nearly choked on his champagne. Beam's face was bland, but his eyes were amused and sardonic. "Well, why not? She never wanted to come out here in the first place, but . . . Frankly, if we hadn't, she'd be dead by now. Chronic bronchitis, the English disease, so to speak. She needed the hot dry air, but she couldn't stand the vegetation it produced. So we found a way to irrigate the land and we employ four gardeners full-time, and she can cut roses all year round. It's worth it." He grinned suddenly. "She only gets the gnomes to tease me, I think. Damn ugly things."

"You have some fine paintings."

Beam looked at him with approval. "You like them? I'm pleased. Our Spanish friends think them not quite the thing—all art stopped with Goya as far as they're concerned."

"I know." Charles nodded, smiling benignly.

"You like it here?" Beam asked curiously.

"What, in Alicante or Spain in general?"

"Spain."

"Oh yes, I've never wanted to be stationed anywhere else."

"He says the Spanish are like Outer Mongolians," Holly said, coming up. Beam looked bemused.

"I meant they aren't like . . ." Charles could have strangled her. "They have unusual attitudes, a kind of remoteness . . ."

Beam looked at him for a moment. "I think the analogy is a good one, Charles. They *are* very special, and it's grown from their isolation."

Relieved, Charles nodded. "It's taken me ten years to learn that, and it will probably take me another twenty to learn to understand why."

"At least," Beam agreed with a smile, and turned away to fill other glasses.

They all filtered out to the rear patio, which was wide and overlooked the rose gardens. Sure enough, there were all the plaster gnomes Dick Beam had warned him about—sitting and standing and fishing in the lily pond.

Somehow—although it was only a trick of light and shadow—the little gnomes' eyes seemed to follow the company as they gathered around the enormous paella pan resting over the fire-pit on a special tripod as Juanito circled it, adding bits and pieces to the already fragrant and simmering golden mass of rice, meat and vegetables. He was wearing a white jacket and his gestures were theatrical. He seemed absorbed in the progress of his cooking, but Charles thought he was also well aware of his appreciative audience. Juanito was, and knew he was, a master.

Twenty minutes later, with a heaped plate on his lap, Charles's expectations were confirmed. It was superb. He glanced around him after a few minutes, and saw Mary Partridge had sat down next to him. She wasn't eating, just pushing her food around on the plate. Her mouth was tight.

Charles leaned over. "If all this is getting a bit much for you, you've only to say. I'll be glad to run you home."

"No, no . . . I'm fine," she demurred. "Really. I'm just not . . . very hungry."

"That's a shame. It's wonderful stuff, the best I've ever had."

"I know. Juanito is famous for it." She glanced at him, her eyes shadowed. "They're giving Reg a bland diet, aren't they? Nothing . . . like this."

"Oh yes, very bland. Too bland, I gather. He says you do it much better." He regretted relaying the compliment when he saw her eyes fill with tears. She blinked them back, then looked around the patio at the others, eating, drinking, talking. On the opposite side, Holly and Mel Tinker were side by side on the low wall.

"He's very keen on Holly," she murmured. "Mel, I mean."

"He seems a perfectly nice chap," Charles said carefully.

"You don't like him," Mary said.

"I didn't say that. He's a little old for her, maybe, but I gather he has money and he's American, of course . . ."

"And you don't like him," Mary said again. It was getting too dark to see her face clearly, but he could hear her amusement. "He's only thirty-eight, actually."

"Oh?" Charles put his plate down on the bricks of the patio. The paella, though superb, was very rich. He'd had enough for the moment.

"I admit, he's a little . . . overwhelming. Perfect clothes, but the voice a little too loud. Handsome, but a little too pushy. A little over the top, as they say?"

"Perhaps."

"Then you probably wouldn't have liked David either. He was the same.

Oh, not loud and overbearing, I don't mean that. But he did everything to extremes, especially when their marriage began to break up. All the clichés came out—driving too fast, drinking too much. It was as if he'd read a book on how to behave when distraught. Reg got quite disgusted with him at one point—there's always been an element of competition between them."

"That's natural between father and son, surely."

"Oh yes, but David was supercompetitive. Everything was a challenge to him, but he was quickly bored. He could do so many things, but he never had the patience to learn them well. The process of learning always involved failure, you see, and he never would put up with that for long. He wanted everything right away, and he wanted it *all*. Almost as if he knew he wouldn't have enough time in the end . . ."

In other words, Charles thought, he was immature and greedy. Aloud, he said, "A passionate spirit."

Again he felt that aura of amusement. "You're very kind," she said. "Holly's a bit like that, too, perhaps that's why they never really got on. Too much competition again. But she's always had a streak of common sense under it all. He never did. She's more . . . solid than David was."

"Was David ever in trouble with the law—before this painting thing?"

"Only once, when he was about seventeen. He was—'busted' I think the word is—for trying to smuggle some marijuana into the country on his way back from a working holiday in Mexico. It was only a little bit, but there was quite a fuss because of Reg's working for Customs and Excise."

"Did it make any difference to Mr. Partridge's career?"

"No, of course not. I think he got teased a lot . . . but it was only a couple of cigarettes—reefers?—and they didn't even prosecute in the end."

"Was that because of Mr. Partridge?"

"It might have been. He never said it was."

"Who said what was?" came a voice out of the shadows. The fire was dying down, but they hadn't lit the *linternas* yet. It was Nigel Bland.

"We were talking about David and that thing with the marijuana, years ago," Mary said. "Was it because Reg pulled strings that David was let off?"

"It might have been. It never got to us, as a matter of fact."

"You meaning Scotland Yard, or you personally?"

"Either. I worked liaison with C and E—that's how Reg and I met. We go a long way back, don't we, love?" Nigel put an arm around Mary.

"We do indeed." She smiled up at him.

"Ummm . . ." Nigel seemed to have something on his mind. "Holly's been talking about the two of you playing detective, Charles."

"Oh?" Charles got out his pipe and began the ritual of filling and lighting it after asking Mary if she'd mind.

"Yes. I'd go a bit carefully if I were you."

"I intend to, sir, believe me."

"There are a lot of funny types who've settled around Puerto Rio," Bland went on musingly. "Some of them wouldn't appreciate your being too nosy, if you know what I mean."

"Like the Neufelds?" Charles asked quietly.

He saw Bland's head come up, only a silhouette against the lanterns that were now being lit by one of the servants. He was reminded of a bull in a field spotting an intruder. "Why do you mention them particularly?"

"First name that came into my head, I suppose," Charles said evasively. "Holly described them and they seemed . . . rather mysterious. And they were the ones who saw the lights come on in the penthouse."

"Or said they did," Mary muttered.

"You think they were lying?" Charles asked.

"Yes. No. I don't know. Reg said he didn't remember turning on the lights at all, as it happens. Frankly, I'm surprised they noticed *anything*, considering what they were probably doing."

"Sorry?" Charles asked, a little lost.

"Well, it's obvious, isn't it?" Mary said disparagingly. "Sick husband, beautiful young wife, healthy young male nurse . . . it's classic."

"I've always thought Fritz was a poof, myself," Nigel said. He laughed. "At least the Neufelds give us all something to wonder about. A place like this thrives on gossip, Llewellyn, you have no idea."

"Oh, I can guess," Charles said. "But what reason would they have for lying, if they did lie?"

"Did they need a reason?" Mary asked.

"Whoa, now, girl . . . just because Mrs. Neufeld was always giving Reg the old come-on . . . ."

"She gives everyone the come-on."

Nigel sighed. "Not me, unfortunately. Always a bridesmaid, never a bride. Story of my life."

Tinker loomed up suddenly. "Listen, Llewellyn, about this little expedition of yours. I want to come too."

"What expedition?" Charles asked guardedly.

"To see these things of Holly's ex. Seems to me—"

"My God, what's she been saying?" Charles demanded.

Holly, on the other side of the patio, apparently had heard him. "What

I've been saying all along—that the police aren't going to do anything, so somebody else will have to. *Us.* We're the only hope Reg has."

"I don't understand," Mary said to Charles in an urgent undertone. "What's this about an expedition?"

"Apparently your son's things are still in the garage of his studio," Charles explained in a low voice. "Holly wants to go through them to see if there's any clue there."

"But . . . she sent all that back to London."

"Apparently she didn't. She said she couldn't face it, so she just locked them up in the garage and walked away."

"Well, she should have told us, we could have done it for her." Mary sounded reproachful. "We'd have been happy to do it."

Holly was continuing her diatribe against López and all the other policemen within a thousand-mile radius. The *linternas* were all lit now. Reactions were varied, to say the least. Mary looked a little sick, Bland irritated, the Beams rather shocked, the colonel approving, Helen Bland and Alastair Morland rather puzzled, and Tinker . . . Tinker's expression was hard to read. It was, Charles finally decided, looking up, a mixture of alarm and pride. He'd seen that look before on the face of an American man whose wife had just made some outrageous statement or other. One could practically see the cogs whirling and the gears clashing as their instincts warred within them. They were calculating the advantages of staying quiet as against the disadvantages of letting their women make fools of themselves. Tinker seemed to be taking a middle road.

"That's a brave plan, Holly, honey, but doing things like that could be dangerous in a foreign country, you know. I don't think I like the idea of you gallivanting around, girl. Really, I don't."

She glared at him and started to speak, but Nigel Bland spoke first.

"Holly, if I'd thought there was anything to be done in that line, don't you think I'd have done it already?" he asked gently. "After all, I *was* trained for it."

"Well, then, why haven't you?" Holly demanded.

"Because I know my limitations," Nigel said. "My Spanish isn't all that good to begin with, and I could end up making things difficult for everyone. The Spanish are quick to take offence, you know."

"That's what Charles keeps saying," Holly said, slightly abashed.

"And he's right," Dick Beam said. "You should listen to him."

"Holly, please be careful," Mary said. With a sinking sensation, Charles realized that Mary knew Holly better than anyone else at the gathering. She seemed to have automatically accepted that if Holly said she was going to do something, she would. He'd been hoping that the passage of time would alter Holly's determination. Apparently that wasn't going to be enough.

Morland cleared his throat. "But what on earth can you actually do, Holly?" he asked in his soft, clear voice. "Surely the police have covered every possibility?"

"Everything they've had access to, maybe."

"What haven't they had access to then?"

"Oh . . . some things of David's, for instance," Holly said airily.

"What things?"

"Oh, junk I couldn't face going through after all the trouble."

"What trouble?" Tinker asked. The people in the gathering who knew the history looked at one another as Tinker charged in where angels feared to tread, and tried to pretend they were somewhere else.

Holly came across the patio, her eyes flashing dangerously.

"When David was arrested for forgery," she said.

"David? Your husband? He was a criminal?" Tinker looked dumbfounded.

"That's right. Why did you think they arrested Reg, anyway?" Holly demanded, looking at him as if he were an idiot.

"I . . . thought it was . . . personal," Tinker stammered. He looked supremely uncomfortable.

"You mean you've assumed all along that Reg was guilty?"

"No . . . no, of course not!" Tinker registered reproach. "I just didn't like to pry, is all." He lowered his voice. "Didn't think you'd like to talk about it."

"You mean as if we had an imbecile child hidden in the attic?" Holly asked sweetly.

"Holly!" Mary said reprovingly. "Mel was only trying to be kind."

Holly regarded him for a moment, then relented. "I suppose so. Sorry, Mel. I'm a little worked up about all this."

"Why, that's all right, honey," Tinker said, relieved. "Let's forget it. Let's enjoy ourselves, hey? More wine all round." The others chorused their enthusiasm with a trace of hysteria, trying to overcome the awkward moment.

"I don't want to forget it," Holly said in a low, dark voice, and went towards the house. Above the hubbub, Charles turned and met Mary Partridge's eyes. She'd heard it, too.

"Don't let her get carried away, Charles," she pleaded in a whisper. "She means well, but her heart rules her head sometimes. All she wants is for everyone to be happy, for everything to be perfect. That's all it is, really."

"That was Hitler's excuse, too," Charles said miserably. "Let me get you some more wine." He took her glass and joined the throng around the table. There were bowls of desserts there, too, for people to help themselves. And plates of *galletas* and *pastelillos* and *turrón*. Charles took a plate and put a selection on it for Mary, and started back across the patio. The gathering had become a little louder . . . much to the distress of Dot Beam, who apparently envisaged something along the restrained lines of a Royal Garden Party. Her kindly horse-face was wrinkled as she sought to soothe with helpings of trifle, and Dick Beam had his sardonic mask on again. No wonder we usually keep ourselves apart from this lot, he seemed to be thinking. His eyes met Charles's and he flushed slightly, as if caught out.

Charles glanced at his watch twenty minutes later, wondering whether he should leave, when a frenzied barking out in the darkness stopped everyone in mid-conversation. It sounded like mayhem, but was quickly identified as Queenie among the peacocks.

"But I locked her in the car . . ." the colonel said, wringing his hands. "Didn't I, Alastair? We both did."

"Well, she's out now," Dick Beam said grimly. "I did ask you not to bring her, Jackson. We never allow dogs." He bustled off, calling servants and demanding more *linternas*. "You'd better see if you can call her," he shouted back over his shoulder.

"Oh, dear," the colonel said, looking on the verge of tears. "Alastair, *do* something . . ."

Charles felt a tug at his sleeve, and turned to find Holly standing there in a shadow. "Come on," she whispered. "Now's our chance."

"For what?" Charles asked.

"To get away. Come on!"

They were driving through the trees before Charles had the nerve to ask.

"You let Queenie out, didn't you?"

"Yep." She seemed very satisfied at the result. Behind them, beams from torches were crossing and recrossing as the servants and the guests ran around trying to catch the dog, whose merry barking soared above the screeching of the harried peacocks. "She won't hurt them, she's a lamb. She only wanted to play."

"You've ruined the colonel's social life for good, as far as the Beams are concerned," Charles said sternly.

"He'll survive. He doesn't like them anyway, he's told me." She grinned. "That's why he brought Queenie in the first place, if you ask me."

"Well, we're away," Charles said, stopping at the mouth of the road and looking up and down the highway. "Now what? And why the sudden dash, anyway?"

"Mel wanted to come along. In another ten minutes, they'd *all* have wanted to join in the fun, like some bloody Enid Blyton adventure, *The Secret Seventeen* or *The Mystery of the Middle-Aged Muddlers.*"

"Instead of which, we have *The Timorous Two,*" Charles said, turning right toward Puerto Rio and, beyond that, Espina.

"The Timorous One, you mean," Holly muttered, but remained silent the rest of the way.

David Partridge's studio had been down near the old harbour. The sea had receded from Espina long ago, and the town itself was now high above the sloping beach. A commercial harbour had been built on the other side of the spit of land that thrust out from the rocky escarpment, for fishing was still a source of revenue for the small town. Much of it, however, had become sport fishing with tourists in the summer months. Only in winter did all the boats go out together.

For many years the old harbour had been more or less deserted, but with the advent of tourism, the old buildings had been taken over by entrepreneurs and remodelled into holiday flats. New buildings in the old style had been added, and David's studio was apparently one of these. Holly indicated the windows of the studio, dark now, as it was nearly eleven-thirty. "I guess they've gone to bed."

"Friends of yours?"

"Not really. Friends of friends. I've been meaning to look them up since I arrived, but . . ." She shrugged and pointed to a narrow dark opening beyond the end of the building. "You have to go through there to get to the garages."

Cautiously, Charles drove the Seat through the gap and down the narrow passage, which eventually opened out into a large paved area onto which faced a line of garages. "The last one," Holly said. "Right at the far end."

He parked the car in front of the door which was painted—or had been painted—bright orange. The colour leapt at him before he turned off the headlamps. "I presume you've brought the key?" he asked, pointing to a padlock.

"Of course." Holly got out and stood looking around. "It hasn't changed much."

Charles closed his door and leaned on the roof of the Seat. The salty air from the sea mixed with the more tangy odours of petrol and oil and the smell of cooking from some of the buildings overlooking the small yard.

Holly went over to the door and he followed, standing there resignedly as she searched for the keys in her vast handbag. She handed him a small box of tissues, a bottle of nail varnish, a Spanish phrase-book, a purse, a cheque book, a large hairbrush, several skeins of wool, a small Spanish doll and an empty aspirin bottle. "Here it is," she finally said, taking out a key on a tag and holding the mouth of the bag open so he could dump all the things back in. "Thanks," she said and reached for the padlock, then froze.

"What's the matter?" he asked.

"It's already open," she said in a small puzzled voice.

"Here, let me," he said and, removing the padlock, he bent down and lifted the door, which swung up and out, forcing them to step back.

The garage was empty.

"Are you sure this is the right one?" he asked after a moment.

"Of course, the number's on the tag. My God, it's been ripped off!"

"Well, it has been sort of ignored for over two years," Charles said. "Somebody must have noticed . . . or maybe one of your tenants?"

"Oh, I don't think so. They'd have said something . . . I know them all, personally. I mean, nobody has any trouble renting a place like this once the word gets around. I never had to advertise, it was always friends, or friends of friends." Her shoulders were slumped, and she looked about half the size she'd been a few minutes ago. Even her hair seemed to droop.

"Is there a light?" he asked. There could have been something left; the place was only faintly lit by the overhead lamps around the yard.

"Just inside, on the left."

He found it after a moment, and turned the switch. Light bounced out for a few seconds from a dusty bulb hanging in the centre of the space, and then there was a *phhffft* and it went out. Even so, it had been sufficient to see that the entire space was empty and clean—almost as if it had been swept out. "Sorry," he said.

She gave a mirthless laugh. "No reason for you to be sorry," she said. "God, I feel so let down . . . I was so *sure.*"

"Never mind, we'll find another way," he said, in an attempt to reassure her, and then stood there, horrified at what he'd said. What on earth was wrong with him? Next thing he knew, he'd be offering to slay a dragon. "Come on. It will be after midnight before we get back."

Disconsolately, she walked back towards the car while he closed the door and, rather pointlessly, replaced and shut the padlock. He was just about to start the engine when there was a shout.

"Alto, mierda! Alto, alto, descarado!" A short, angry man ran out onto

the concrete apron, waving his arms. Charles paused, half in and half out of the car.

"*Que hay, abuelo?*" Charles asked, startled. Holly, too, was standing amazed on the other side of the car. The little man puffed up to Charles and grabbed his jacket, releasing a flood of garlic-scented abuse.

"*Vaya más despacio, por favor,*" Charles pleaded, trying to make some sense of the strongly accented outrage.

The old man, still angry, looked at the car, blinked up at Charles, and released a fresh torrent of Spanish, waving his arms and taking Charles by the sleeve, dragging him back to where the concrete apron was edged by a fence. The old man pointed at an area of fence that was flattened. The ends of the splintered wood showed white as they lay on the remains of a small vegetable patch. Several large green pumpkins lay split open, clearly crushed by a car's tyres.

"*No fuimos nosotros,*" Charles protested.

"*Sí, sí, misma garaje!*" the old man shouted.

"What on earth is wrong?" Holly asked nervously, looking around as if expecting a mob to arrive with torches and lynch them.

"Somebody backed into his garden," Charles tried to explain over the old man's complaints. They were not so outraged now, but had more of an air of self-pity about them, as he regarded the destruction of his autumn crop. "About an hour ago, somebody in a green van came to this garage and cleared it out. They were in a big hurry and backed into the fence as they left."

"Tonight!" Holly exclaimed.

"About an hour ago," Charles repeated. "They left too fast for him to catch . . ." He paused and turned to the old man.

"*Vió la matriculación?*"

"No." The old man was regretful.

"He didn't see the registration plate," Charles said. Something struck him. "*Español? O extranjero?*"

"*No estoy seguro,*" the old man muttered, jamming his hands in his pockets. "*Es lástima, verdad?*"

"*Verdad,*" Charles agreed, sympathetically. He took the man's name and address, and said he would be in touch, because they would be making an insurance claim and there was no reason why the fence and the lost vegetables shouldn't be on it too. He gave him some money "on account"— thereby removing any stigma of charity.

They drove away, the old man watching them suspiciously, but fingering the money Charles had given him as a source of consolation.

The road back to Puerto Rio seemed longer than the road coming, although it was the same road. There was only one.

"Any of them could have used the phone," Charles muttered.

"Who?" Holly asked, startled, for he'd been silent for some time. "Oh, you mean someone at the party?"

Charles nodded. "Somebody was worried about what we were going to find. The trouble is, what was it?"

"I can hardly remember what was in there now. Reg might remember more, he has that kind of mind."

"Well, we'd better go and see him in the morning and see if we can work out what it might have been. Something important, obviously, because they moved fast to get it before we did."

"But it was only junk . . . painting gear, clothes . . . Look out!"

Charles had been looking out. In fact, he'd had his eye on the glaring headlamps that had been following them since they left Espina. They'd loom up, then drop back, then loom up again, as if the driver of the other car had wanted to pass them, but thought better of it each time. The road was twisting, but Charles had been maintaining a good speed. He'd presumed the other driver had finally accepted defeat and settled back, content to match his pace. Now, however, on the worst curve of all, the shadowy figure behind the other wheel had decided to make his move.

And there was simply not enough room.

Charles swerved, hit the horn and brakes simultaneously, but it was no good. With a shattering, shuddering crash and a grind of metal, the front wing of the other car hit the side of his own, twice, and sent him straight towards the fence at the side of the road.

The dry wood of the palings snapped, the car teetered for a moment on the edge of the drop, then started its long slow slide down the ravine. Faster and faster it went, gathering speed. Charles opened his door, grabbed a screaming Holly's arm and jumped, hitting the scratchy bushes in a painful tangle of arms, legs, elbows, knees.

The car continued down the slide, rolling from side to side now, as it hit rocks that had preceded it down the hill over the years. At last it hit a boulder. It would have turned over, but had nearly reached the bottom of the ravine and ended on its side in the dry bed of the creek. There was a long pause, broken only by the slide and skitter of small rocks and clay and sand following after the car. Then there was a *ping* and a sudden *whoosh,* as if from some invisible bellows.

The darkness disappeared as the car began to burn.

And the bright night grew hot.

CHAPTER 8

The first face that Charles saw as he came to was that of Holly bending over him. It seemed a wonderful way to wake up, gazing into those turquoise eyes that had grown all dark with concern.

And then the pain hit him.

"Bloody hell," he mumbled. The pain had been caused by his trying to move. He didn't try it again, except his mouth, to ask her if she was all right.

"I'm fine. I landed on you."

"So I notice. Where are we?"

"At a clinic in Espina. An ambulance brought us here."

"Who called the ambulance?"

"The Guardia officer who came by a few minutes after you passed out."

"Oh." It couldn't have been Moreno, that was certain. Moreno would have driven right on by.

"Charles?"

"What?"

"You saved my life. I was terrified, I couldn't move . . . you grabbed me . . ."

"Did I?" He tried bending his arm. Big mistake. "I really don't remember doing anything, to tell you the truth. Was I very brave and noble and all that?"

"No. You just started yelling and cursing and grabbed me and we shot out into the bushes."

"And rocks. There must have been some rocks." He tried the other arm. Another mistake.

"Yes, lots of rocks. I'm afraid your car was totalled."

"Was what?"

"Umm, what do you call it? Written off."

"Wonderful. Beautiful. Perfect ending to a perfect day."

"Don't be such a crab. We're alive, aren't we?"

"Speak for yourself. Personally, I think . . ."

"You're only bruised, the doctor said. And a little concussed. Fortunately, he speaks English. Oh yes, and a couple of your ribs are cracked, but not very badly."

"What about my right leg? I can't move my right leg!" His voice rose suddenly in an undignified yelp of panic.

She glanced down. "Oh, for heaven's sake." She did something with the bedclothes. "There. It was only caught in the sheet. You *are* a baby."

"A minute ago I thought I was a hero."

"Yes." She straightened up and looked thoughtful. "Charles."

"Still here."

"That other car pushed us over on purpose, you know."

"I'm quite aware of that, thank you. It was a red car."

"Was it? I didn't notice."

"Do you know anybody with a red car?"

"Lots of people. Mel's car is red . . . a red Mercedes convertible."

"This was a saloon."

"You're very observant."

"It had been behind us from the minute we left the harbour."

"Did you get the licence number?" she asked eagerly.

"Damn, I knew I'd forgotten something," he said sarcastically.

"Shame."

"Indeed." This time, when he moved his body, it wasn't so bad. It was still agony, but the agonies had sorted themselves out. There was a small agony in his left knee, a medium agony in both elbows, and quite a respectable-sized agony in his chest. Also, his nose itched.

Being alive was not all that he'd hoped it would be as he leapt out of the falling car.

"We're on to something," Holly said in a stage whisper. "I told you."

"Do you think they have something like Novocaine for your whole body?" Charles asked plaintively.

"Oh, stop complaining and listen," Holly commanded. "Really, Charles, you are so *feeble.* Don't you see? Somebody is afraid of us!"

"Oh, goody," Charles said, closing his eyes. "Isn't that swell?"

A couple of hours later, Charles stood teetering on the steps of the clinic and shivered. His ribs told him this was not a good thing to do, but he couldn't stop. Dawn was just breaking over Espina. The ramparts of the old castle on the hill were gilded with the sun's light, but the air was cold.

"What do you suggest we do now?" Charles asked. "Hire a bicycle?"

"Nigel should be here any minute. I rang Mary and she rang him."

"Good old Nigel," Charles muttered. When she turned on him and opened her mouth, he beat her to it. "I know, I'm an ungrateful bastard and feeble with it. Where's my backbone and my stiff upper lip and all that? Scattered over that ravine, I should imagine."

"I didn't ask."

Now she was angry. Apparently he wasn't being all he should be. No wonder David Partridge had moved to Spain. She probably figured *he* should have shaped up, too. Instead he'd shipped out. Probably Mel Tinker would have said something wonderfully inspiring about it being the dawn of a new day, in which they'd seek truth and justice, which was the American way.

They stood there in silence, shifting from one foot to the other until Nigel arrived.

"You don't look too bad," he observed as they climbed in.

"This is not my body you see before you," Charles growled. "It's a plastic facsimile they ran up in the basement. It doesn't fit."

"We were forced off the road on purpose, Nigel," Holly reported in some triumph. "Somebody tried to kill us!"

Nigel's eyes met Charles's in the rear-view mirror. "That so?"

"Well, I'm not so sure now. It could have been an accident. Spanish drivers are pretty wild . . ."

Holly emitted a strangled sound of either derision or frustration. "He's just scared."

Nigel glanced at her. "Aren't you?"

"No."

"Then you're a fool," he said flatly.

"Well," she amended, "I'm a *little* scared, but mostly I'm just damned angry." She told him about the empty garage. "Don't you see, Nigel? Somebody didn't want us to find what was there, and somebody doesn't want us to go on looking for the real killer."

"Presumably the killer himself," Charles said drily.

"You should leave these things to the professionals," Nigel said.

"Who? The Judicial Police? This lazy López Charles keeps talking about?"

"It's not laziness," Charles protested from the back.

"What is it then?" she asked without turning around.

"Well, it's more like fatalism. The Spanish have a saying: If God wants to help me, he knows where to find me."

"And if he doesn't?"

Charles shrugged, and nearly screamed. It wasn't his ribs so much as the way the adhesive strapping pulled at the hairs on his chest. He wondered why he felt so entirely rotten, aside from the bruises and the shock, and then remembered he'd had practically no sleep. A coma didn't count as sleep, did it? Well, unconsciousness, then. Not the same thing at all. Holly and Nigel were talking in the front seat. They seemed to have everything in hand. He wasn't needed.

"Charles!"

"What?" He jerked his head up from where it was resting against the window. "What? What?"

"You were sleeping!" Holly said in an accusing voice. "The doctor said you weren't to be allowed to sleep for at least twelve hours . . ."

"I was just resting my eyes," he mumbled.

"Nigel thinks we ought to tell your precious López about this."

"Good." Charles closed his eyes again. "You tell him all about it. He'll like that. He likes to be told things. All the facts at his . . ."

"No, Charles, *you* need to go."

"Won't," Charles said sulkily. "Can't make me."

"Two disasters!" López said with concern. "I had been informed about the accident, but not the robbery. Thanks be to God you were not badly hurt."

Charles considered dying right there in his office, but decided it would be bad manners. Better to wait until he got outside in the street.

"But don't you see?" Holly said eagerly. "It means that someone tried to kill us."

"Señorita, with the greatest respect, it need mean nothing of the kind," López said. "The robbery and the road accident may not be connected in any way."

"Oh, come *on*," Holly said, her voice heavy with sarcasm.

Charles saw López's eyes narrow, and roused himself. "It does seem a rather high order of coincidence, Esteban."

"But what was in this garage that is so important?" López asked Holly. His eyes said he appreciated her, but not her interference. "And why did you not come to me about it?"

Holly gestured impatiently. "Why should you waste your time on it unless there *was* something important?" she asked. My God, Charles thought, she's improving. That was almost a compliment. "That's why we wanted to take a look first. If there had been anything, we'd have brought it to you."

In fact, Charles was dismayed to find, she'd improved too much. *That* was an out-and-out lie.

"I still do not quite understand what it is you are—or were—trying to do, Charles." López's eyes, when they turned to him, were full of reproach. Don't you trust me, old friend? they seemed to say. Don't you know I will do my best to be fair, despite the fact that the father-in-law of this impossible girl is a murderer?

"Holly feels there may be some connection with Graebner's death and the forgery case of some years ago," Charles said.

"But yes, clearly that is so. Señor Partridge threatened the man's life at that time," López agreed. "That was the cause of the hatred."

"No, you don't understand," Holly broke in. "We think there was some-one *else* involved, someone who doesn't want—"

"Graebner took the full blame, señorita, it is in the records. He implicated no one else . . . save your late husband, of course," López said, a slight warning edge in his voice.

"Maybe he was paid off to do that," Holly said promptly. "Didn't it ever occur to you that it must have taken a lot of people to—"

"It would have gone easier with Graebner if he had turned evidence against any other, señorita," López said. "Yet he did not, and he was the kind of man who would have done anything to save his own skin, by all accounts."

Holly glared at him. "I don't think you're taking this seriously enough."

"Oh, but I am," López said, glancing at Charles. "I can see that you want to do anything you can to release your father-in-law from the charge of—"

"Up to and including throwing myself off a cliff, I suppose?" Holly asked sweetly. "Do you think I'm making all this up? Do you think *I* made Charles drive off the road?"

Charles got up and took her arm, helping her, rather abruptly, to her feet. "I'm sure Esteban doesn't think anything of the sort," he said hurriedly. He could see the look of anger gathering in López's face. The fact that she was pretty wasn't sufficient to overcome the Spaniard's instinctive dislike of a female who didn't know her place. "We've reported the accident. I'm cer-tain that all proper investigations will be made concerning the other car and driver. Meanwhile, we're tired and upset, and everything will be better after we've had a bit of a rest and—"

"Don't be such a mealy-mouthed fat-head," Holly said, pulling away. "I want to get—"

"We'll be in touch, Esteban, as soon as we have a list of the things that were in the garage," Charles said, moving towards the door. "Thank you for seeing us."

Back in the car, Holly threw herself into the front seat beside Nigel. "There was no need to hustle me out of there like a kid," she complained.

"I told you to keep your mouth shut."

"What did she say?" Nigel asked, amused.

"I didn't say *anything.*" Holly sulked.

"It wasn't what you said, but the way you said it . . . you as much as told him he was a fool."

"Well, he is." She turned to Nigel. "The smug bastard isn't going to do anything, Nigel. It was as plain as plain."

"On the contrary, I think he is already doing something," Charles said from the back seat. His tone was thoughtful.

"Why do you think that?" Nigel asked, turning around.

"Because he said he'd been informed about the accident. Normally he wouldn't be; the GC handle road accidents. If he was informed, it was because he'd *asked* to be kept informed about us. I find that very encouraging."

"You would," Holly said in disgust.

López was smiling. "Bas, I want to hear the minute the GC have anything on this red saloon. Also send someone to interview this caretaker, or whatever he was, about the people who ruined his garden last night." Bas was making notes furiously. "Ring Señor Ribes again and tell him that we are still looking for the files on the Graebner-Partridge case."

"But they are there, on the desk; I got them—"

"Tell Señor Ribes we are still looking."

"Yes, sir."

"Convey my deepest apologies."

"Yes, sir."

"And did you get the information on those officers from the GC?"

"Yes, sir," Paco said in a low, miserable voice. The ordeal had been even worse than he'd anticipated.

"Where is it?"

"Also on your desk."

"Ah . . . yes." López lifted up one file and found another. "Did they give you a difficult time?"

"I . . . prevailed."

López smiled. "One day you will learn that to prevail is as important as to pounce. Steady pressure is what we are after here. If you are learning to apply it on one level, you will learn to apply it on all. Do you understand?"

Paco swallowed, took a deep breath, and spoke. "I don't understand anything, sir. I don't understand why we are doing half the things we are doing; and if Señor Llewellyn is such a good friend, why you do not trust him; and if there is danger, why you allow it to continue when already a man is dead, and—"

"Sit down, Paco," López said sharply and Bas, with a stricken expression on his round ugly face, sat. Now it was over. He had gone too far, and his career was destroyed. His mother would kill him. His father would curse him. His sisters and brothers would laugh at him. "Why haven't you asked me all this before?" López asked.

"I didn't think it was my place, sir."

"But that is exactly what it is, Bas, your place. I thought you would never get around to taking it." López smiled. "Now that you have, I will explain."

Reg was horrified to learn of the accident. Although it seemed impossible, he grew even more pale. "My dear girl, you must stop all this nonsense at once!"

"Stop what?"

"Trying to find out things. Trying to play detective. Why, you might have been killed!" The danger to her seemed to be more real to him than his own, and yet nothing had changed. He was still in jail. Still charged with murder. And still unwell.

"If Spain hadn't abolished the death sentence a few years back, you might have been too, by now," Holly shot back. "I didn't get killed anyway, because Charles saved me."

Reg turned to him. "Dear boy, what can I say?"

"You can tell her to stop getting up people's noses and go home and tend to her damned sewing," Charles said wearily.

"It doesn't appear to have much effect," Reg observed, looking at Holly's flashing eyes and clenched fists. She looked ready to hit someone.

"I know. Keep trying," Charles said.

"No, instead try to remember all the things of David's we packed up after the funeral," Holly said, with a scowl at Charles.

"What possible use would that be? You have it all in London, don't you?"

"No . . . I chickened out at the last minute. It's been in the studio garage ever since," Holly said, hurriedly. "I just couldn't face it."

"Well, but you should have told me. I'd have done it for you," Reg said. "My goodness, it's not as if I didn't have the time."

"Anyway, you have a better memory than I have," Holly said briskly. "Now, what did we put into those two big cartons, for a start? The sketch books went in the bottom, but . . ."

Over in the corner, Charles snored softly.

They pretended not to hear. And he pretended not to listen.

Twenty minutes later the list was finished, and read as follows:

Clothing in three suitcases—1 blue plastic and 2 brown leather
About twenty unfinished original paintings
Seven incomplete copies of Goya Caprichos
Four empty frames
Frame moulds and materials
Three cartons of unused paints
Stretchers, canvas, wood scraps, et cetera
A portable radio/cassette player, not working
Mattress and box spring
2 odd chairs
2 cartons of books
1 carton of miscellaneous "junk"—toiletries, et cetera
2 cartons of personal papers and records, cheque stubs, et cetera
4 lamps
Beach equipment—1 chair, 1 umbrella, 1 windbreak, 1 mat
Typewriter, portable
Tennis racket, squash racket, golf clubs
Weights

In short, not enough to tempt a rag-and-bone man, much less a thief.
And yet it all was gone.

CHAPTER 9

"What do you mean by 'weights'?" Charles asked that evening. He'd spent
the day asleep, and had hoped Holly would do the same, but she had rung
him up at four to make sure he'd come around to dinner. The pain of the
telephone bell piercing his brain had been so intense, he'd agreed before he
realized what he was doing.

He'd wrapped a plastic dry-cleaning bag around his chest to protect the
bandage while he washed, but it had got wet, anyway, and now it felt cold
and sodden in the breeze from the sea. Next, he supposed gloomily, it would
be pneumonia.

Oh well, they had a cure for pneumonia, didn't they?

Unfortunately, they didn't have a cure for Holly Partridge, which was a
much more severe affliction. She showed little sign of being either tired or in
pain, although Charles was sure she, too, must be aching from the crash.

There she was, sitting across from him on the patio of the penthouse, the last of the sun catching in her glorious hair—bright-eyed, chirpy, and ready for anything.

It made him feel twice as bad.

"You know," she said patiently, gesturing in the air as if pushing at something heavy overhead. "Dumb-bells. David thought he was too skinny and was always trying to build himself up. He was very athletic."

He didn't want to hear about David's muscles and David's golf handicaps. "And frame moulds—what are they?"

"Oh, David made all his own frames. Most young artists do now—especially the poor ones. He used fibreglass to duplicate old mouldings."

Charles grunted. He didn't want to hear about David's clever economies or abstruse skills or his meaningful struggles with artistic expression during their marriage. He especially didn't want to hear about their marriage.

"I see. What about these personal papers? Could there be anything in there?" He was gazing at the list, which kept flapping in the breeze.

"No, it was mostly old bank statements, tax records, art catalogues, commission records, that kind of thing. We went through them at the time and weeded out anything that needed attention. What was left was all out-of-date stuff. Just dross, but it needed to be kept for a couple of years because of taxes."

"And the tape recorder? Could there have been a cassette in it?"

She leaned back against the blue-and-white-flowered cushions of the patio chair. "What, with some kind of message on it, you mean?"

"I know it sounds far-fetched, but . . ."

She shook her head. "It was empty. I looked. I took *all* the cassettes David had. Some of them were mine anyway."

Charles scanned the list again. "Could there have been anything stuffed in the mattress? I'm told David's share of the proceeds was never found."

"Because he never had any money. There were only a few hundred pounds in his account when he died."

"The number of a Swiss account? It could have been written down someplace; all you need is the number and . . ."

"That might be, if he'd had any money from Graebner, which he didn't." Her voice was angry. "All he had was the commission money for the copies, and that had been spent."

"How much?"

"According to his bank statements, six thousand pounds."

"And it was gone? What did he spend it on?"

"Well, knowing David, I'd say some went on women, some on drink, some on clothes, some on gambling . . . and the rest he spent foolishly," Holly said snidely.

From the kitchen came the clatter of Mary Partridge preparing the dinner. She sounded angry about it, he thought. Maybe she hadn't wanted him to come. Or maybe she hated cooking. He let the list drop and lay back, wincing. The list was too general. Whatever they were searching for could be very small, very insignificant. And anyway, it was gone.

"Hi! You suffering, too?" came a call from the next patio.

Charles opened his eyes and saw the small, wiry figure of the colonel outlined against the red sky. "Good evening, sir."

"Got it too, did you?"

"Got what?"

"The Valencian quick-step," came the reply. "Up all night after that damned paella of Beam's, sick as a dog. From the look of you, you had the same."

"No, we didn't. Had an accident with my car, instead."

"You don't say. All right, are you?"

"More or less."

"We wondered where you'd got to last night. Once all the excitement had died down, that Tinker chap started looking for you. He was fit to be tied when he realized you'd gone off without him."

"I know," Holly said. "He rang me at lunch-time."

"Jealous, isn't he?" The colonel cackled. "Thought he was, the way he carried on about poor old Charles there."

Poor old Charles smiled to himself.

"Do him good," the colonel said, bending down to pick up his watering can. "Too fond of himself, if you ask me. Had the gall to tell me I should keep Queenie on a lead. Still don't know how she got out . . . unless she opened the door herself. Wouldn't put it past her, clever girl."

Charles could see Holly's face flushing slightly. "She didn't do any damage, did she?"

"Got a mouthful of feathers, that's all," the colonel crowed. "Ever see a peacock run? Funniest damn thing I ever saw. Well, must get on, must get on . . ." He moved off down the line of geranium pots, bearing their water of life.

"So Tinker was jealous, was he?" Charles asked, amused.

"Don't be silly. He'll probably be around later. He usually is."

"How wearying for you, poor flower," Charles remarked.

Mary appeared in the open doorway. "Dinner's nearly ready, you two. Better wash your hands."

"Yes, Mummy," Holly murmured with a grin.

"You know," Charles said, getting up carefully, "you said David did well out of his copying, but I don't think five hundred pounds a picture is much return for the amount of work he must have put into it. In fact, he came up short, didn't he? He did thirteen pictures, a baker's dozen, that works out at—"

"Would you rather eat out here?" Mary asked patiently.

"Why not?" Charles said. "It's warm enough still." Belatedly he remembered his manners. "Let me carry the things out for you."

"Thank you." He dutifully followed Mary into the kitchen, but Holly didn't move. When he appeared with the first tray-load, she was gone.

"Holly?" He looked around, but she was nowhere to be seen. His stomach clenched, and he started towards the patio's edge. It wasn't possible, she simply couldn't have . . .

"Hey, look at this!" came Holly's voice from behind him. Charles nearly jumped out of his skin.

"Don't *do* that!" he shouted, turning.

She stared at him, startled. "Do what?"

She was carrying the fake Bosch pressed against the front of her sweatshirt. Her legs were bare below ragged cut-off denim shorts, her knees were scraped, like a child's, and her red curls were blowing every which way. She looked like Orphan Annie.

"Don't disappear like that!"

"I didn't disappear, I just went inside to get this. What's the matter with you, Charles? You really are an old fuss-pot."

"I suppose I am." He was suddenly embarrassed. He could hardly admit he thought she'd jumped over the edge in a fit of grief, could he? Fuss-pot, maybe. But an *old* fuss-pot, surely? Was he? He turned away, only to encounter the interested stare of two sets of eyes and one pair of sunglasses, behind which, presumably, a third pair of eyes lurked. They were turned in his direction, at least, and were on the face of a man in a wheelchair on the patio of the third penthouse.

Mr. Neufeld, I presume, Charles thought.

The wheelchair was near the parapet at the front, facing the sea, but Neufeld's face was turned towards them as he watched their activities with apparent interest. After a moment the head turned away, and the sunglasses faced the sea once more. The hands folded on the blanketed lap twitched once, and then lay still.

The other two sets of eyes were more interesting—at least, the pair belonging to the tall, elegant blonde was. Dark-blue and huge, they were openly assessing him, up and down. Mrs. Neufeld was a beautiful woman all right, and even at this distance exuded an animal sexuality that was like the perfume of tropical night flowers—intangible but all-pervasive.

The third pair of eyes belonged to the male nurse and their message was also plain: Keep off.

Seeing Charles's glance meet Mrs. Neufeld's across the intervening space, he stepped forward and asked her some urgent question in a low voice. With a faint, final smile, the lushly curved Mrs. Neufeld abandoned her survey of Charles and put a hand on the manservant's arm. Her husband's back was turned. The situation was clear. They might have had signs over their heads —"cuckolded husband," "cheating wife," "jealous lover." He sighed, and went over to the table to put down the tray. "Look at what?"

"This picture of David's. What you just said reminded me of something. It's pretty fantastic, but . . ." She was energetically prying at the back of the frame with a knife from the tray. "Damn." The knife had slipped, cutting her slightly.

"Here, let me." Charles took the picture and the knife from her. He removed the panel pins and pulled the wooden backing away from the frame. Holly took her thumb out of her mouth, wiped it impatiently on the side of her shorts, and took the picture back. She stared at it for so long, Charles became impatient. "Well, what is it?"

"This canvas is too new," she finally said.

Charles peered at it. "Looks pretty old to me."

"Old, yes, but not old enough. Remember, Bosch was painting nearly five hundred years ago. This canvas isn't anywhere near that."

"Does that make a difference?"

"Yes. For a start, I expected the picture to be relined . . . a lot of old paintings grow fragile or become damaged over the years, and need to be relined with modern canvas so they won't fall apart. Then only the edges show their true age. Sometimes forgers maltreat a copy and 'restore' it—so the buyer thinks he's getting a real bargain, when really the whole damn thing is a fake. Or they'll take an old *bad* painting on canvas of the right age and overpaint it, then treat the new work with heat lamps and so on until it matches the canvas. That's what he seems to have done with this one. Maybe he just couldn't find a canvas old enough and hoped the buyer would be too thick to know better."

"Is it really that easy to fool people?" Charles asked.

"Oh boy, is it." Holly grinned, leaning the picture and frame against the inside of the parapet and going to help Mary with the casserole she was carrying. "Pictures are authenticated by what's called 'provenance'—a proveable record of its history, either through bills of sale or wills or contemporary accounts of such and such a family owning such and such a painting, and so on. There's a thriving business in fake provenances, along with fake paintings. Museums have ways of authenticating paintings by scientific means, obviously, but the ordinary collector has to depend on provenance or on the reputation of his dealer or on the opinions of experts. And believe me, experts these days are very cautious. Honest experts don't hand them out like gum drops. Crooks do. Graebner did."

"This table is getting very battered," Mary said suddenly.

Startled, Charles and Holly looked at her as she spooned food onto their plates.

"We only got it last spring and look at it . . ." She seemed strangely upset by it. "I must ask Reg to . . ." Mary's fork faltered in mid-air.

"I'll be glad to . . ." Charles said quickly.

"I can do it," Holly said at the same time.

Mary put her fork down. Her tears spilled out so quickly they dropped onto her plate before she could get her napkin up to her face. She stood up abruptly. "I don't feel much like eating," she said. "You two go on—I'll just lie down for a bit. Please . . . go on." She ran for the solacing shadows of the penthouse. After a moment they heard the bedroom door slam.

"Blast," Charles said, half under his breath, jabbing his fork into the nearest piece of beef and splashing tomatoes and peppers all over the top of the table.

"Maybe I'd better see . . ." Holly started to get up.

"No," Charles commanded. "Let her cry—it will exhaust her and she'll sleep. You go on telling me about faking pictures."

"But she . . ."

"Go on, tell me," he said sharply. After a moment of hesitation, she sat down obediently and picked up her fork.

"She's only hanging on by a thread, you know."

"Tell me about the bloody pictures, dammit," Charles said.

Holly swallowed. "All right. Where was I?"

"About expert opinions and how they don't give them out," Charles said, doggedly. "Why are they so cautious?"

"Well, to start with, you're up against the Old Masters themselves in trying to place a picture. A lot of them had pupils who copied their work in order to learn. Some of the pupils were very good. For instance, there was a pupil of Velázquez named Del Mazo, who could not only copy Velázquez, but also Tintoretto, Raphael, Titian . . . he did it as a living, just as David did. He worked for King Philip IV of Spain, as a matter of fact, and he married Velázquez' own daughter, so he was well thought of. You see, in those days the only way they could see masterpieces was to send a court painter to copy them and bring them back. Everybody did it. And those pupils also sometimes painted in backgrounds on the big pictures, or had their own copies corrected by the Masters—all that makes it very difficult, right?"

"I guess so."

"So first of all you get attributions to 'the school of,' okay?"

"Yes."

"But that's not the whole problem. You see, not all those court painters indicated their works were copies. Sometimes they even fooled the Masters themselves. And to make matters worse, they were doing their copies at the same time the originals were done, or damn near it. Which means not only are their canvases the right age, but also their pigments, solvents, varnish and so on. David said there were a lot of those contemporary copies in museums that'd paid big prices for them as originals, and couldn't afford to admit their mistake. David always said if you could put a copy and an original side by side, after a time you could tell the real thing. The copy would sort of 'fade away,' as he put it. But how often do you have a chance to put a copy next to an original? A lot of them are in private hands—even secret collections—so you can dupe a buyer into thinking the one he's buying is 'it.' Who's going to tell him differently? Especially when a lot of those masterpieces in private collections didn't get there too honestly in the first place. The Nazis stole a lot of paintings that are now starting to show up here and there. They stole a lot more that may never show up on the open market. Experts know where some of them are—but not all, believe me. Fakers depend on that—and on fallow periods."

She was forcing her words out and the food down, but he was gradually getting her mind off Mary and onto the picture again. "Have you ever heard of a forger called Van Meegeren?"

"Isn't he the one who faked Vermeers?"

"That's right. The experts had always predicted that somewhere there might be some Vermeers with a religious content—something Vermeer should have been painting at a particular time that seemed to have been fallow. If he'd been painting at all, that is. Van Meegeren obligingly produced some Vermeers to fill the gap. And did them brilliantly too—even those experts were fooled—until he asked them to suggest a subject and painted it for them right there in his jail cell. Experts have become even more cautious since Van Meegeren, believe me."

"But real pictures *do* turn up in attics from time to time," Charles said.

"Yes, I know. Just often enough to keep the grabbers happy." She turned around in her chair to look at the fake Bosch leaning against the parapet. "I wish I knew what David had planned to do with that picture. It was obviously meant to be a late Bosch—his early things were all on wood panels. But if he was going that far . . . why not start with an older canvas? It just doesn't make sense—unless I'm right, of course."

"Right about what?"

"About that baker's dozen you mentioned. About the fact that David painted exactly thirteen pictures. An odd number, isn't it?"

"An unlucky number," Charles said softly.

"For some," Holly agreed, putting down her fork. The food was congealing on both their plates, and on the one in front of Mary's deserted chair. "She can't take much more, Charles."

"I realize that."

"Most people don't. She makes such an effort and she's so convincing. Everyone thinks she's strong, but . . . it takes a lot out of her, smiling and pretending. Reg teases her in public, but underneath what they have is so wonderful . . ." She looked away. "With David and me it was guerrilla warfare—nice in public, but in private always looking for the weak spot, the unguarded flank, an inch of advantage." She sat up straight, impatient with herself. "Sorry. I don't know why I said that. It doesn't have anything to do with anything." She tried a bright smile. "I think I'm going to cry now."

"I really wish you wouldn't," Charles said, looking at her and reaching for his wine at the same time, with the usual results. She laughed and mopped vigorously. The bad moment passed.

"Did you do that on purpose?" she asked.

"I don't think so. They call me the Gerald Ford of the *Corps Diplomatique.*" He smiled self-consciously and looked around. On either side the curtains of the other two penthouses were drawn and their patios deserted. It was growing dark and they could have been alone above the world. The bright diamond lights of the other buildings in the distance could have been set there by a jeweller for their pleasure. The sea was invisible now, but its sibilence was still audible. He poured more wine into their glasses. "What do you know about the people at the party last night?"

"Not a lot. They're Reg and Mary's friends, not mine."

"Well, one of them certainly is no friend of yours or mine."

"You mean . . ."

"I mean that one of them must have arranged the robbery and the accident. Or perhaps two of them. Or maybe *all* of them. But until you announced our intention of going through David's things in the studio garage in Espina, nobody except you knew they still existed. Not even Mary and Reg. *They* thought you'd sent it all back, right?"

"Yes, but . . ."

"But what?"

"How would they know the garage?"

"Most of them were living here when David was here, weren't they?"

"Yes, I guess so."

"If not, they could ask someone who *had* been living here—just casually, of course." He leaned back and looked up at the sky, thinking. "I mean, damn it all, when we disappeared during the Great Dog Round-Up, it wouldn't have taken a genius to figure out where we'd gone. Especially since you'd virtually announced it with letters of fire. All it would have taken was a phone call to a confederate in Espina . . ."

"All right. But if they cleared out the garage, why try to kill us? I mean, they must have gotten what they were after. Our problem is, we don't *know* what they were after."

"Let's go over them one by one. First of all, obviously there's Colonel Jackson. He said he wasn't here the night Graebner was killed. How do we know that?"

"Because I presume the police checked his alibi—he goes to the movies every Tuesday night. He leaves Queenie with the manager and collects her afterwards, and they both go to have a drink. The manager is ex-Army, too."

"And that's what happened on that Tuesday? Same as always?"

"Yes. If it hadn't, they'd have bothered him more, wouldn't they?"

He had to admit that was true. The Guardia would have certainly checked out the colonel's alibi thoroughly as a matter of course, seeing as he owned one of the other penthouses. And the same must be true of the Neufelds. "All right, what about the others?"

"Who, for instance?"

"Well, what do you know about Morland?"

"Oh, for heaven's sake, he's a retired vicar," Holly said impatiently, getting up and walking to the parapet to look out over the lights below. "And he has multiple sclerosis. It's in remission at the moment, but it will come back. Inevitably." She was silent for a moment, then spoke with venom. "Why is it that the worst things always happen to the best people?"

He sighed and got up to join her there, glad of the chance to stretch his legs. "I don't know," he admitted. "Maybe it's just that we notice it more when it does. What about Tinker?" he added casually.

"What about him?" She moved away slightly and put a hand up to brush her hair away from her face. He'd seen her do that before—when she was embarrassed.

"When did you meet him?"

"Oh, about two hours after I landed in Spain." Her voice was a little wry. "We stopped off at the club on the way back from the airport. Reg and Mary kept on their membership at Montana Sol when they moved here—most of the English community use it as a social centre. It's very nice, with . . ."

"I know it," he said. "What about Tinker?"

She waved a hand slightly. "Oh, he was there, with Nigel and Helen, and they introduced us. He's rented a beach house a little down the coast."

"He said he'd opted out of the rat race," Charles recalled.

"Yes. Anyway, he's got plenty of money and obviously means to enjoy himself. He took one look at me and sort of—rolled over me like a wave. I didn't encourage him, he didn't need it, but I didn't exactly *dis*courage him, either." When Charles didn't say anything, she went on, slightly defensively, "Well, why not?"

"Why not, indeed?" Charles agreed neutrally.

"The thing is, as you've probably noticed, he's taken to considering me 'his' girl."

"And are you?"

"I'm not anybody's girl, and I don't intend to be," Holly said in a flat voice. "I've come to the conclusion that I was born to be solitary. Like you."

"Have I come to that conclusion?"

She turned towards him, her face faintly visible in the last light of dusk. "I think you have, yes."

He nodded. "The difference being that you see it as some kind of triumph, whereas I see it as a failure," Charles said softly.

"But there have been women in your life, haven't there?"

"I didn't exactly take monastic vows when I joined the FO."

"But no one now?"

"Is that important?"

"No—I just wondered. Do you ever get lonely?"

"Do you?" he countered.

"No."

"Neither do I," he lied.

"Right." She was silent for a minute. "But I do like to enjoy myself, so I went out with Mel Tinker."

"He seems a perfectly nice man."

"Then why are you asking me about him?"

"I'm asking you about *everyone,*" he pointed out gently.

"Well, ask me about someone else then." Now she sounded petulant.

"What about the Blands?"

He sensed her instant withdrawal. "Now look, they're Reg and Mary's oldest friends. It was when they came over to visit the Blands that they first fell in love with Spain. My God, Nigel was a policeman!"

"There are always a few bad apples in the barrel," Charles said.

"*Not* Nigel!"

"All right, calm down. Not Nigel then. The Beams?"

"I don't know much about the Beams—the other day was the first time I'd met them. I'd *heard* about them—Reg met Mr. Beam at some kind of local residents' meeting, and they hit it off. I gather that makes Reg some kind of genius, but people have always taken to him. Always."

"The Beams are a rather mysterious couple," Charles mused. "Sort of old-line residents, with a lot of pull in both the English and Spanish camps. They seem to grow money the way other people grow geraniums."

"So one gathers. Did you see those pictures on the walls?"

"They *are* the real thing?"

"Yes, they are. You know, *he* could be the one behind the art fraud. Reg only got to know him about a year and a half ago . . . my God, Charles, he could have engineered that meeting with Reg."

"What for?"

She was silent for a moment. "I don't want to say . . . just yet. I'm not very sure of my facts."

"Look, I thought we were supposed to be working together on this."

"Oh, we are, but I don't want to make a fool of myself. If I'm wrong, you'll think me an absolute nincompoop, and I don't want you to think that. Any more than you already do, that is."

"I don't think you're anything of the kind," he said quietly.

She gave a little self-conscious laugh. "Oh yes, you do. You think I talk too much and fly off the handle and have no control over myself . . ."

"If any of that's true, and I'm not saying it is, it's because you *care* so much. And you think I don't. I can see where that would be frustrating. I *do* care . . . but I'm a little slow to commit myself until I'm sure I've considered everything. Perhaps that's why I've always missed out—I always waited to be sure. Too sure . . . too late."

"Maybe you should take a chance once in a while. You might be surprised."

He took her in his arms suddenly, kissed her and let her go. "Is that what you mean?"

"Not exactly . . ." Her voice was a little unsteady, and she shivered. "It's getting chilly out here. Let's go in."

Charles followed her. She was kneeling in front of the fireplace as he closed the sliding doors, and flames began to leap from the match she'd applied to the neatly laid tinder.

"I think I know what this is all about, Charles," she said.

"Maybe you'd better risk making a fool of yourself and tell me then," he suggested, sitting down on the sofa and taking out his pipe and tobacco pouch.

She turned away, picked up a knitted afghan that was folded on a chair and slung it around her shoulders. She began to pace in front of the fireplace, with the afghan fluttering around her bare legs like a cape. He hid his smile in the actions of filling and lighting the pipe.

"I wanted to do some reading up on this because I'm not sure, but I guess I'll have to tell you because most of the books at the library will be in Spanish, won't they?"

"Seeing as it's a Spanish library, hardly surprising."

"Yes. Was there a war in Spain just before the turn of the century?"

"There have been dozens of wars in Spain. Do you mean the Carlist uprisings in the 1870s?"

"Yes—Carlist, I remember David saying that word. Carlist. Well, they robbed the Prado of some Goya paintings that have never been recovered."

"Did they? I don't remember reading about that."

"Well, I'm certain that's what David said. He also said that the experts are pretty certain they're still around someplace—and obviously worth a fortune. David was always prowling junk-shops, saying if he ever found one he'd be rich. It was partly a joke, and partly an obsession. All right?"

"Yes," he said automatically, puffing at his reluctant pipe.

"Well, David painted twelve pictures for Graebner. And how many Goyas do you think were stolen from the Prado by those Carlist people?"

"Twelve?"

She shook her head. "No. Thirteen. David always referred to them as the Baker's Dozen. Twelve pictures for Graebner's client *and* the Bosch. And all on old canvas."

"Are you saying that those twelve pictures that the valuers called 'fakes' in America are actually Goyas?" Charles demanded.

"I don't know. And I have no way of knowing, because I don't know where they are now. Presumably still in Texas. I only know where one is. Where it's been all along—here, with Reg. And hidden away, because Mary couldn't stand the sight of it."

"But why?"

"I suppose Graebner must have come across the pictures," she said. "I don't know how or where—a lot of things were hidden by the Nazis during the war—we'll never know, I guess. The point is, *he found them in Spain.* He must have. If he'd tried to sell them here, the government would have confiscated them. Oh they might have paid him some kind of compensation, but nothing like the prices he could get at auction or a private sale. So he had to get them out of Spain."

"Which he did. As forged originals," Charles pointed out. "And got a big price for them."

"The valuers said they were fakes. But they had no reason to look *underneath,* did they?"

"Are you saying the American buyer *knew* the Goyas were under there?"

"I don't think so. If he had, he would have been getting quite a bargain, since one really fine Goya might command that price alone in auction. Especially with a romantic history attached. No, Graebner got greedy, that's all. He probably only hired David to paint cheap fakes on top of the Goyas, but when he saw how good they were, he got someone else to put on the signatures and sold them as originals to the American. I don't know what he planned to do at the other end, when the pictures actually arrived. Buy them back, perhaps, or steal them. Stealing them sounds more likely. Of course, he never got the chance."

"Why didn't the Bosch go with the rest?"

"I don't know. Technically it would have been the most difficult to do. Or maybe . . ." She stopped in the middle of the floor, her red curls standing up on end, her eyes blazing in the firelight. "Of *course.*"

"What?"

"Graebner never paid David, there wasn't anything in his bank account; he gave him the thirteenth Goya instead. And David put the Bosch on top of it, to get it out of the country for himself. And that's why Graebner came back here . . . he knew David was dead, and he wanted the last picture for himself. Don't you see? That's it. That *has* to be it."

"Holly . . ."

"What?" Her eyes were shining, she was delighted.

"You've just given Reg an even better motive for murder."

Her face went white so suddenly that he stood up, thinking she was going to faint, and put his arms around her. "Hey, take it easy . . ."

"He didn't know, he didn't *know* . . ." Her voice was muffled in his jacket lapel. "He would have done something about it if he'd known, but it's just been here in a cupboard, all along."

"Then if Reg didn't know, and didn't kill Graebner, then you're right, someone else *is* involved, and that someone else stole the things from the garage."

"But they didn't find this picture in the garage," Holly said. She had pulled back slightly to look into his face. Now her eyes widened with horror. She was looking behind him. Charles turned.

Fluent in four languages, he could only make a gurgling noise in his throat as he looked straight into the muzzle of a gun. He had never realized before how big a hole there was in the muzzle of a gun. The same size, presumably, that it would make in him. About a yard wide and a yard high. The gun was held by a man dressed in black, with a black Balaclava over his head, and only the glitter of his eyes showing. Behind him stood another, and behind that one, another one.

They all had guns.

And one had something else. Something white, like a bandage or a handkerchief, and a bottle. He came towards them, unscrewing the cap.

Charles struggled, but it was no good. The FO had never trained him to deal with chloroform.

And chloroform is very quick.

CHAPTER 10

"If you're going to be sick, señor, do it in here."

Paco Bas shoved a plastic bowl next to Charles's face. Charles moaned again, and opened his left eye. The bowl wavered and changed shape. He could see every mark and scratch on its green surface.

"Go away," he mumbled. "Let me die in peace."

Paco grinned and moved away while Charles spent a few minutes alone. He staggered to his feet, finally, and lurched down the hall to the bathroom, leaving the unused bowl on the floor where he'd lain. He only just made it. Afterwards he felt better. Not a lot. But better. After a wash and gargle, he felt better still. Except for the knot of anger in his stomach and the knot of confusion in his brain. When he opened the bathroom door, Paco Bas was leaning against the wall opposite, his arms folded. He smiled.

"It was the chloroform, señor."

"I know what it was," Charles snapped, then sighed. "Sorry. Where is López?"

"Right here," López said, coming out of the master bedroom.

"Holly? Mrs. Partridge?"

"Lying down. They, too, feel sick." López looked around the hall, and then walked into the sitting room. The fire had gone out, and as they entered it settled with a little sigh into grey ashes. Charles stood there for a minute trying to figure out what had changed in the room. The green plastic bowl still sat there, incongruously, in front of the sofa.

"The walls, Carlos. They took the pictures from the walls. Here and everywhere in the flat. A clean sweep," López finally said.

Charles stared at him for a moment, fighting the urge to be sick again. "Did she tell you? About the Goyas?"

López smiled and nodded. "She did. Unfortunately, there is no longer any proof, one way or the other. Until, of course, we can trace the paintings in America."

"But . . ." Charles's eyes went towards the sliding glass doors. Beyond them, in the first light of dawn, he could see a faint line of footprints in the dew-hazed tiles. The footprints went over to the parapet and back again. And where the Bosch (or Goya?) had stood, there was only a line. And another for the frame. Both picture and frame were gone. "Oh," Charles said.

"What?" López looked puzzled.

"They got *all* the pictures," Charles said miserably.

"Yes, as I said. A clean sweep."

"How long have you been here?" Charles asked, sitting down on the sofa with a thump. "How did you find out?"

"Miss Partridge called me," he said, and smiled. "Not without difficulty, you understand, but she *is* persistent. She called the doctor, and the doctor called me. He's with them now."

"Were they hurt? You said they were just lying down . . ."

"They are feeling sick and upset. It was a very frightening experience."

"You're telling me," Charles muttered. "Three enormous men . . ."

López grinned. "She said they were quite average."

"Guns, they had guns. I don't *like* guns." He was aware that he sounded childish, and it made him even angrier. "For heaven's sake, Esteban, this is turning into something very nasty indeed; perhaps *now* you'll believe someone else besides Partridge is involved. Somebody pretty dangerous . . ."

"They didn't hurt you."

"They tried to kill us by sending us off the road," Charles pointed out.

"Ah, *sí,* but *last* night they did you no harm. They only made you sleep while they did what they had to do. They didn't even tie you up, Carlos."

"My, my . . . what gentlemen," Charles said sarcastically.

"And now, presumably, they have what they were after, so the danger is passed," López said. "I don't think you have to worry anymore."

"Not worry? What about Partridge? What about the murder charge?"

López's face tightened. "This does not change anything, Carlos. We still have the weapon with his fingerprints and Graebner's blood on it. Pictures make no difference, there."

"Well, someone *else* could have used the sword . . . someone who got into the flat." Charles waved his arms around. "I mean . . . suppose Graebner came up here to see Partridge, and got no answer because Partridge had already left. Then he heard the lift coming up and, being a cautious type, ducked into the stairwell so as to see who it was. And it was Partridge who went in . . . leaving the door ajar behind him. After all, he only intended to be in the flat for a moment, right?"

"Go on," López said, with a glance at Bas.

Charles was warming to his theory more every second. "I mean, I must have been working this out subconsciously and it fits, Esteban. Suppose Partridge left the door ajar, as I say, and Graebner slipped in behind him and hid in the kitchen or the bathroom until Partridge left again."

"What for?"

"To search for the picture, of course."

"Then Graebner took the sword off the wall, using gloves, of course, stabbed himself in the heart, hung the sword back up, went out onto the patio and threw himself off . . . is that right?" Paco asked, a half-smile on his face.

"No, of course not," Charles snapped.

"Perhaps he let someone else in," López suggested.

"Yes . . *yes!*" Charles said gratefully.

"And *he* stabbed Graebner?" Paco asked. "And then threw him over the edge?"

"Yes!"

"And then left the flat without the picture he'd come for and killed for?" López went on. "My goodness, what a wasted effort."

"Maybe he was interrupted."

"The Partridges didn't return until midnight."

"Well, maybe he *thought* he was going to be interrupted," Charles persisted.

"Maybe he had an appointment somewhere else," Paco said.

"Yes, of course . . . at that same bridge party," Charles said. "Don't you see? It had to be someone who knew the . . . someone who could have . . .." He was slowing down.

"Someone who knew the picture was here all along? And, despite count-
less opportunities to steal it—as the Partridges were often out—chose this
night and this night only to do so?"

"Well, but . . ."

López was shaking his head. "No, my friend, it does not hang together.
Only Graebner knew that Mr. Partridge had the picture, because Graebner
knew he had been at the studio when the original arrest was made. He heard
David Partridge call out to his father to look at the picture—in *English.*
Neither of the Guardia officers who arrested them spoke English. I
checked."

"He could have told someone else."

"In which case they would have stolen it long before. Oh no, my friend.
Graebner was not that kind of man. He stayed silent all the while he was in
hospital, had no visitors, kept himself to himself. Brooding, I'm told. If he
spoke at all, it was only of revenge. I'm sorry. All you have said is interesting, but none of it is proof. And now that even the last picture is gone . . ."
He shrugged.

"But you'll have someone check those pictures in America?"

"But of course. If Miss Partridge's theory is true, they must be found and
recovered for the nation. Think of the joy, of the excitement . . . you can
be sure I will check."

"Well, that's something."

"*Sí,* it is something. And, of course, we will endeavour to find the thieves
who broke in here last night, that goes without saying. A great deal does
remain unanswered about the case, with that I do agree. But the proof
against Mr. Partridge has not changed, Carlos. Nor has my mind been
changed about him. I think he is sicker than we know. And I do not think he
cares anymore about what happens to him. He killed, knowing perhaps that
he would not live to be tried."

"You mean . . . he has cancer?"

"No, I have no evidence of that. Nor does the doctor think so. But
continuous pain, a son dead, time passing—all these things can change a
man, Carlos."

"You're wrong, Esteban. You're *wrong.*"

"Then we shall have to agree to disagree, my friend," López said, his eyes
cold. Charles had never seen him look like that. But then, Charles had only
seen him across dinner-tables and circulating at parties and, occasionally, at
the embassy. And they had always been on the same side then.

"Can you tell me if the Guardia were careful about checking the alibis of
all who might conceivably be concerned in this?" he asked desperately.

"The people on either side—Colonel Jackson and the Neufelds. There's something funny about them, you know, Esteban."

López nodded. "Your instincts are still intact, I see. The colonel's alibi has been verified. There is a great deal wrong with the Neufelds, Carlos, but nothing we can prove. Believe me, we have tried, and we are still trying. Also, the Israelis are trying. This surprises you?"

"Nothing surprises me anymore," Charles said wearily, going over to the sliding doors and looking out at the patio and the growing roseate light of dawn. The sea stretched flat and metallic to the horizon, and the parapet blocked off all the ground below, save for the jutting cliffs of the coast far to the left. The dew was drying off the tiles already, and he could barely see the prints that led away from the door. But he could still see them. He turned back into the room and reached for his cigarettes. The pipe was wrong now. The pipe was for reflection.

"Who do you think Mr. Partridge would kill if you let him out on bail, Esteban?" he asked quietly.

"I think perhaps himself, Carlos," López said softly.

"Not with a wife still to look after, a wife he loves very much," Charles said. "That's a ridiculous thing to say."

López's face tightened, and belatedly Charles realized he'd broken about ten of his own rules about dealing with the Spanish. "My word is final, I'm afraid. I'm sorry you see it as you do," López said stiffly. "Paco."

Paco Bas stood up and they started for the door.

"Aren't you going to fingerprint the place or anything?"

"They wore gloves—is that not so?"

It was so, Charles remembered. Holly must have told them. "Do you think you will find them? Or the pictures?"

"We will try." López's voice was cold. "The minute we have anything to tell, we will be in touch. With Mrs. Partridge." With a curt nod of the head, López went out. A moment later Charles heard the outer door close, and after that, the sound of the lift descending. He stood where he was, waiting.

After a moment, Holly appeared in the kitchen doorway. He had caught a trace of her scent and had known she was out there, listening.

"You see?" she said angrily. "There's no sense talking to them, no sense at all. Their minds are as closed as little fists. You can't . . ."

"Where is it?" Charles asked. "Where's the picture, Holly?"

CHAPTER 11

"It's under Mary's mattress," Holly said reluctantly. "I put it there while she was in the shower. How did you know I still had it?"

He gestured towards the patio. The footprints were gone now. "Someone in bare feet went out and got the picture. Those men wore shoes—I remember them clearly, because when I went down, my nose was right up against them."

"They never thought to look out there. They must have been told to steal every picture in the place, and that's what they did. They stripped the walls and searched everywhere else they could think of. But it never occurred to them that people might have a picture out on the patio . . . well, people don't usually, do they?"

"And now what do you intend to do with it?"

"I want to take it to . . ."

Mary Partridge suddenly appeared in the hall doorway. She looked ghastly. Pale and trembling, she clutched her dressing gown in front of her. Her hair was in disarray, and her face looked old.

"I don't want to stay here, Holly. I can't stay here, knowing . . . strangers . . . have touched . . . everything . . ."

Holly went over to her instantly. She put her arm around her shoulders and guided her to a chair, then knelt beside her. "Oh, I know how you feel, love, really I do. But you can't go back to England now, not with Reg . . ."

"Oh, I don't mean go back to *England,*" Mary said. "I'd never leave Reg —no matter what. But I don't want to stay in this flat anymore. Not without him. Not now that . . ." She fretted with the tie of her dressing gown. "Oh, Holly, I'm just so grateful I was asleep . . . that I didn't *see* them. They must have just put the thing over my face . . . and I never . . . it must have been awful, seeing them . . ."

"They were just ordinary thieves," Charles said quickly. "There have been a lot of robberies lately along the coast."

"Look, why don't you go over to Nigel and Helen's for a few days?" Holly suggested brightly. "They've been asking you to, and you know Helen will spoil you rotten. It's just what you need."

"But I just thought I'd move in downstairs, with you," Mary said in a puzzled voice. "Don't you want me?"

"Well, of course I'd want you, silly. But I think you'd be better off at

Helen's, because I have to go away for a few days, and you really shouldn't be alone, you know."

"Where are you going?" There was real panic in Mary's voice, and she reached out to clutch Holly's arm as if to hold her back.

"Oh, Charles and I have to go somewhere for a couple of days, that's all."

Mary looked up from under her lashes at Charles, and he thought he saw suspicion and a little reproach there. He was taking her girl away. He smiled, and wondered what the devil Holly was up to now.

"With Charles?" Mary asked uncertainly.

"That's right."

"But where? Where are you going?"

"Alicante," Charles said.

"Valencia," Holly said at the same time. There was a stricken moment of silence, then she spoke quickly. "Well, we *might* have to go to Granada, but Charles hopes the lawyer in Alicante will be able to take the case."

"I don't understand. I thought he'd got a lawyer for Reg," Mary said fretfully. She looked from one to the other, and then flushed. "It doesn't matter," she mumbled. "I'll go to Helen's. I'd better pack some things and call them." She stood up and hurried out, not looking at either of them.

Charles stared after her. "You know what she thinks, don't you?"

"That we're going off on a dirty weekend together." Holly sighed. "Well, let her."

"Just out of interest, where *are* we going?" Charles asked.

"Oh, we're going to Madrid, of course," Holly said, standing up.

Charles wrapped the picture in brown paper while Holly packed her things. She came up and they put the package in between layers of clothes to protect it, for without the frame it was a bit fragile (and without the frame was the only way they could get it in the suitcase).

Nigel and Helen arrived just as Charles was rewinding the ball of string for the third time. They were not alone.

"Are you all right, honey?" Mel Tinker asked, bursting into the lounge and going straight to Holly. "My God, if only you'd let me come around the way I asked . . . they wouldn't have gotten away with it."

"There were three of them," Charles said.

Tinker looked at him. "I don't see any bruises on you," he said disparagingly. "Didn't you even *try* to stop them?"

"As a matter of fact, he did," Holly said. "But they used chloroform."

"Chloroform?" Nigel asked. "That's a little old-fashioned, isn't it?"

"We lag behind the times, here in sunny *España,*" Charles said apologetically. "No doubt back home they're on to tranquillizing darts."

Helen bustled in. "She's all packed. Is that suitcase to go?"

"Yes, but not with Mary," Holly said. "It's mine."

"Where are *you* going?" Tinker wanted to know.

"Valencia," Charles said.

"Alicante," Holly said at the same time.

"Well? Which?" Tinker demanded. "And why?"

"Alicante first, then Valencia," Charles said quickly, before Holly could think of some other variation on the theme. "Although we may be able to do the entire thing from Alicante."

"Do what entire thing?"

"Get Holly's passport renewed," Charles said, noting that Holly didn't even try to explain, leaving everything to him. And about time, too. "She's let it get out of date, and she has to renew it in person. Normally that means Madrid, but we're hoping to short-cut that . . ."

"Thanks for looking after Mary for me, Helen," Holly interrupted. "She's really in a bad way."

"Don't worry about her," Helen said. "Here, Nigel, help her with that case."

"It's all right; I'll take it," Charles said.

"I'll take it," Tinker said, grabbing it from him with alacrity. "And I can take her to get this passport thing done. I have some clout myself." He took the case with such violence that one of the catches came undone, half-tumbling the contents out. Charles grabbed it back, pushing the clothes and the edge of the package back inside and reaching for the string.

"We were just about to tie that up," he said pointedly. "The catch is broken."

"What's that?" Tinker asked, as the package showed briefly between something denim and something lacy.

"A mantilla for my aunt in Idaho," Holly said. "I have to mail it today, or she won't have it in time for her birthday. Don't let me forget, Charles."

"Right," Charles said.

"I said, *I'll* take you," Tinker repeated mulishly.

"No, you won't," Holly said briskly. "It's all settled. I'm going to stay with Charles and his wife until we get this straightened out."

"Oh," Tinker said, in a mollified voice. "You married, Llewellyn?"

"Oh yes," Charles said vaguely, knotting the string.

"Five children and another on the way," Holly said brightly. "He showed me pictures."

"Now isn't that nice?" Helen beamed at him. "A nice, reliable family man. Isn't that nice, Nigel?"

"That's nice," Nigel said sardonically. "Very nice, Charles."

The doorbell rang.

"Now who can that be?" Holly wondered.

"I'll go," Charles said quickly, avoiding her eye. He opened the door and there stood Alastair Morland.

"Hello," he said cheerfully. "Thought I'd drop by and see how things were going."

"What things?" Charles asked.

"Well, Reg and Mary and . . . things. You know."

"Charles, I think . . ." Holly stuck her head out of the lounge door. "Oh, hullo, Alastair. Come in. Let him in, Charles."

Charles sighed and stepped back. "Welcome, one and all."

Alastair looked at him and then at Holly. "Look, if it's an awkward time, I can . . ."

"No, come in . . . Charles, you're the most unfriendly man I've ever met," Holly said.

"He does rather seem to like throwing people out." Morland grinned. "Is it another party, Charles?"

"Just about," Charles said, closing the door. "Parade, picnic, and fireworks to follow. Come one, come all." He trudged after Morland. Nobody paid any attention to him at all, so he sat down in the corner and finished the sandwich he'd made himself while waiting for Holly to pack.

The others were filling Morland in on the latest events. Charles watched him closely, but he seemed genuinely surprised and dismayed. "My God," he kept murmuring, which seemed appropriate, Charles thought, seeing as he was a retired vicar. Tinker sat back and kept his mouth shut for once, his eyes on Holly. He had a tight look about the face, and spared one brief glance towards Charles when Holly was talking about the masked men. Wouldn't have happened if I'd been looking after her, the look said. The look might have worried Charles if he'd given a damn what Tinker thought of him. He looked back unperturbed, and chewed his sandwich.

Morland, it seemed, had just called to collect Colonel Jackson for their weekly shopping trip to Espina, and had come around to see if Mary needed anything. They explained that Mary was going to stay with Helen and Nigel to get a few days' rest.

"Well, I don't mind saying all this is beyond me," Morland said. "One dreadful shock on top of another . . . it's sinful."

"Kind of makes you think someone doesn't like them, doesn't it?"

Charles put in blandly, wiping crumbs off his lap and standing up. "With enemies like that, who needs friends?"

"Is that supposed to be funny?" Nigel asked.

"Are you implying one of us had something to do with this?" Tinker wanted to know, sitting up.

"You said it; I didn't," Charles observed, with a big smile for everyone. And the doorbell rang again.

This time it was Maddie, arms full of groceries and eyes full of avid interest. "I have brought supplies," she announced, sweeping in dramatically. She put the bags and packets on the closest level surface and turned to them. "Where is Mary?" she demanded, stripping off her gloves. "Well?" She looked from face to face.

"I'm here," Mary said in a weary voice, coming in.

"But . . . you look dreadful," Maddie said, in tones of sepulchral horror. "Like the walking dead."

"Thank you," Mary said with some irony.

"You should be in bed. Let me . . ."

"No, thank you. I'm fine."

"Well . . ." Maddie looked around suspiciously. "What is going on here? Why are you all looking at me? And what are the suitcases? Are you going away?" This to Mary, who ignored her and sank into a chair. Maddie kept turning in the centre of the room. "What is different here? Something is wrong."

"They were robbed last night," Alastair said eagerly, either not seeing or choosing to ignore Holly's glare. "Masked men came in and stole all the pictures in the place."

"But . . . have you the police phoned?" Maddie demanded, her grammar going a little askew in her excitement. Her very bright blond hair was beginning to wisp down around her face, escaping from the bun on top, and a line of perspiration had begun to bead her upper lip. Her eyes rolled.

"Yes, Maddie. Everything that should be done has been done," Holly said. "Thank you for the groceries, but we're going away for a few days, and won't need anything."

"Going? Where?" Maddie demanded.

"Valencia," Holly said.

"Alicante," Charles said.

"Granada," Mary said. There was a brief silence.

"Anyone for Barcelona?" Nigel inquired brightly.

CHAPTER 12

Charles drove the Partridges' old VW Beetle to a small clinic he knew of near Espina that catered to wealthy foreigners. It was ten miles inland—a strange, isolated building in the old style, with nothing around it for miles. Here, away from the sea, the air was hot and dry and still, and the rackety sound of the VW's engine was an intrusion into the bright, secret morning.

"Why *five* children, for heaven's sake?" Charles demanded.

"Six, when the next one arrives. It seemed like a nice round number." Holly smiled to herself.

"My hormones thank you for the compliment," Charles growled. "I presume you were trying to put Tinker's mind at ease concerning any time we spend together?"

"I was trying to get him off your back," Holly snapped.

"Going off your fellow-countryman, are you?"

"I don't like to be crowded—I'm claustrophobic."

"I see." He pulled up and turned off the engine. What had seemed silence as they passed along the winding narrow road proved to be a little less than that. The clinic stood on a rise, and from the ochre fields that dropped away and rose again on the terraced hillside all round, there came a soft, rustling rattle of dried grasses and the steady burr of cicadas. There was a slightly metallic smell emanating from the clinic, cutting the fragrance of grass, onions and fertilizer.

The building itself dated from at least a hundred years ago, but the cubes of air-conditioning units on each window indicated it had been brought forward in time for its demanding patients. It was tall and narrow and had a startled look, as if this were not what it had planned for itself all that time ago. There were only three other cars in the gravelled car-park. They had been parked widely apart, as aloof as the clinic itself. In the distance, in the folds of the hills, small groves of olive trees made silvery-green patches of shade that promised coolness, but there was no respite here. Only the fist of the sun, the dust settling on the bonnet of the car, and the promise of a headache if one lingered outside too long.

They went in, and after a word with the director—an angular mustachioed Englishman with a faintly military air—a bored Spanish X-ray technician took a few "snaps" of the painting. He thought they were crazy.

But then, working in this particular clinic, he thought all foreigners were crazy.

"Is this an asylum?" Holly whispered to Charles on the way out. It was so silent, she thought, as if everyone were locked in his or her room.

"No, of course not. They would hardly have an X-ray department in an asylum, would they? This is a general medical and surgical clinic, privately run."

"By whom?"

"A friend."

"A friend of whom?"

He scowled at her. "A friend of Her Majesty's Government."

Was Charles more than he seemed? It would be nice to think so, but she doubted it. He was so self-contained, so hard to read. It was very exasperating.

They opened the doors of the car, the windows, and the envelope in that order. Charles held the thin plastic sheet up to the windscreen. "Looks like oatmeal to me," he said doubtfully. But when he looked at Holly, he saw it meant more to her.

"It is," she whispered. "It *is!*"

"What, oatmeal?"

"No, idiot. Look . . . here . . . and here. See those shadows? Now look at the picture itself." She held it in her lap and he glanced from one to the other. "See? There's nothing in the Bosch to match those shadows, is there?"

"No, I guess not."

"So there *is* something underneath."

"Not necessarily a Goya, though. It could be anything."

"I know. The next thing we need is to find out just what Goyas were taken. Where could we find that out?"

"*We* probably couldn't. But López could."

"No, thank you. What about the library?"

"We could try."

But the library in Espina, although cooler by far than the clinic car-park, had little to add. They did find a mention of the theft, but no listing of the pictures.

Charles, back in the car, hesitated. "As it happens, I do know somebody at the Prado who might be able to tell us what we want to know. I could call him."

"Is he safe?"

Charles looked at her. Over the pale skin was a glow of pink, and her red hair was charged with electricity. Excitement emanated from her like perfume, and he could feel it going to his head. Keep calm, he told himself.

"Well, he's not exactly a retired vicar, like Morland, and he's bound to be curious, but it should be all right," he said in a mildly reproving tone that didn't penetrate her armour of self-satisfaction an inch. "He's one of the senior curators—intelligent, articulate, and very charming."

"I don't trust charming men," Holly said, wrapping the picture up again in the brown paper and leaning over the seat to replace it in her suitcase.

"You trust *me*," Charles said.

"Exactly."

They went to the *fonda,* getting some sideways glances as they went up the stairs to Charles's room. Holly noticed the lips of the lady behind the desk tightening with disapproval.

"They think I'm your mistress or something," she whispered to Charles's back. "She and Mel ought to get together."

He went into his room and sat down on the bed, leaving her to close the door. Private telephones in the rooms were one of the things that made him choose this particular inn. Such luxuries were usually reserved for the big hotels, but Spaniards, too, were beginning to demand these modern amenities. He put through the call, then covered up the mouthpiece. "There—we can't be doing anything so terrible if I'm on the phone, can we? This will save your honour."

"I can look after my honour myself, thank you," Holly said, going to the window and looking out into the dusty little courtyard below. A man sat there, half-asleep in the shade of a small olive tree, a bowl of pea pods resting in his lap, another bowl beside him on a rickety table. The second bowl was empty. So was a glass that had obviously held red wine. He looked very peaceful, the man with the bowl of peas. A grey cat was sleeping at the base of the tree, curled into a knot between the gnarled roots. Charles's room was baking hot, and Holly opened the window to get some air. The tiny noise it made stirred the man, and he began desultorily breaking open the pods and chucking the peas into the empty bowl.

The cat didn't stir.

A sudden spate of Spanish told her Charles had got through to his friend at the Prado. There seemed to be a great deal of conversation before she heard the name Goya mentioned. After a minute, Charles pointed towards the bureau and made "bring-me" gestures that became quite frantic. Holly bought him his notebook and sat down in the one chair, watching him write quickly. When he'd finished, he tossed her the notebook, and then went on with the conversation. Holly inspected the list. The names meant nothing to her. "Hannibal Crossing the Alps" was one, then several portraits—"Don Pedro Rodriguez, Conde" and "Don Francisco Xavier Larriatigui," and several general titles—"The Water-Seller," "La Prendería Camios," "Children with Drums and Trumpets," and "The Smugglers." That last would be suitable, she thought amused. Charles was still chatting, and he raised his eyebrows in a gesture of impatience as the man at the other end of the line talked on. Finally, he put the phone down. "Whew," he said. "Six years of news in ten minutes—must be a world record. The list any good?"

"What's 'La Prendería Camios'?" she asked.

"Sorry—literally, 'the Shirt-Sellers,' but Alfredo said it had actually been a street scene showing the Rag Fair."

"Oh. And what's this—'La Maja Roja'?"

"The Red Maja. I don't know. Maybe a picture of a woman dressed in red?"

"Maja means whore, doesn't it?"

"Not exactly. 'Courtesan' would come close, I think."

Holly took the X-rays out of the manila envelope and held them up to the window. No . . . it didn't . . . She sucked in her breath suddenly.

And turned it sideways.

Now the shadows made some sense. Head and shoulders . . . yes!

"Look," she said in a choked voice. He got up and came over to stand beside her. He looked at the X-ray. Finally he glanced at her and raised an eyebrow.

"Well, can't you *see* it?" she demanded. "For heaven's sake, don't just stand there, say something."

"All right," he said quietly. "I admit there *could* be something there."

"Oh, wow, thanks a lot!" She glared at him while below, in the courtyard, the old man looked up from his task with interest. People arguing was more interesting than pea pods.

"And what do you propose to do about it?" Charles went on. "You said yourself you can't remove the paint."

"No, but an expert could," she said with determination. "And all the experts are in Madrid."

"All becomes clear—at last," he said. "And what if that picture *is* a Goya? What do you propose to do then?"

"Are you obliged to report this to anyone?" she asked suspiciously. He was just standing there, with his hands in his pockets, giving her no clue.

"Obviously, I *should* . . ." He looked out of the window. "But it's your decision. We may never know the true history of the picture. There might have been some kind of clue in your late husband's papers, but *they're* gone. All we're left with is the picture itself, and that's mute."

"You mean someone might have had it in a private collection, and David and Graebner might have stolen it. That's what you're implying, isn't it?"

"It's a possible explanation." He smiled slightly. "Of course, the former owner would never be in a position to claim the loss or press charges, without having to answer some questions himself, would he?" He rubbed the back of his neck. "The point is, you don't *know* that it's a Goya in its present state. No one could say you do."

"What did you tell your friend?"

"Oh, that I'd come across a mention of the theft in an old book and wondered if it was true. Said next time I was up there I'd make a search of the Rastro."

"What's the Rastro?"

"Madrid's equivalent of the Paris Flea Market," Charles said. "Alfredo doubted that would be useful—he seemed to think they were long gone. Said something about Argentina." He looked at her quizzically. "What are you going to do with it, Holly?"

"It could be worth a fortune."

"Theoretically."

She thought for a while. "I see what you're getting at. If I leave it as it is, I could take it out of the country quite legitimately as a copy, because to all intents and purposes I have no reason to think it's anything but a copy. Once I had it out, I could have it cleaned and if it *was* a Goya, that would be just my good luck. I could sell it to the highest bidder, quite legitimately."

"That's right. You could."

"But that won't get Reg out of jail, would it?"

"No."

"Whereas, if I get it cleaned here in Spain, and it proves to be a Goya, López might realize that Reg knew nothing about it, and he might be more willing to investigate the people who've been trying to get it from us." He watched her, waiting. "But if I do that, I can't ever take it out of the country, because it belongs to Spain. They'd seize it."

"You'd be given a fair compensation."

"Fair isn't a fortune."

"That's true. And there's no guarantee that it would convince López one way or the other. It might do no good at all."

She sighed. "It's really Reg's picture, you know. I think I'd like to talk to him about it. Maybe he thinks the money would be more useful. The trouble is—he's so damn *honest.*"

"No," Charles said. "The trouble is, *you're* so honest."

He waited, his car parked outside in the near-empty street, smoking his pipe and watching the few passers-by. He'd found a place under a lone tree, grateful for the shade, and thrown his jacket into the back. He'd also checked out of the *fonda* because either way, he was moving on. Reg would be moved to Alicante in the next day or two, that was certain. The whole wheel of justice would slowly grind on, and he could do nothing but try to keep pace with it, calling encouragement to Partridge from the side of the road as the days went on. The one thing they had, the only thing, sat in its brown paper wrapping inside Holly's suitcase. And if it proved to be a Goya, they'd be no closer to getting Reg out from under a charge of murder. Only López could do that. They had to convince him it was necessary. Would one picture do that?

Holly came out of the jail and stood at the top of the steps, looking up and down the street for the car. It didn't take her long to spot the Partridges' old yellow VW Beetle. She came down the steps slowly, and he tried to tell from her walk what the decision had been. She looked smaller and thinner and the red curls clung damply to her forehead as she got in beside him.

"Madrid," was all she said.

CHAPTER 13

"What are those black bulls on the hillsides?" Holly asked half an hour later, as they sped inland. She'd noticed the black silhouettes on practically every other hilltop, as big as hoardings, made presumably of painted wood.

"Advertisements for sherry and brandy."

"They don't say so."

"You're supposed to know, without being told."

"That's so arrogant!"

"No. That's Spain."

"Why do all the children in the villages look so old?" Holly asked.

"They come into the world starved and they know they'll leave it starved, with little in between except hard work."

"How do they know?"

"Their parents tell them every night."

"But that's dreadful!"

"No. That's Spain."

"Why are the Spanish such rotten drivers?"

"Because they never see anybody's point of view but their own. When they want to change lanes they change lanes. If you blow your horn they're surprised and disappointed, because you should have realized they were going to do it."

"But that's anarchy."

"No, that's—"

"Don't say it!" Holly shouted, startling Charles so much he very nearly sent the VW off the road. "Is being 'just Spain' your explanation or excuse for everything in this benighted country? It's so . . . fatalistic."

He grinned. "And that is also Spain. Sorry, maybe I've been here too long after all." He glanced at his wristwatch, ignoring her growl. It sounded savage, but she was smiling. At least his inanity had distracted her a little. "We can get something to eat soon. Places will be opening up again."

"This siesta thing is so awkward," she complained. "It's the damnedest way to . . ." She paused, and sighed. "I know, it's Spain."

"And it makes good sense, especially in summer. I don't suppose you've noticed, living with Reg and Mary in the Puerto Rio cocoon. I'll bet you still went on eating breakfast at eight, lunch at one, tea at four, and supper at six, just like at home, didn't you?"

"Well . . ." She looked at him and laughed. "That's England."

They stopped at a *posada,* set well back from the road next to a petrol station. There were a few tables set outside, but they opted for the cool, dark interior. The wailing croon of Julio Iglesias wafted from a radio in the kitchen, barely audible above the clatter of pans. The proprietor seemed surprised to see them, but shrugged. Beer and sandwiches? If they wished to poison themselves with heavy meals in the heat of the day, why not? He could accommodate them—and the *servicios* were down the hall, there, señora.

When Holly came back, she found Charles standing in the doorway looking out, an odd expression on his face. "What's wrong?" she asked.

"Nothing." He came back to the table and sat down.

"Well, you don't look like it's nothing."

"I just thought I saw a car I recognized slow down outside, then drive on, that's all."

"Which car?"

"A red Mercedes convertible."

"Mel Tinker? It couldn't have been. He thinks we've gone to Alicante."

"I wonder. When Mrs. Partridge blurted out Granada like that, he looked very suspicious."

"But we explained all that . . ."

"Uh-huh. What's more, I don't think he was very convinced by your 'wife-and-five-children-with-another-on-the way' gambit, either. A married man is no less apt to make a pass at a girl like you than a single one."

She took a bite of her sandwich. "But if we were intent on getting into bed, we'd hardly need to drive off to Alicante, when I have a perfectly good flat of my own. I admit, Mel *is* rather fond of me . . ."

"Or pretends to be, in order to keep track of you."

She glared at him and put her coffee-cup down with a bump. "You do have a talent for giving with one hand and taking away with the other, don't you? Is that Spanish, too? My God, I hate this country."

"You do?" He was startled. How could anyone hate Spain?

"Well, it's cruel, and hot, and . . . glaring. The Spaniards are always yelling at one another . . . I mean, *listen* to them." She tilted her head back towards the kitchen, from which came the sound of voices raised over the radio and the clatter.

Charles listened for a moment. "They're discussing the price of chickens —they're agreeing that it's outrageous." A phone rang, and the shouting stopped.

Charles held up his hand, suddenly. He turned his head so as to hear more clearly. The voices had started up again, as loudly and seemingly as angrily as before. Charles frowned, then stood up abruptly.

"Come on."

"But I haven't finished . . ."

"Come on." He practically dragged her out to the car and made her get in. As they pulled away, rolling the car windows down as quickly as they could to blow out the hot air that had accumulated, Holly noticed the proprietor run out of the *posada* and stare after them.

"You did pay him, didn't you, Charles? He's waving at us."

"I know." Charles went up the road a short distance, reversed, and started back the way they'd come. As they passed the *posada*, Holly saw that the proprietor had gone inside.

"You're going the wrong way," Holly protested.

He turned off the road abruptly and the VW lurched and bounced over the poor surface for some way. When they'd rounded several turns and were out of sight of the highway, he pulled over to the side of the road and switched off the engine. "We'll wait here a bit."

"Why?" There was a stream nearby. She could hear it, but not see it.

"Because that telephone call was for us. That is to say, it was someone asking to speak to the 'American girl.' "

"But I never opened my mouth—how could he know I was American?"

"*He* didn't—he was about to ask if you were—but whoever was calling knew it."

She stared at him, amazed. "Then it *was* Mel's car?"

"I think it must have been."

"And he's following us because he's jealous of *you?*"

He ignored her incredulous tone. "Or because he's trying to keep track of the picture he must have figured out we have."

"Then you think . . . Mel . . . is the one?"

"I don't know. I just don't see any other reason for him to follow us, except his supposed jealousy, and I really don't see him behaving so wildly over that. Do you?"

"I don't know."

"Well, think about it, while I find another route to Madrid." He reached for the maps. About five minutes later he started up the engine, thrusting the maps into the gap between the seats. "We'll have to go north. I suggest we stay the night in Cuenca, then go north to Guadalajara and drop down to Madrid from there. Is your 'jealous lover' very familiar with Spanish roads?"

"I have no idea," said Holly in a small voice. "I think he's only been in Puerto Rio for a couple of months. He may have been somewhere else in Spain before that, but he's never mentioned it. I got the impression he came straight there."

"Like a homing pigeon?" Charles asked, glancing into the rear-view mirror.

"Maybe." She sounded resentful. "You know, he wasn't even in town the night Graebner was killed. He was in Alicante."

"Doing what?"

"I don't know."

"You said he was with Nigel Bland when you first met him. How long had he known them?"

"I don't know."

"What kind of a firm was Tinker Electronics?"

"I don't know."

"Does Nigel have anything to do with Tinker's firm?"

"I don't know."

"You seem pretty reluctant to suspect someone you know nothing about," Charles said irritably. "Isn't it better to suspect a stranger than a friend?"

"He *is* a friend."

"Uh-huh. He's a 'friend' of Nigel's, too."

"Do you honestly think Nigel could have something to do with all this?" Holly asked a little while later, when they'd crossed the stream on an old wooden bridge and eventually picked up the main road to Cuenca.

"It could be."

"But I told you . . . Nigel and Reg are old friends."

"We're talking about an awful lot of money—from the fraud, and maybe from that picture back there, if it *is* a Goya. Even old friends can turn."

"And Mary's with them, right now!"

"Oh, don't worry about that. They aren't interested in her. It's that damn picture, that they've been after all along."

"But Nigel knew about the . . ." She paused. "No, he didn't. They were back in England when David was killed. They didn't come back until after the funeral. But surely Reg must have told him about the picture then?"

"Not necessarily. Mary made him keep it hidden, remember? He may have tried to spare her feelings—especially since he knew it wouldn't do any good, once David was dead and Graebner had changed his plea. Anyway, you said that your father-in-law had taken several of David's pictures. Maybe only Graebner knew there was a thirteenth Goya. He apparently spoke of revenge in prison, if he spoke at all, so I don't think he'd have told any of his former partners about it. After all, it was the only thing he had to bargain with. And he didn't tell his killer either, because the flat wasn't robbed that night. In fact, nobody did anything until you mentioned David's things being in the garage. Nobody knew about that stuff—not even Reg and Mary. But the minute it was mentioned, it was taken. What they were looking for wasn't there, so they took all the pictures in the penthouse, hoping to find the right one. But it *still* wasn't found. They were flummoxed —until good old Nigel and good old Mel saw that brown paper parcel in your suitcase and realized they'd missed one somehow. Do you see it now?"

She was silent.

Charles took his eyes from the road briefly, to look at her. Head down, deep in thought. "Do you suppose when my flat in Hampstead was ripped off they were looking for the picture? It happened about a month after I'd gotten back from the funeral, and a couple of days after the few things I *did* send back were delivered."

"I wouldn't be at all surprised," Charles said. "It fits. Was Nigel still in England then?"

"Yes." She sounded on the verge of tears. "But how do we prove all this?"

"I haven't the faintest idea," Charles said. "I wish I did."

Cuenca, perched high on the ridge between the ravines of the two rivers, was bathed in blood-red sunlight when Holly first saw it. They'd had to pass through two tunnels first, and she was unprepared for what awaited them on the other side.

"My God, Charles, look at those houses—they're hanging over the edge of the cliff!"

"Las Casas Colgadas," Charles said. "The Hanging Houses of Cuenca. They're famous. Three of them have been joined together to make a museum. You should see it someday. Really good modern Spanish painting."

"I didn't know there *was* such a thing as modern Spanish painting—I thought everything ended with Goya."

"Didn't David ever mention the museum at Cuenca?"

"He might have—I don't remember." She turned away to stare at the old town as Charles drove up and down the narrow streets looking for an hotel he remembered only vaguely, but which he knew was the best in Cuenca. Finally he drew up in front of an archway they'd passed several times. Beyond it, on the other side of a tiny courtyard, a second door stood open, a tiny brass plate beside it. "My goodness, they don't exactly shout out for customers, do they?" she said.

"Wait here," he said, getting out. "They may not have rooms—it's a tiny place."

She looked around when he'd disappeared into the shadows beyond the second doorway. The houses on both sides of the little street were almost faceless, except for the magnificent carved wooden doors that were so commonplace in Spain. A small balcony hung above the cobbles here and there, but for the most part the old buildings kept their secrets well. She could hear voices occasionally, but she couldn't see anyone anywhere. Feeling stifled, she got out of the car and took a deep breath. The heat of the day was draining away from the town rapidly, and the street was like a canyon, deep in shadow. Charles reappeared.

"I've taken two rooms, but I'm afraid they're on opposite sides of the hotel."

"Does that matter?"

"No." His mouth quirked. "It's just another example of residual Spanish morality at work. Try not to giggle."

"I don't giggle," Holly said, offended.

He dragged their suitcases out. "You might, when you see the lobby in this place."

She very nearly did, for every wall was covered with elaborately framed pictures.

And each one was a copy of a Goya.

They decided to visit the museum when they learned it would be open until seven. Charles parked the car and then met Holly at the top of the canyon-like cobbled street. Using the hotel clerk's instructions, they eventually came to a path that ran along the wall of a cathedral, then turned into a cul-de-sac. "That's it, I remember now," Charles said, going towards one of the medieval doors set into the surrounding walls. Since it was the only one ajar, and it had next to it a small sign saying *museo,* it seemed a fair assumption. Out of breath, Holly followed him in, not expecting much, and found herself pleasantly surprised.

Most of the work was superb, and Charles had to drag her away from several of them. Her fingers itched for a sketch pad to make notes of the ideas that were flooding her. There was a fire here that one didn't often see in French, English, or American Abstracts. The earth colours and the textures . . . she felt exhilarated and ashamed that she had never sus-pected this outpouring of raw, restless talent from the conventional Spanish. She wasn't surprised that David had never mentioned it, although she felt sure he would have come here. How aware it must have made him of his own shortcomings. What a slap in the face it must have been to see that men *not* schooled in the studios and art colleges of Europe could paint so well, so freshly.

The three buildings that housed the museum were interconnected, and stairs went up and down unexpectedly, little corners were revealed sud-denly, and surprises abounded. "This is how a museum *should* be," Holly enthused. Charles was beginning to weary, but she seemed to grow more enthusiastic with every step. When they came to a small room that con-tained textiles, she refused to go any farther. She just stood there silently in the centre of the room.

"Just give me a moment . . ." she said vaguely.

Bored, he wandered over to the window, involuntarily stepping back when he realized it hung out over the six-hundred-foot drop to the Río Hueca below. It was barely visible beneath the tangled vegetation that lined the banks, but he could hear its distant chuckle. A glint here and there between the leaves, no more, revealed its course. Straight ahead he could see for miles in three directions, and he felt rather like a bird in flight, for nothing came between him and the sky.

As for the land below . . . He stiffened suddenly, looking down. Below and to the left he could see the road leading up from the second tunnel, the one he and Holly had taken an hour before.

Coming along it was a red Mercedes convertible.

CHAPTER 14

Holly's feet never touched the ground.

"What's wrong? What is it?" she demanded, as Charles literally swept her out of the museum and into the cobbled street outside, holding her arm in a wrestling lock.

"Tinker's here. I just saw his car coming up the road below," Charles said, half running through the archway and down the twisting snake of road that led back to the hotel. "I want you to pack your case . . ." He was fumbling in his pocket, and produced his room key. "And then do the same with mine." His foot slipped on the dusty path and they nearly went over the edge of someone's doorstep into the gloomy shadows of an inner courtyard. Dusk was falling fast. "Try not to let anyone see you, but if they do, say . . . you've had bad news . . ." He skidded to a halt at the top of the street where the hotel entrance was visible half-way down. "Do my case first, then yours. Wait in your room until I come for you. Don't answer the door unless it's me. I'll knock two short, two long, and two short. Got it?"

"For heaven's sake, Charles, this is crazy!" Holly protested.

"I'm sure Graebner thought so, too," Charles said. "Shut up and do what I said."

The thought of Graebner was enough. Until this moment Holly had been going on adrenaline alone, keeping memories well back in her mind, trying to ignore them. Now all she could see was the huddled shape under the canvas the Guardia had thrown over Graebner's body in the torchlight. The way one claw-like hand had poked out at a corner. And the way the thin lines of blood had drained towards the earth around the palm trees, had soaked in, glistening . . .

She shut up.

"He'll take a while to work his way around to this hotel, but not long. There aren't that many good places in Cuenca, and with your red hair
. . ."

She looked at him helplessly.

"Damn," he muttered. "How *could* he have found us?"

"I don't know," she wailed.

"All right, go on. I'll get the car." Charles disappeared into the shadows of yet another narrow cave-like passage. She hurried down to the hotel and was relieved to see no one at the desk. She reached over and got the key to her room, then hurried up the stairs, turning towards Charles's room rather than her own, and with fumbling fingers opened his door and stepped inside.

Ten minutes later, she emerged and started down the hall furtively, towards her own room, carrying his case. As she crossed the landing she glanced down and her heart gave a painful jerk in her chest, then started to pound heavily.

Mel Tinker was standing at the desk, talking to the clerk.

How on earth had he found them so quickly? Was it mere chance that had led him to this hotel, or was he simply starting at the top of the town rather than the bottom? More importantly, he was now standing directly in Charles's way. There was no lobby, as such. The minute Charles turned into the hotel from the street, Mel would spot him. There was nothing she could do.

Oh, God, she could see the clerk nodding. After all, all Mel had to do was describe her. How many red-haired Americans could one expect to find in a small Spanish town on an autumn night?

Panic-stricken, and yet feeling oddly disoriented by having to flee from someone she'd regarded until now as a friend, Holly stepped back and sidled across the landing to her own room. As far as the desk clerk knew, she and Charles were still at the museum. Maybe he would send Mel after them. Please, God, let him go to the museum, she thought, putting Charles's case down in order to unlock the door of her own room.

Stepping inside, she reached for the light switch, and encountered the back of a hand instead. Before she could scream, another hand came over her mouth.

"For God's sake, don't bellow," Charles hissed in her ear.

She went limp in his grasp, and he had to tighten his arm to keep her from slipping to the floor. "And don't faint, either. There isn't time." He removed his hand from her mouth.

"Mel's downstairs," she managed to gasp.

"I know, I saw the car parked outside. Let's hope the clerk sends him to the museum."

"How did you get past him?"

"I climbed in your window, Juliet," he said. He nodded across the room at the french window, which opened onto the balcony that encircled the inner courtyard. She went over and looked out. As far as she could see, the only way he could have made it was by flying. He came over and stood beside her.

"I'd like you to think I'm Icarus, but the fact is, I parked the VW on the other side of the wall and climbed up onto the balcony."

"And are we supposed to go out that way?"

"If we have to . . . yes."

There was a knock at the door. "Holly? You in there?" It was Mel Tinker's voice. Holly and Charles stared at one another, and he made a gesture for her to remain perfectly still. "Holly? Honey?"

He sounded so friendly, so concerned. Charles scowled, and Holly made a face at him.

"Holly? It's Mel, honey . . ."

There was another voice, speaking in Spanish. Tinker answered, and then they heard footsteps moving away. Holly let go of the breath she didn't know she'd been holding, and saw that Charles looked puzzled. "What's wrong?" she whispered.

"He spoke Spanish, not the way he . . . it was as good as mine."

"What did he say?"

"What?" Charles stirred from his trance. "Oh, the clerk remembered about the museum and Tinker asked for directions. Come on, we'd better move. Take the picture out of your case before you pack, by the way."

"Why?"

"I'd rather put it into a less conspicuous place—just in case that *is* what Tinker is after."

When she'd finished, they went to the window. The balcony was not an easy way out or in, for it encircled the courtyard at a height of some twenty feet, on three sides only, and had no stairs leading down. Furthermore, the rooms that looked out onto it were separated by little cross-bars, added when the house was converted to an hotel, so they had to climb over one after another to get around to where the end of the balcony hung over the wall. There was a drop of about five feet to the wall itself, which was only about twelve inches wide and broken in places. Holly halted in dismay.

"It's all right," Charles urged in an undertone, glancing at the nearest window, which was lit, but fortunately both curtained and closed. Voices could be heard within, however, murmuring idly. "I'll go first."

"Oh, God . . ." Holly said, swaying. "I can't stand heights."

"That's not a height," Charles said irritably. "It's a drop."

"Oh, don't . . ." She closed her eyes.

"Well, you've just failed the audition for Superwoman," he muttered, and swung one leg over the balcony railing. "Look, hand me the stuff and I'll take it to the car. Then I'll come back for you."

She tried not to watch him teeter along the wall with a suitcase in each hand, but she couldn't look away. He never missed a step, and moved lightly and steadily along, as if he'd trained for it all his life. He put the cases on the roof of the VW, then came back for the painting. He dropped down on the other side of the wall, and she swore she never heard a sound. After a moment Charles's head popped back up and he grinned at her, his very slightly crooked teeth white in the moonlight. His hair was over his forehead, his shirt was open at the throat, and he looked rather like a highwayman coming for Bess, the innkeeper's daughter. She stood there looking down at him as he came back and waited for her to join him.

She just stood there.

His smile abruptly blinked out, and his arms dropped to his sides. With a sigh, he lifted them again and gestured at her to climb down to him. She couldn't move. He waved again, looking behind him and around the courtyard. "Hurry up," he whispered impatiently. She shook her head. She could hear him, muttering and cursing to himself as he climbed back up. He made a grab for her and she shrieked involuntarily. They froze, locked together on either side of the balcony, waiting. The voices behind the curtains of the lighted window had stopped suddenly. They could hear someone asking something that could only have been, "What was that?"

Charles tugged at her as the latch to the french window was undone, and she climbed over the balcony's edge and into his arms. He pulled her down and they crouched below the lip of the balcony, clinging to the edge of the floor and balancing on the top of the wall.

Holly tried to make her mind a blank.

After all, how far could it be to the cobbled street below the wall? Ten feet? Fifteen? Twenty? What was the worst that could happen? A broken ankle? Arm? Back? She moaned into Charles's neck, and he tightened his hold on her. After about ten or twenty seconds, they heard the window close again, and the voices resumed their earlier rise and fall, with an edge of idle conjecture. Whatever they'd heard, they were agreeing, it couldn't have been important.

"Okay, now down onto the roof of the car," Charles's voice said in her ear. He sounded very calm. Awkwardly, she disentangled herself from him and somehow scrambled down to the car and then dropped to the cobbles. Unbelievingly she looked down at herself.

Nothing broken.

Charles dropped lightly beside her, straight from the wall, eschewing the intermediate step of the car-roof. She hated him. He grinned at her again, and opened the passenger door with a flourish.

"Señorita?"

The VW's engine seemed deafeningly loud in the narrow, twisting little streets. "Which way are we going?" Holly whispered.

"At the moment, down," Charles said in a normal voice. He nosed the car out of one street and into another slowly. Twice he had to back out of turnings that led nowhere, but finally came to what seemed like a main thoroughfare. On the far side, railings edged it, and the street lights reflected on water.

"Now which is that, the Hueca or the Júcar?" he muttered to himself.

"You're asking me?" Holly said.

"There's no time to look at the map," he said.

"Left."

"Left it is."

About ten minutes later, he began to curse. They'd passed a Firestone station, but it was closed. There didn't seem to be any signs at all on the road. He pulled over and switched on the interior light, wrestling the maps out of the gap between the seats.

"Oh hell," he finally said. "We have to go back the way we came."

"Doesn't this road go anywhere?"

"No, nowhere we want to go, anyway. It takes us miles out of our way, and the only alternatives are cart-tracks. Apparently, we're missing some fantastic scenery, according to the map. Isn't that a shame?"

"Oh yes, a great shame. I love scenery almost as much as I love climbing down drain-pipes and . . . ahhhh!"

He'd started to turn the car back, but she shrieked as he completed the circle and continued down the road even faster than before. "I can't take much more of this!" he informed her at the top of his voice. "I'm a desk man —this isn't exactly my idea of fun."

"But what—"

"Your bloody boyfriend's behind us, closing fast," Charles said in a harassed voice, hunching over the wheel. "He's got twice our speed and power, we'll never outrun him . . . how the bloody hell does he *do* it?" He glanced into the rear-view mirror. No doubt about it, the Mercedes was coming up on them. He could see Tinker's shadow behind the wheel, faceless, menacing. Something of Holly's hysteria communicated itself to him, and he felt his muscles begin to flutter. Ahead, a dirt road to the right offered itself, and without a moment's hesitation he slewed into it, nearly precipitating Holly into his lap. The car rocked violently in protest. There was a muffled bang, and suddenly it was all over the road. He couldn't control it. It skidded and swerved and the wheel jerked out of his hands as they bounced from one bank of the road to another and finally came to an abrupt halt in a great scattering of gravel.

Holly, struggling upright, stared at him.

"Flat tyre," he said. "Come on."

It occurred to her, quite clearly despite the panic of the moment, that Charles always seemed to be dragging her out of things—cars, hotel rooms . . . whatever. All around them loomed stunted trees and rocks, thrown into relief by the sudden glow of the Mercedes' headlamps.

"Once more into the bushes, dear friends," Charles growled. They scrambled up the bank and then fell over the other side in a dusty, stony slither, coming to a bumpy stop between two of the twisted trunks of the olive trees. Overhead the feathery leaves briefly showed green in the glow of the Mercedes' headlamps. Then that winked out as the Mercedes came to a stop beside the VW and the engine was cut.

"I think I'm going to be sick," Holly whispered.

"Not now—later," Charles whispered back.

"Holly? Charley? What the hell are you running away for?" It was Tinker's drawl, echoing strangely. It sounded as if they were in a gigantic auditorium. Charles tugged at her hand, and they began to move as quietly as they could down the slope, and away from Tinker.

"This is downright silly," the voice came after them.

From the splatter of gravel, it sounded as if Tinker was coming after them, too. They moved faster now, not worrying about the noise, and promptly fell over a tree root. Then a fence. Then a rock.

"I really think we ought to talk," Tinker called.

Charles thought so too, until he heard the sound. He'd never heard it in real life before, but hundreds of Saturday mornings at the Palace Royale cinema had set it deeply in his memory. The sound of a gun being cocked. Holly must have been a film-fan too, for he felt her stiffen beside him.

"He's got a gun," Charles said wonderingly.

"What on earth would he need a gun for?" Holly asked.

"I really don't think I want to know," Charles said. "Come on."

They stood up and began to run in earnest, and as their eyes became accustomed to the darkness, they ran into things less often. Behind them they could hear Tinker running too. He wasn't shouting now. They didn't stop to reason, only propelled forward by the blind unthinking panic of the chased and hunted. Suddenly Holly stopped, stared and screamed.

Directly in front of them was a dinosaur.

CHAPTER 15

Holly took her hands away from her face.

The dinosaur was still there.

"Oh, pull yourself together, it's only a rock," Charles hissed in her ear. All around them, barely visible in the faint glow of a rising moon, loomed monstrous twisted animals, buildings, and human shapes, seemingly conjured up out of some sorcerer's demented imagination.

"Come on, keep moving," Charles whispered. He tugged at her arm and she came obediently, terrified lest he leave her, more terrified lest Tinker find them.

"What is this place?" she hissed as he dragged her along.

"La Ciudad Encantada—big tourist attraction. Just a bunch of rocks weathered into funny shapes, that's all." There was an incongruous guidebook tone to his voice—as they were now crouched under a giant toadstool like a couple of fieldmice hiding from a cat.

Holly jerked and tried to climb inside Charles's jacket as Tinker's voice came out of the darkness quite near them, distorted by the night air and the rocks.

"This is stupid," the voice said conversationally. "What good is the picture to you with Graebner dead?"

It sounded so reasonable, that voice. One could almost believe it.

Perhaps Graebner had believed it, too.

Charles tightened his arm around her and tugged gently. They straightened up and moved away from the voice, but big rocks mean little rocks, and they betrayed their movements with sibilant voices as they cascaded down the slopes and valleys beneath their giant brothers.

"You have absolutely nothing to be afraid of, you know. If you'll just come out where we can talk this over . . ."

Charles wanted to be brave and masterful, but the fact was that his knees felt like water, and so did his bowels. He was shaking and he was sweating and he wished they were anywhere but there. Alicante, London, my God, even Cardiff on a wet Wednesday night. *Anywhere*.

He had two choices, really. He could keep on crawling around there like a coward, or he could stand up and fight.

They kept on crawling. Until they came to a barrier and sensed the yawning chasm beyond it. End of the line. The moonglow showed the tops of trees far below. He'd been there once, a long time ago, and recalled the view by day—the silver snake-coils of the river, the rocky outcroppings, the distant horizon under a blue sky with high flat-bottomed clouds drifting overhead.

Now there was only darkness, a sense of space, and the faint faraway tinkle of the river tumbling over the stones, hundreds of feet below. Charles took a deep breath and sighed.

"Stay here," he told Holly. He sounded very tired.

She clutched his sleeve. "Don't leave me here, please . . ."

"Get behind one of the rocks and wait," he said, and with a few steps he was gone among the monster shapes. Holly, hugging herself in the chill that rose from behind the fence, couldn't stop shaking. The voice was getting closer.

"Holly, come on, honey . . ."

She wanted to answer. She wanted to shout angry accusations, call him dreadful names, but she stayed very small beneath the big table-shaped rock, and didn't move. At least, not at first.

Charles, after removing his shoes, found the going slightly more silent, and a great deal more uncomfortable. He could think of nothing positive or constructive, except that as long as Tinker kept talking, he'd at least know where he was.

Tinker, *not* very obliging, fell silent.

The whole place was silent, dark, and menacing.

Mind you, Charles reasoned, crouching next to what looked like a brontosaurus, finding Tinker was one thing, knowing what to do with him was quite another. He was just not the physical type. Desk-bound most of the time, with just the odd game of cricket. He couldn't recall actually striking anyone since that time at university. Sorting out disagreements over contracts and renewing passports was not exactly an exemplary preparation for this kind of thing.

He realized he was procrastinating, trying to get up enough nerve to face the big American.

He really was a *very* big American.

And he had a gun, too.

He began to feel seriously depressed.

It then occurred to him that he'd been standing there for a good three minutes and he hadn't heard a sound out of Tinker. My God, he must have found Holly!

He began to run back, with his hands outstretched to avoid collisions with the rocks, so he didn't see Tinker.

Until he tripped over the body.

Charles went sprawling in the dust with a startled "Oooof!" and lay there for a moment, trying to figure out what had happened. He'd tripped over something soft, not hard. Not a rock, but . . . He got to his hands and knees. Holly? He crawled back and touched the supine figure.

No, Tinker.

And then he looked up.

About ten feet above him, on the flat top of one of the misshapen rocks, was the figure of Holly outlined against the sky. She was staring down at him.

"What are you doing up there?" he asked, nonplussed.

"Waiting for a Number 73 bus," came the quavering reply, and then she crawled to the edge and dropped down with a thump, staggering sideways into him and bringing them both down to ground level beside Tinker. "Where have *you* been?"

"What did you do to him?" Charles asked, not sure he really wanted to know.

"I dropped a rock on him," she said, her teeth chattering.

Charles drew himself up. "*I* was going to do that."

"Well, why didn't you?" She stared at him and then down at the limp form. "I never hit anyone with a rock before. It made the most awful sound." She seemed on the verge of tears. "Is he dead . . . or something?"

Charles bent down and listened. "No, he's breathing. You just knocked him out, that's all." He stood up. "I think we'd better get out of here before he wakes up. He's bound to be a little irritable."

"What about . . . that?"

Charles followed her pointing hand, and saw the dark shape of Tinker's gun lying a few feet from his outstretched fingers. He went over, picked it up gingerly and, walking to the fence, threw it as far into the darkness as he could. There was a moment of stillness, and then he could hear it bouncing off the rocks far below.

"What on earth did you do that for?" Holly demanded, outraged. "We might have needed it!"

"For what?" Charles asked. "Could you shoot anyone?"

"I could shoot *you*, right now," she raged.

"Perhaps that's why I got rid of it." His voice was cold. He turned and marched off, the dignity of his progress marred somewhat by the sharp stones that persisted in cutting into his stockinged feet. After banging his nose painfully he found his shoes and put them on, then continued his march to the car.

"You're cross, aren't you?" Holly said, stumbling after him, her voice hurt and reproachful. "I practically saved your life, you know."

"I'm well aware of that."

"What are we going to do now?"

"I don't know about you, but I'm going to . . ." He paused, then went on walking. His nose had started to bleed, and he wiped it with his shirt tail.

"You don't know what to do, do you?" Holly asked.

"Shut up. Let me think." He banged his elbow on a rock so hard that it went momentarily numb. He massaged it as they walked, and cracked his shin on another just before they mounted the bank beyond which were the cars.

The VW was still slewed crazily half-way up the bank. The Mercedes had drawn up behind it. A few yards ahead, he could now see the entrance to La Ciudad Encantada, barred and locked, of course. He went over to the Mercedes and looked in. The keys were in the ignition. And on the seat, there was a small black and chrome box. He reached in and took it out, carrying it over to the VW to inspect it by torchlight.

"So now I know how he kept finding us so easily," Charles said to Holly, who was sitting in the driver's seat of the VW with her feet outside on the ground, shaking gravel out of her sandals.

"What is it?" she asked.

"Some sort of homing device. I suppose there's a bug on the VW. I would suggest you don't marry him, he'd always know where you were."

"I have no intention of marrying him or anyone else. Won't he come back here when he wakes up, by the way?"

"He won't wake up for a while yet. When he does come back, we won't be around." He felt in his pockets and produced the keys to the VW. "Here, you follow me."

"With a flat tyre?" she asked sweetly.

"Oh." He stared at the VW. "I'd planned to leave it in the petrol station up the road, but . . ."

He went over and gestured her out. Then he tipped the driver's seat forward and crawled in the back. Pulling the back of the rear seat away, he rescued the painting, then replaced the seat. "I'll leave him the keys to the VW, he can have a good time changing the tyre."

"And what if he reports his car stolen?"

"Do you really think he's likely to do that?" Charles asked impatiently.
"He'll probably follow us to Madrid, but without any help from his
friends." He dropped the box of the homing device onto the ground and
smashed it with a few well-aimed kicks.

"Goodness, flamenco dancing and everything," Holly said mockingly.

He merely glanced at her, picked up his things and went over to the
Mercedes, holding open the door until she'd collected her big handbag and
joined him. Then he slammed the door, went around to the driver's side, got
in, started the car and backed out onto the highway.

He stopped at a petrol station outside Madrid to clean himself up a little
before going to the embassy. He could hardly walk in with blood all over his
shirt, could he? He'd extracted a rumpled shirt from the bundle, and now
changed into it. He washed his face and stared at himself in the mirror. His
eyes were bloodshot from driving all night, and there was a bruise coming
up on his cheek. His nose was swollen, giving him a clownish appearance,
and his hair seemed to have a life of its own, standing on end in several
places.

Our man in Alicante? Dear God.

He went back to the car and got in. Holly had awakened, and apparently
done something to herself in the Ladies'. She looked as bright and fresh as a
daisy, her curls springing bouncily in the sunlight. He'd been hoping she'd
be gone when he got back, but there she was. She even smiled at him.

"That's a big improvement," she said cheerfully.

"Mmmmm." He started the car and joined the line of early morning
traffic on the *autopista* leading into Madrid. They'd managed to miss the
rush-hour in Guadalajara, but not this one. And this one was always twenty
times worse than any other in Europe, he thought. To take part in it was a
further demonstration of what had to be an unsuspected death wish in
himself. All through the night he'd driven down the dark highway in the
Mercedes, wondering what had impelled him to get into this mess. A death
wish seemed the only rational answer. By dawn, he'd begun to accept it
fatalistically. This was the way it was going to end for him. Caught up in
some stupid, meaningless rigmarole involving stolen paintings and murder
and men with ulcers sitting in jail trying to be brave. Nothing noble or
inspiring about it. Just another damn mess. Llewellyn's Last Mess, the One
That Finally Got Him. He swerved to avoid a bright-blue Citroën driven by
another hapless male bent on premature suicide.

He felt terrible.

Holly looked at him. Poor Charles. He'd been quite nice about everything until last night. Now he was sulking because she'd been braver than he had. Or so he assumed. She'd tried to explain how afraid she'd been, that was the only reason she'd had enough guts to drop the rock. Well, if he wanted to sulk, that was his choice. She'd tried to be civil, hadn't she? He had the jaw for it, anyway. With a jaw like that, you'd have thought he would have taken on ten Mel Tinkers. Well, he just wasn't the physical type, that's all. Some men were, and some weren't. He was sensible. He was intelligent. She wished he weren't so angry. She looked around.

"This looks like downtown Chicago," she complained. "Except for the signs being in Spanish." Charles said nothing. He really was a pain, sitting there, she decided. "I thought Madrid was supposed to be such a beautiful city."

"Parts of it are."

"But not this part."

"No."

She sighed. "Be funny if it wasn't a Goya, wouldn't it?"

"Hilarious."

"Oh well . . . if you're going to act like *that.*"

"I'm not acting like anything," Charles said through gritted teeth. "I'm driving the car. I can't carry on a sprightly conversation with you and drive this car in this traffic at the same time. I'm not . . ."

"All right."

"I don't *have* to go on with this, you know. I'm doing my best."

"All *right.*"

A few minutes later, she spoke again. "This is more like the Madrid I expected." They had turned out of the stream of traffic onto a wide, graceful street, tree-lined, with huge houses set back in park-like surroundings on either side. Some distance ahead, a fountain sparkled in the centre of the roadway. The traffic swirled around it, and Neptune looked down at it benignly from his own carriage, drawn by two aquarian centaurs, half horse and half fish. Thin jets of water rose over the cascades surrounding him, and some of the drifting mist blew onto the windscreen of the Mercedes and glittered in Holly's hair.

"That's the Prado," Charles muttered, nodding his head in the direction of a long building, faintly pink, with a classical facade of tall columns and sculptured bas-relief.

"Why are we stopping here?"

"We aren't. I just thought you might like to see it, that's all. We're going on to the embassy."

"The embassy?"

"That's right. I have a friend there who lets me use his flat from time to time. If we go to an hotel, Tinker might be able to find us. And Brad's flat has an underground garage, so we can hide the Mercedes. Just in case Tinker tries to find us that way. All right?"

"Fine. Did you think I'd object?"

"I never know what you're going to do," he grumbled.

"No," she agreed. "Neither do I."

Charles found Bradley behind his desk, an unusual occurrence in itself. "Can I stay at the flat tonight—maybe tomorrow night, too?"

"If you must," Brad said with a grin.

"I . . . I'm not alone."

"Well, well, back among the living, are you? Congratulations."

"Nothing like that."

"Which is what you always said." Bradley removed the key from his drawer and handed it across. "As it happens, you're in luck, old boy. I have to go to Valencia this afternoon—won't be back for a couple of days. Isn't that handy?"

"Yes."

Bradley frowned. "You don't seem exactly knocked over by your good fortune, old man. Don't tell me she's an ugly second cousin from Swansea or something?"

"Something. Thanks. I'll drop the key off here."

"Righto. Good luck." Bradley watched Charles's drooping figure leave the office, and reached for the phone. He dialled, waited, and finally got through.

"I say . . . Baker . . . he's just been in. What do I do now?"

CHAPTER 16

The Rastro reminded Holly of Camden Lock on a Sunday morning, except for the buildings that rose over the bustling, crowded stall-lined streets. She couldn't figure out what it was that made it seem so un-English. Finally she got it.

"It's the awnings," she decided. "They make it look so—jaunty. Like a seaside resort." She was glad she'd changed at the flat, leaving her legs bare and putting on a light dress. She was gathering admiring glances, and turned to see if Charles noticed. He did not. He was pushing his way through the crowd impatiently, leaving her to follow behind as best she could. He looked uneasy.

"What's wrong now?" she asked.

"I don't know. I feel as if we're being watched."

"We are," she said smugly. He stopped and stared at her, then looked around furtively.

"How do you know?"

"A woman usually knows when she's appreciated."

An expression of extreme disgust passed over his face. "Oh, *that.* Aren't you used to that by now? It's your red hair, that's all. I thought you were serious." He turned on his heel and once again breasted the crowd like an impatient tugboat. Finally, exasperated by the slow-moving browsers, he took her by the elbow and propelled her into a side street. "We'll cut through here, it's faster."

After the bright hustle of the Rastro, the street seemed dark and mean, sidling between haughty grey buildings that had no interest in them or anything else. Charles stalked along and she pattered after, carrying the painting in the plastic carrier bag. At least it was a little cooler here. He swerved to the right, through an alleyway and out into another narrow street. At the mouth of it, to her left, she could see the Rastro in the distance, sunlit and busy. But they turned right.

"I think it's the next one. Yes, Calle de Gavilán. Hawk Street. *Numero treinte y uno* must be up here."

They finally arrived at a narrow doorway next to a small display window that contained some oil paintings and a lacquered box. Despite the lack of light between the buildings, the picture in the centre of the display glowed richly. It was a Madonna and Child, with a background of landscape only faintly indicated in browns and yellows.

Even Charles was stopped. "That's rather nice," he said. "Looks like a Raphael, doesn't it?"

Holly giggled. "On behalf of my late husband, I thank you."

Charles stared at her. "You mean . . ."

"I posed for it. Don't you see the resemblance?"

He leaned closer to the window. The face of the Madonna was uncannily like the face reflected beside his own in the glass. The hair styles were different and the expressions certainly were. No Madonna ever wore the look of mischievous satisfaction that Holly had at that moment. And yet the resemblance was perfectly clear. My God, what a coincidence, he thought, wondering how David had managed to keep her still or serious long enough to catch that wistful sadness in the Madonna's eyes.

Inside, the small space was crowded with pictures and redolent with the smells of hot wax, turpentine, linseed oil, solvents and varnish. It was a very old-fashioned smell somehow. Had it not been for the very modern electronic till next to an equally modern telephone, they could have imagined themselves in a previous century. Equally disappointing in that respect was the man who stepped through the curtains at the back in response to the gentle tinkle of the bell over the door. To be in keeping with his surroundings he should have been a wrinkled old man with a stoop and a cough. Instead he was a broad-shouldered young Spaniard in a bright-red polo-necked pullover and jeans, with dark, tightly-curled hair and a gold earring in one ear. He glanced at Charles briefly, then settled his eyes on Holly, where they stayed.

"*Puedo ayudarle?*" he asked with a charming smile.

Charles cleared his throat. "We have a painting that we think may have another painting underneath it," he said, before Holly could speak. "Could you remove the top layer of paint for us?"

"May I see the picture?"

"He wants to see it," Charles told Holly. He took the picture from the carrier bag and put it on the counter. The young man produced a pair of scissors, cut the string and pushed the brown paper aside.

"*Madre de Dios!*" he exclaimed, switching on a strong narrow focus light to illuminate the canvas. "You want me to destroy this?"

"Yes."

"Do you know what it is, señor?"

"It is a very excellent forgery," Charles said. "We feel there may be a more valuable painting beneath. You were recommended by Alfredo Braganza as a restorer whose work and discretion could be trusted." He had called Alfredo from Bradley's flat. Without going into much detail, he'd explained the situation and said he was inquiring for a "friend." He had no doubt that Alfredo's interest would be even more piqued, but he'd rather risk that than entrust the picture to some dishonest firm they didn't know.

The young man made a graceful, deprecating gesture. "He is very kind."

"How long will it take?"

The young man shrugged. "A couple of weeks, perhaps three."

Charles wasn't shocked. Both Holly and Alfredo had told him this might be the case. Holly spoke up.

"Do you speak English?" she asked. Charles had been speaking in Spanish.

"Yes, señorita."

"You see, we really are in the most frightful hurry," Holly said in a small, wistful voice that made Charles stare at her in amazement. "It's terribly important that we find out exactly what's underneath the picture. A man's life could depend on it," she added, with what Charles thought was quite unnecessary melodrama.

The young man straightened a little and gazed into her eyes. "I will do my best, señorita. But I must be very careful . . ."

"Mr. Braganza said you were the best he knew," Holly murmured. Charles felt like vomiting, but the young man blossomed. From the expression in his dancing eyes he was quite aware that he was being manipulated—what he seemed to appreciate was the effort. And the source.

"For you, señorita, and for Alfredo, I will put everything else to one side and begin work immediately," he promised.

"Thank you," said Holly demurely, lowering her eyes.

"We'd like to call back in a day or two to see how the work is progressing," Charles said brusquely.

"I will have hardly begun," the young man protested. "I must determine the thickness of the overpainting, the state of the varnish underneath . . ."

"Of course you must," Holly said. "There are so many possibilities, aren't there?"

"The possibilities are endless, señorita," the young man purred. "As are the variations . . ." Nobody thought he was talking about art restoration.

"Thank you, we'll be in touch," Charles said, starting for the door. As his eye fell on the picture in the window, he paused. "By the way, how much is the Raphael?" he asked negligently.

"The Madonna and Child?" the young man asked, straightening up a little at the possibility of a sale. "It is very beautiful, is it not?"

"Oh, very," Charles agreed, wondering what outrageous price this sloe-eyed mountebank would ask.

"Unfortunately, it is not genuine," the young man said, coming around the counter to pluck the picture out of the window. He put a long arm over the brass rail from which the velvet drapery hung. "It is an excellent approximation, painted by a very good friend of mine who passed away two years ago. One of your countrymen, as it happens."

"You . . . knew David?" Holly asked in amazement.

The young man stared at Holly, dumbfounded, and then looked again at the picture in his hands.

"But . . . you are she! You are Holly? David's wife?" he demanded, his whole demeanor changing. He seemed instantly younger, and the deliberately cultivated air of sexuality dropped away from him like a discarded cloak.

"The Bosch is David's too," Holly said, her face drawn up as she scrabbled in her memory. "Of course . . . *Gavilán,* the name of the street! David always used to refer to his friend in Madrid as 'the Hawk' . . . Jaime, isn't it?"

"Yes, it is I!" the young man said, delight illuminating his undeniably hawk-like features. "He would always stay with me when he was copying at the Prado. He spoke of you often and so sadly . . ."

Charles turned away irritably. Obviously there was now going to be a massive reunion scene, with reminiscences of David flowing in all directions. He stared out of the window bleakly as the other two chatted.

Jaime's English was excellent, they had no need of a translator. He felt quite extraneous. Outside, in the narrow street, a man walked by the shop slowly, his eyes not on the paintings in the window, but looking within at Jaime and Holly. Charles, in the shadows to one side, stepped back even farther and looked at the man with a frown. He'd been in the Rastro, too—quite near them at times. Not a Spaniard, either. Something indefinable about the clothes he wore said "foreigner."

After a moment's pause, the man walked on, leaving Charles to ponder. Eventually he stirred himself. "We really must be going."

"But you must stay and have a meal with me," Jaime said. "You must."

"Well . . ." Holly hesitated.

"Thank you for your hospitality," Charles said. "But we have some other calls to make. Perhaps when we return?"

"Very well," Jaime said, but his gaze softened when he looked again at Holly. "You promise this?"

"Yes, of course. I'd love it."

"We must go," Charles said again.

"Wait," Jaime said. "I want you to have this." He held out the Madonna and Child.

"Oh, no . . ." Holly protested.

"But I insist. It is of you, after all. Who better to have it?" He went to the counter. "Look, it will fit into the same paper easily. It is fate . . . you must have it."

Holly watched as he wrapped the picture in the brown paper with a flourish, slipped it back into the plastic carrier and handed it over to Charles. "You will carry it, señor, it is heavier than the other." He glanced at the fruit and vegetable cartoon on the side of the carrier. "This is good," he said. "To carry a picture through the Rastro from this direction is risky. Our name is known there."

It took Charles another seven minutes to get Holly out the door. Through the window Jaime watched them go, then sighed and took the picture they'd left back through the curtains to the workroom.

As the curtains closed behind him, the man who had been watching from outside walked past again. Ahead, Holly and Charles turned into the bright bustle of the Rastro.

He followed.

They returned to the flat, having stopped in the Rastro to purchase some things for lunch. Charles was almost too tired to eat, having had no sleep and several nasty moments since the previous day. Holly, too, had had the nasty moments—but she'd slept in the car.

"I want a bath, before I do anything," he announced.

"After you," Holly said demurely. He grunted and disappeared in the direction of the bathroom. They'd had no real time that morning to do more than park the Mercedes in a dark corner of the basement and drop their luggage in the hallway. Now she looked around with pleasure.

Charles had said Peter Bradley had an independent income, which was reflected in the furnishings. The flat was a high one in a modern block, but it was graced by beautiful Chinese carpets and an assortment of antiques. The view of Madrid was fantastic. She thought of her little flat in Hampstead, overlooking the tiny back gardens of the other houses, and smiled. Not the same at all.

Above the green expanse of Retiro Park below, she could just make out the black figure of a man on horseback, which Charles had said was a statue of Alfonso the Twelfth, looking down with some evidence of disdain at the Retiro Pond, full of rowboats and pedalos, and the shirt-sleeved office workers who were in them, looking for a cooling hour in the heat of the day. With a sigh she turned towards the kitchen and nearly screamed.

She hadn't heard the sound of the door opening above the sound of Charles's bath running. But it had.

And a man stood there looking at her.

A very big man.

CHAPTER 17

"Well, well—I see Charles is keeping up to his former standard," the man said, smiling. He came towards her, hand outstretched. "I'm Peter Bradley."

Holly almost collapsed with relief. "Oh . . . I'm Holly Partridge. Charles is in the bath. We just got back from the Rastro."

"And you expected to have the place to yourselves? Sorry." Bradley grinned. "You will. I just have to have a quick word with Charles before I go. Okay?"

"Well, of course." She wasn't quite sure why he felt he needed her permission. "We were just going to have some lunch—will you join us?"

He laughed and shook his head. "I can just imagine how that would go down with Charles. Thanks, but when we shared this flat we had rules about that sort of thing; I'm sure they still apply."

"Charles . . . lived here?"

"Sure. Didn't he tell you that? I've still got a few of his shirts hanging around someplace. The ones the lipstick wouldn't wash out of." He saw she looked puzzled, and shrugged. "You're American, aren't you?"

"Yes, that's right."

"Don't think Charles ever knew an American girl before," Bradley mused. "The one nationality he missed." He grinned again and turned towards the bedroom. "Glad to see he's catching up in style. I was a bit worried about old Charles, stuck down there in Alicante. But he hasn't changed."

"Changed?" All this was mystifying Holly—from the way Bradley was talking, you'd have thought Charles was some kind of . . . *Charles?*

Bradley went into the bedroom and raised his voice. "I like your lady, Llewellyn!"

There was a moment of silence, followed by a gurgling of water from behind the bathroom door. "Peter?" came Charles's voice, rather thinly.

"The one and only." Bradley winked broadly at Holly, then closed the bedroom door.

She stood staring at the blank panel for a moment, then shook her head. Let him think what he liked, he was obviously an idiot. She could hear them talking as she put the lunch things out: fresh bread, butter, olives, two kinds of sausage and three kinds of cheese, fruit, wine, and some very nasty-looking pâté he had crowed over and paid the earth for in a dark little shop she wouldn't even go in. It was, he said, an experience. Eyeing it, Holly thought it would be one she'd forgo. She jumped when Bradley's voice came from behind her.

"I'm off now," he said, looking at her oddly. "Sorry if I was a bit out of line, earlier. Charles explained you were just up here on business." The grin reappeared briefly. "Although how he can limit himself to business around someone like you, I don't know. Maybe he *has* changed, at that. Nice to

have met you, anyway. Coffee percolator is in the cupboard over the sink."
With a wave, he went out.

A few minutes later, Charles appeared in the kitchen doorway, his hair still damp and roughly towelled, his feet bare beneath his trousers. "That was Peter," he said, in a preoccupied voice.

"He introduced himself," Holly said, busy with the percolator.

"He came to warn me."

She turned, the filter in one hand. "Warn you? About what?"

"He wasn't sure. He'd been told to report if I turned up in Madrid."

"Report it to who?"

"A man named Baker in Alicante."

"Is he your boss?"

"No, but he'd like to be. Peter did as he'd been told, but then he started to worry about it. He doesn't like Baker any more than I do, so he came to see if I was in trouble. He felt pretty bad about having told Baker, I think."

"Well, if it was an official order . . ."

"That's just it. It wasn't. Baker had just phoned him rather casually early this morning and said if he saw me to let him know. Peter just thought it was —well, he didn't think anything of it. Until he saw me looking . . . 'harassed,' he said. Did he say anything to you?"

"He seemed to think you've changed," Holly said.

"Changed? In what way?"

"Oh, the implication was you've gotten past it," Holly said lightly, and turned back to the percolator.

Charles seemed bemused and distracted during the meal. Several times Holly caught him looking at her in a peculiar way. Other times he seemed mesmerized by the view out of the window. Finally, over the coffee, he spoke.

"Peter said I should watch my back. Whatever's going on, he only knows part of it and I know none of it. Peter went to all the right schools, he believes in fair play—which means he couldn't leave me unarmed—but nor could he tell me too much. Poor sod." He shook himself slightly. "Maybe I'm just over-reacting, but I can almost feel a knife between my ribs already. I'm so tired I practically drowned in the bath. I'm going to catch up on my sleep, if you don't mind."

"Will my taking a bath disturb you?"

"The crack of doom wouldn't disturb me," he said.

After her bath, she'd intended merely to rest on the bed in the guestroom, but when she opened her eyes again it was late afternoon and Charles was tapping on the door. "Holly?"

"Wait a minute."

She tugged on her robe and went out to find Charles frowning at the vista of Retiro Park.

"I've just been on the phone to Puerto Rio," he said, turning. She couldn't make out his face, but he lifted his hands helplessly. "Nigel Bland told me Reg has been taken to the hospital. He began vomiting blood late last night—presumably about the time we were running around in circles with Tinker."

"Oh no . . ." Holly sagged against the nearest chair. "Is it—very bad?"

"I'm afraid so," Charles said very gently. "They may have to operate."

"Don't blame yourself," Charles said suddenly.

Holly sat hunched into the corner of the Mercedes, her coat wrapped tightly around her. The night wasn't chilly, but she felt cold, so cold. What if Reg died? Accused as a murderer but never tried. Just as David had been accused and never tried. Accusation would live on, no one would ever know for sure that either one of them had been innocent. It was so terribly unfair. She'd wanted to help—but maybe rushing off to Madrid to find out about the painting had been the wrong approach. Maybe they'd have been better advised to stay in Puerto Rio . . .

"You can't be everything to everyone all the time, you know," Charles went on. "You're just an ordinary human being, not Wonder Woman."

"I never said I *was.*"

"You're the type who always *wants* to be, though," he said, turning the car smoothly into a curve and putting the headlamps up to full beam. It was true night now.

"I see. You're a psychiatrist, too," Holly said defensively. "How wonderful. Free personality analysis on the move. All right, then, tell me—were you 'exiled' from Madrid because of your womanizing?"

He turned to look at her and nearly went off the road. "Who told you that? Peter Bradley?"

"Nobody told me, I just made a wild guess. They say things about compulsive womanizers, you know. Especially the ones who never marry."

His hands tightened around the wheel. "You know what you need?"

"Let me guess, either a good hiding or a good screw, that's usually the line, I believe." She wanted to hit back at him because he'd hit her own weakness so squarely.

"No." His voice was calm. "What you need is someone to look after you."

"Hah!" She stared out of the window fixedly. ,

"I was moved to Alicante because I had an affair with the wrong man's wife," Charles said very softly, staring out at the highway rushing towards him. "I nearly came apart at the seams when she ended it. I finally went down with hepatitis, which probably saved me, because I was too ill to object when they transferred me. I think now it was done more to help me than punish me. People like Peter Bradley seemed to care . . . I'll never know why. My body healed, but the rest of me has taken a little longer. Neither a clever story nor an original one. People fall in love with the wrong people all the time."

Holly felt too wretched to answer.

"If I recognize someone else who's trapped in the land of thin skins, it's because I used to live there myself. Lonely place, isn't it?" Charles asked.

When she still didn't answer, he sighed. Wrong again, Llewellyn, he told himself. Still not taking any prizes for insight, are you? "There's a café ahead. I'll ring through and see if there's any news."

The café was noisy, smoky and busy. He headed for the phone after ordering some coffee and sandwiches to take away. By the time he'd finished talking, the food was ready. He paid and went out into the night, all the more cool and quiet because of the contrast with the lively scene he'd just left.

"I spoke to Nigel and he suggested we go straight to the *clinica* in Espina. They're definitely going to operate."

She gave an odd, dry laugh. "Kind of a rough way to break jail."

He smiled grimly. "A little drastic, perhaps."

She sighed, suddenly exhausted as the adrenaline drained away. "What are we going to do about Mel when we get back?"

"I don't know. Surely that depends on how he plays it?"

"But we don't *have* the picture anymore—we can't give it to him if we don't have it."

"Yes, but what worries me is the way he may go about asking for it." He made her drink the hot coffee, but when she refused the sandwiches, he tossed the bag onto the back seat and drove on.

Back at the café a man who'd driven in after the Mercedes pushed past the group around the television broadcast of the game between Real Madrid and Juventas, and went to the pay telephone at the back.

The receiver was still faintly warm where Charles had held it.

CHAPTER 18

López put down the report from Interpol and looked bleak. "All that time," he whispered to himself, "waiting." Tilting his chair back, he stared at the brilliantly shined tips of his shoes. It gave him no satisfaction to be right. None whatsoever.

Nor did it give him satisfaction to have found the one absolute and total vindication of Reg Partridge's innocence. Because it might be too late, even now. And, as yet, it proved nothing else.

Bas came in. As he shut the door, there were several sharp explosions from outside. For a moment both of them stiffened, then they relaxed and exchanged sheepish grins. "The fireworks," López said. "Every year a little earlier."

"It's only the children," Bas said indulgently.

López pushed the Interpol letter over the desk towards him. "Tell me what you think about that."

Diffidently Bas picked up the report and looked through it. He stopped, stared and looked at López in astonishment. "This is true?"

López nodded. "This evidence is incontrovertible."

"But what made you ask for this in the first place?" Bas was lost in admiration.

López smiled sadly. "I suspected it when I read the background of Graebner. He'd been a smooth type, a fast-talker, a true con-man. Yet in hospital he was consumed with bitterness and revenge. He spoke of retribution with the eagerness only a man who has been betrayed and destroyed could feel. The change was monumental."

"But who killed him, then, if not Partridge?"

López smiled, bleakly. "You tell me, Paco."

Bas looked stricken. "I think it could only be one man."

"But you are not sure?"

"No."

López sighed. "Then we will have to make him tell us, won't we, Paco?"

They began to encounter the traffic about five miles out of Espina. The roads were busy, both going into and coming out of the town, and as they dropped down, it got worse. Charles glanced at his watch. Nearly ten o'clock on a Saturday night. All right, he'd accept that there might be an increase in traffic, but not to this extent. He was about to say something about it to Holly when a great arc of red, green and white spangles burst in the sky overhead and, a few moments later, the dull *thump* of the explosion reached them.

"Is there a fiesta today in Espina?" he asked.

"What?" She hadn't noticed the firework, and had been lost in dark thoughts of her own, staring at the hypnotic line of red lights on the cars ahead.

Another firework lit the sky, the signal for the beginning of festivities. "A fiesta, in Espina. We seem to be caught up in it," he said, as the line of cars lurched forward through the narrow streets and stopped yet again.

"Oh. I think so. I remember Reg and Mary talking about it last week. Before . . ." She waved her hand vaguely. "The last one of the year, I think they said."

"Wonderful," Charles muttered. "Look, there isn't going to be much parking room left . . . I'll get you as close to the hospital as I can, then drive around until I can find a place to leave the car."

"Why don't you put it in David's garage?" she suggested. "God knows there's room enough now." She fished in her handbag and emerged triumphantly with the key on its tag. "Can you find it again?"

"I think so." He looked around. "Look, the *clinica* that they took Reg to is right down that street—can you find it? It's called the Clinica Leonides. If you get lost, just keep asking, *'Dónde está la Clinica Leonides?'* . . . okay?"

She repeated the phrase to herself several times. "Okay." She didn't sound too certain. "Will you come there?"

"As soon as I've parked the car."

After several false turns, Charles eventually located the studio garage and put the Mercedes inside. It was a little too long to allow the door to drop closed completely, but he didn't think anyone would notice. He put the padlock on the hasp anyway, as camouflage, then walked back down the alley to the road that edged the old harbour.

From the town above he could hear the roar of the crowds and the music from the bands, but here by the sea it was peaceful except for the crash of the surf, which was rather high. He sat on the broken harbour wall for the length of time it took to smoke a cigarette, then flicked the stub out over the choppy water, where it fell between two bobbing, rusty buoys.

Picking his way carefully over the broken cobbled streets, he worked his way up into the town, and eventually emerged into the Plaza Mayor, where the crowd was the thickest, the noise loudest, and the excitement at its peak. All around him enthusiastic celebrants shouted and laughed, waving their leather *botas* full of wine, and running a great risk of upsetting the boiling oil of the *churros* vendors onto themselves and the street. Somehow, it never happened. The plaza was a seething mass of people, food vendors, musicians and dogs. Dogs were everywhere, nipping in and out between everyone's ankles, snapping up the bits of food that dropped with the eagerness of seasoned titbit hunters. Aside from the *tapas* sellers, vendors of all kinds offered dolls, noise-makers, small fireworks and a myriad of items suitable to the occasion. Charles marvelled at what they thought suitable. He tried several alternative paths through the crowd before he realized that the fiesta procession was passing directly between him and the hospital.

Even if he got to the front of the crowd, he knew he'd either have to wait, or hope to find an opportunity to run across the parade itself. From the comments around him, everyone seemed to be worried that the weather was going to break soon. He'd noticed the sea had seemed on the verge of getting unpleasant, and the wind was certainly picking up, too. This seemed to have increased the pace of everything—from the parade to the number of times the *botas* were raised. By the time he had reached the front of the crowd and could see the parade dancing along, he'd had several streams of wine from the leather *botas* directed over his jacket by accident, along with many invitations to open his mouth and save his clothes. Twice he'd accepted, rather than risk an insult, and as a result his stomach was telling him there was soon going to be trouble if he wasn't careful.

The mood of the crowd was cheerful, if a little hectic, and they good-naturedly made way for him each time he said he was trying to get to the *clinica*. He'd proceed ten feet, and then have to raise his voice in an appeal once more to a new set of grinning faces and fresh offers of wine and food. It was Spain at its best—and for once he could have done without it. It would have been so much easier if they'd all been at home watching the latest dubbed episode of *Dallas*.

The smells of food and wine and sweat encircled him, and he wondered if he was going to disgrace himself. He clutched at a lamp-post as the scene swam before his eyes.

"*Borracho*—hey, *borracho*—so soon, you give up?" asked a cheerful voice, as a hand thrust a leather *bota* under his nose. "If something is going down, nothing can come up, hey?"

Charles looked into the encouraging, jolly face of a stranger and smiled weakly. "No, thanks, *amigo* . . ."

"But yes . . . if you are going to have a 'head' tomorrow, make it one worth having." The man laughed, offering the wine again.

"I . . ." He waved a hand and stared desperately around, seeking escape, then stared, his rebellious head and stomach forgotten.

Across the gap, between the gigantic heads and the marching band, he saw the bandaged head and broad shoulders of Mel Tinker above the crowd. Another gigantic head intervened. When it had passed, Charles searched the crowd.

But Tinker had disappeared.

Holly was watching the procession from the window of the *clinica*. Despite three cups of coffee, she was in danger of falling asleep simply through exhaustion. After a nightmare of turning streets and imperfectly understood directions, she'd arrived at the Clinica Leonides, only to find that Reg was in surgery. Mary was nowhere to be found.

The nurses had been extremely kind, and many of them spoke English. They'd shown her to the waiting area and promised to let her know the minute Mr. Partridge was out of theatre. She was not allowed into his room to wait, because a policeman was in there. There was another in the operating theatre, too, apparently, which seemed to afford the nurses a great deal of amusement. They said they expected to see him brought out on a stretcher at any moment.

Her head jerked again, and she turned away from the window. Perhaps if she just took a few minutes on that inviting chrome-and-leather sofa . . .

"Holly?"

The voice awakened her and she sat up blinking. Outside the windows the fiesta seemed louder than ever, and the room was lit by the bright random glare of fireworks. Cracks and booms and splatters of caps echoed across the square.

"Oh, hi," she said. "I just dozed off. Where's Mary?"

"They sent me to get you. I'm afraid Mary isn't very well . . . she collapsed a little while ago."

"Oh no, not Mary, too?"

"I don't think it's anything too serious, but we'd like you to come. Thought you might be here by now. How's Reg?"

"Still in surgery. Shouldn't somebody wait here?"

"They'll let us know as soon as there's news—I left the number at the desk. Come on, my car's outside."

Charles searched the crowd carefully, then spotted Tinker moving towards the far side of the square. He hadn't been seen, but as he stared, Tinker turned around and looked back, as if he'd felt Charles's eyes on him.

Impulsively Charles grabbed the *bota* the man had been offering him and lifted it in front of his face, turning slightly sideways so he could keep an eye on Tinker. He caught a bit of the wine in his mouth, but spilled most of it, pretending ineptitude. The owner of the *bota* laughed and laughed, finally taking the wineskin back to display his own expertise. The minute he lifted it, head back and eyes closed, Charles darted between a head of Don Quixote and another of Esmeralda, narrowly missing bringing the latter down by treading on the fluttering silken "skirt" that fell from the neck to the ground, covering the legs of the man inside.

"Ole!" shouted the crowd, as the huge figure curtsied and stepped in front of Charles again, flirtatiously. He tried to pass on the other side, but again the swirling brightly coloured silk barred his way.

"Ole!" shouted the crowd again, laughing madly at this impromptu display.

This was ridiculous. Any minute now, Tinker might turn round to see what all the fuss was about. Through the gap in the neck of the papier-mâché head, covered by gauze, Charles could see the bright, delighted eyes of its carrier. This was novel sport to break the long, hard trudge.

Taking a resolute breath, Charles raised his hands to his head to form horns, and bent double. The crowd cheered as the big figure with its grotesque head and bulging bosom danced away and awaited his next move. He pawed the ground with one foot, bull-like, with the approval of the crowd, and then darted forward. Again the big figure coquettishly swayed in front of him blocking his way, and the roar of the crowd was deafening. Three more times Charles made an attempt to pass and, at last, found himself enveloped in the soft clinging folds of the silk as he passed beneath the skirt and came slap up against the laughing man inside.

The sexual connotations of his "penetration" were not lost on the crowd, and they shouted obscene suggestions to him as to what he might do with what he discovered under the lady's skirt, whether he was capable of doing it, and whether "she" would appreciate it.

Charles was nose to nose with the hot, perspiring Spaniard who carried the head, and couldn't think of a single thing to say, always assuming he could even be heard above the noise outside. The man grinned at him and shrugged.

"You're a good sport . . . give it a few seconds and then get out again," he shouted.

Charles nodded and grinned inanely. They walked along for a few paces, he backward and the Spaniard forward, and then he made his exit out the back of the "skirt."

"*Ole!*" shouted the hysterical crowd, and as he pushed his way into them, enthusiastic hands clapped him on the shoulders. Further comments on the apparent capacity of his sexual equipment were drowned by the approach of the next brass band. He was left to anonymity at last.

Tinker hadn't turned around, and what was more, he was nearly out of the square on the far side. It was only his height that gave him away. He entered a side street, and Charles hurried to catch up with him. Several times he thought he'd lost him, only once again to glimpse that head above the crowd. The bandage was as good as a beacon in the half-light of the *linternas* that lined the roadway. The farther they got away from the square, however, the more difficult it became for Charles to follow unseen. Tinker was obviously nervous, and kept glancing behind him, forcing Charles to duck into doorways. He was running out of doorways when he saw Tinker enter a small office building overlooking the harbour.

There was no sign in the building to indicate what business was carried on within, although it was partly given over to garaging facilities, to judge from the big door farther along.

Carefully, for there was no cover for him, Charles edged along the opposite side of the street until he was level with the lighted window on the ground floor—the only lighted window in the building. Inside he could see Tinker talking to two men. One was a sinister-looking type with a scar down one side of his face and one blind eye.

The other was Nigel Bland.

CHAPTER 19

He had to get inside and hear what they were saying.

Brushing the dust and confetti from his jacket, he waited until the street was empty, then approached the building at an angle, stepping through the glass door that gave onto the small reception area.

That was the simple part.

There were three doors opening off the reception area, but he knew which one he wanted. He could hear the voices from within, but he couldn't make

out what they were saying. He tiptoed over and put his head close to the
panel, pressing his ear gently against it.

As slowly and as elegantly as in a dream, the door swung inward, and he
went in with it, making a lunge for the knob just too late. He had an
impression of three faces turning to stare at him as he teetered there, off-
balance.

"Llewellyn!" Bland said, startled. "What the hell are you doing here?"

Charles did the only thing he could do.

He shut the door.

As he ran out into the street he heard the office door bang open and hit the
wall. He heard the men running after him. He was scared witless. People
didn't chase people, except in the movies. Dammit, people didn't chase *him*,
ever. Nevertheless, there he was, running like a terrified kid, and he didn't
even know why.

He did know he didn't like it. But that didn't seem reason enough to stop.

He headed back towards the crowded Plaza Mayor. Safety in numbers,
that was the thing. If they caught him in the deserted side-street they could
kill him easily and no one would know. His heart was pounding and his
chest hurt. He simply wasn't cut out for this kind of nonsense. He *hated* it.
And it was the second time in two days, too.

The injustice of it all weighed on him heavily.

Darting between two matrons in tight black dresses, he joined the throng
in the plaza. The parade was just finishing, and the sounds of the last band
filtered back from the far side of the open space as the last huge head and the
float with the cross on it disappeared between an office building and the
cinema.

He pushed his way into the throng, deeper and deeper, risking a glance
back over his shoulder. He saw Tinker's bandaged head swivelling around
like a lighthouse, and then the big man spotted him and plunged like a
swimmer into the crowd. Charles ducked into the shadow of an empty stall,
his feet crunching on the crumbs and sugar of the *churros* it had sold—long
since consumed. He stood there, trying to catch his breath, hoping that he
could circle around it as Tinker passed by, and then go back the way he had
come.

Suddenly there was a deafening explosion and a glare of reddish light
flooded the plaza, exposing Charles to view at the same moment Tinker
drew level with him. Their eyes met for a moment, and he saw the big
American's eyes widen in recognition, and then he changed direction and
came straight for him, saying something to the men with him.

As the crowd cheered and the fireworks continued their deafening and magnificent display directly over the Plaza Mayor, Charles bolted again. The crowd oohed and ahhhed at the coruscating wonders that bloomed overhead like novas, reflecting their light from the underside of the racing clouds onto the upturned faces, shining eyes, and open mouths of the spectators. The flower-faces of the crowd turned in unison, a garden in momentary thrall to each new sun that appeared and faded, only to be replaced by another, more gaudy, showing a different hue or pattern of trailing sparks. The noise of each successive explosion echoed around the plaza, repeating and bouncing off the buildings and one another until it seemed there was constant thunder and lightning coming from the sky overhead.

Charles pushed his way through the gaping crowd, heading towards a nice dark alleyway. He bent low and ducked inside, hoping he'd be hidden, but a particularly brilliant double sun blazed overhead at that moment, revealing his refuge yet again.

Somebody up there didn't like him.

He ran down the narrow alleyway and the noise of the fireworks was instantly halved, giving him the momentary illusion that he'd gone deaf. That illusion was shattered by the sound, the very loud sound, of Tinker shouting his name.

The alleyway turned a corner and stopped. Panic swept Charles as he saw only a wall ahead, high and impossible to climb. He looked to the right and left, finally seeing an even narrower opening between two houses. He darted into that just as the pursuing men came around the corner. The opening was barely wide enough to get through, and his shoulders brushed the walls on either side. Many cats had been there before him, and the acrid ammoniac smell engulfed him as his feet slipped on rubbish and discarded nameless things that had lain there mouldering for years. Ahead there was a small wooden gate.

He climbed over it and found himself in another cul-de-sac. It was back to the square or nothing. He looked back but saw and heard nothing of his pursuers. Probably the gap was too narrow for Tinker to get by—he'd had to squeeze in a few places himself.

Breathing heavily, he went back towards the noise and tumult of the Plaza Mayor, where the fireworks were working up to a blazing finale overhead. As he came near to the opening, he found he could hardly lift his feet, his body felt so heavy. His legs seemed dead from the knees down, and his chest was agony, cramped by the grinding ache of his cracked ribs as he heaved for oxygen to feed his muscles. He staggered a little, looking to the crowds ahead as to a sanctuary. They would hide him. God willing, they would even help to hold him up while he tried to learn to breathe again, as they swayed and were enchanted by the fireworks above. And then the moving crowd was hidden by something that stood quite still. And waited. Tinker.

"Bloody hell," Charles choked, and darted to the right, then the left in a feint he hadn't used since grammar-school soccer. Tinker lunged for him and missed. Charles ducked under his reaching arm and darted through a gap in the crowd, only to find himself blocked by a wagon piled high with oranges, melons, and bananas. He could hear Tinker behind him and tried to skirt the stand, but Tinker launched himself and they both crashed into the stall, scattering oranges and melons everywhere. The crowd shouted and turned towards them, angered at this untimely distraction.

Charles struggled within Tinker's grasp. Suddenly a vast noise rocked the entire plaza.

As the sound rumbled around the wide space there was a moment of stunned silence from the crowd. They froze where they stood, for an instant only.

And then it began to rain.

Dismayed shrieks rose up on all sides and people began to run, oranges split and rolled and melons shattered as the mass of people began to swarm over them, ignoring the two men fighting beneath the remnants of the wagon. Now, instead of the fireworks there was the blue-white flash of lightning. It illuminated Tinker's features, twisted by anger and determination as he hung over Charles and tried to hit him. Charles rolled this way and that, and finally got a knee in, winding Tinker just enough to make him lose his hold. He swung wildly and connected with something—he thought it might be Tinker's jaw, but then again, it could have been his shoulder—and tried to get to his feet. An orange treacherously rolled underfoot and he lost his balance, going onto his hands and knees again in a pulp of mashed melon and seeds.

The scurrying, laughing, sated crowd surged around them, heedless of the fight, not caring about the men or the mess but only pleased to have had the excitement of the festival before the rain came. The thunder cracked again, and the wind began to slash the rain down onto them in earnest as it swept in from the sea.

Charles struggled up, aimed another kick at Tinker's ribs, and turned to run. But Nigel was there and took hold of him, twisting his arm efficiently around his back, and totally immobilizing him in an instant.

"Come on, son, settle down. This whole thing has gone on long enough. Where's the picture?"

Paco Bas came into López's office. It was in darkness, lit only by the fireworks outside. "Sir?"

López, in his chair, turned around to face Bas. "What is it?"

"Señor Llewellyn and Señorita Partridge have returned to Espina."

"Have they?" López didn't seem all that interested. His voice was weary. "How do you know that?"

"Well, I don't know about Señor Llewellyn for certain, but Señorita Partridge came into the hospital a short time ago. Pérez called in that she was waiting there to see how Señor Partridge was."

"And how is he?"

"He's still in surgery, sir. Pérez said the nurse told him it would be at least another half an hour."

"And if he survives, what I have to tell him about his son may send him right back in there again. I have handled this badly, Paco."

"No, sir, I don't believe that. You did what was necessary," Paco said stoutly. As he spoke, thunder rumbled outside, and after a second, rain spattered the windows. "I admit you were taking a chance, but . . ."

"One is not supposed to take chances, Paco. One is supposed to be a reliable, responsible officer of the court. I just thought they might be lulled into thinking they were safe and . . ." He shrugged. "But there are other things at work I didn't count on: this matter of the garage and the pictures at the penthouse. I simply cannot reconcile that with the attempt on the lives of Carlos and the girl . . . it doesn't make sense. Paco, it doesn't make any sense at all."

"No, sir." Paco wasn't worried. He was certain it would begin to make sense soon. Someone like López always won in the end.

López stood up. "Well, one might know it would be raining, but I think I had better go over to the hospital and talk to the Partridge girl. Perhaps by then the surgery . . ."

"She's not there," Paco said.

López stared at him in the flickering glare of a lightning flash. "Not there? You just said she—"

"Pérez told me she'd come, but that she had just left again. With a friend."

Holly closed the car window as the rain began to slant in through the gap at the top. "My goodness, what a downpour."

"Yes, we get some pretty spectacular storms here in autumn."

The windscreen wipers started their rhythmic *slip-slap* and the car's engine purred. The wind blew the rain back along the bonnet of the car in long wavering streaks, the red finish making it look as if the car was bleeding every time another flash of lightning lit the highway.

"This is a new car, isn't it?" Holly asked curiously. "What happened to the Citröen?"

"Oh, I sold it. Got a very good deal on this one and I couldn't really pass it up. Somebody going back to England . . . you can often pick up bargains like that, if you're quick. It's much easier to handle."

"How long have you had it?"

"A couple of weeks, but I lent it to a friend for a few days."

"Oh, that's why you weren't driving it the other night, at the Beams, then?"

"That's right. My friend had it."

"Do I know him?"

"Her."

"Why . . . you're a dark horse, aren't you?"

"A bit, maybe. Still a man, you know, despite . . . everything."

Holly frowned. "I thought Mary was at Helen's," she said.

"That's right."

"This is the way to Puerto Rio."

"That's right."

"But . . . why?"

"Let's just say we have an appointment there."

"I don't understand," Holly said, her voice tightening. "I want to go to Mary . . ."

"All in good time, my dear."

"*Now.*"

"This won't take long."

Holly looked at the familiar profile against the rain-streaked window, and felt a sudden chilling certainty that had nothing to do with the storm outside. Her storm was inside.

"Your friend . . . is she a good driver? Or does she tend to run people off the road?"

The profile became full-face, and the smile was not at all the smile she was accustomed to seeing there.

"That's right, my dear."

As the rain beat his hair down over his forehead, Charles tried to think of some answer that would satisfy Nigel and the others.

"I don't know."

"Come on, son," Nigel said patiently. "We know you took the picture to Madrid. You took it to a restorer in Gavilán Street. We know that."

Charles felt the rain blowing into his open mouth. How could they have known it? He and Holly had left Tinker unconscious in the middle of those crazy rocks, and he'd destroyed the homing device.

"Then if you know all that, you know everything. The picture is a fake, that's all, not worth a penny. We left it there."

"You went into the place with a picture and you came out with it," Tinker said.

"But . . ." Charles stopped. The hell with them. He was exhausted, he was soaked, and he felt sick as a dog. "That's right."

The man with the scar spoke impatiently. "I can't say I enjoy standing here in the rain."

Charles stared into the darkness. When a flash of lightning came again, he saw the face of the third man, marred by the scar, and the drooping lid of the white, blind eye. It was a dreadful face, a villain's face, a Spanish pirate's face, yet the voice was exceptionally gentle and cultured.

And English.

"From what you've told me, this man has been through a good deal in the past few days. I'm sure he would appreciate getting dry and warm. We can discuss it like gentlemen in my office."

"Don't have much sympathy for him, myself," Tinker growled. "Still got a goddamned bump on my head the size of an egg."

"You shouldn't have chased us like that," Charles said.

"Bullshit, that's my goddamned job, Charley."

It was the first time Charles had encountered a thief and murderer with professional pride. He swayed slightly. The weight of the rain on his shoulders was becoming just a bit too much for him.

"Come on, son, lean on me," Bland said.

Charles did, wishing he could whirl on them like some paperback hero, bring them all down with flying feet and fists, and then pelt off into the darkness. As it was, he could barely put one foot in front of the other. Anyway, what was the point? They were probably going to kill him, anyway. They'd killed Graebner, hadn't they?

"Reg is out of surgery, Mary, and the nurse said the doctor's very pleased. He's going to be fine."

Mary started to weep with relief, and put her teacup down on the coverlet. Helen rescued it just before it went over. "Thank God."

"Yes." Helen seemed bemused. "The nurse said that Holly was at the hospital."

"Oh, she went straight there, then. How sensible," Mary sniffed approvingly. Now that she was sure Reg was all right, she approved of everything. "Did you speak to her?"

"No, the nurse said she was there, but had left about an hour ago. With Alastair Morland. She said Holly mentioned something about coming to see you."

"An hour ago? But they should have been here by now, surely?"

Helen glanced out at the storm. "You'd have thought so, wouldn't you? Perhaps the storm held them up. Alastair is so very careful, you know."

"I don't understand . . . *why?*" Holly kept asking.

"Money, sweetie, the root of all that's lovely in life," Alastair said, his hand tightening around her arm as he hurried her into the lobby of 400 Avenida de la Playa.

She glared at him. "You're not a vicar, are you?"

"God, no . . . pardon the blasphemy," Alastair said, winking. "God very definitely no, I should say."

"Let me go . . ." Holly struggled to free herself. "You aren't sick, either, are you?"

"Do I look sick?"

She stared at him, stunned by the transformation. He not only did not look sick, he looked as she'd never seen him look before. His eyes were glittering and his jaw was set. The mouth that had always seemed so sweetly gentle was suddenly hard and cruel. She tried to strike him, but he ducked adroitly, as if accustomed to avoiding such things.

"Now, now, none of that. You'll break a nail or something."

"Damn you . . ."

He pushed her over to the lifts and punched a button savagely. "Never mind me, sweetie. *I'm* the nice one. Wait until you meet the one waiting for you upstairs."

She looked at the lift. "That's not our lift, that's . . ."

"You artists are *so* observant," Alastair said with a sneer. "Too bad you aren't smart as well, isn't it?"

"I don't want to talk about it," Charles said. "I'm sick of the whole business. If you're so bloody eager to get hold of that picture, why didn't you steal it before?"

"We didn't know Reg had it, old son," Nigel said, handing him a cup of coffee. They were back in the office building. Outside the storm continued with unabated virulence. October storms were like that, fast to come and slow to go, with a great deal in between. The rain slashed at the windows like mindless applause.

"As a matter of fact," Nigel went on, "I didn't even know it existed until Mel here came to see me."

Charles glanced at Tinker. Despite the soaking and the fight, the big American looked as formidable as ever. He looked, in fact, even bigger—obviously one of the new miracle Americans that didn't shrink when wet.

"I see," Charles muttered. "I assume you must have been the American end of Graebner's little deal."

Nigel chuckled. "You've obviously got hold of the wrong end of the stick, son." He glanced at Tinker. "I told you we should have brought him in on it from the beginning. Despite what Baker said."

"Baker!" Charles exclaimed. Damn. Of course, Baker. He'd disliked him from the day he'd met him, and now he knew why. The man was an out-and-out crook, *and* using the Diplomatic Service as a cover. It was despicable.

"I didn't know anything about him," Tinker said. "I *still* don't."

"That makes us even, then, doesn't it?" Charles snapped.

"He thinks we're *crooks,"* the scar-faced man said suddenly, as if he'd been visited by a revelation.

Nigel grinned. "I was beginning to wonder about that. You disappoint me, son. You really do," he said to Charles.

Tinker reached into his pocket. "He's obviously no professional. When you had me down, Llewellyn, you should have used the opportunity to search me—but you didn't. Could have saved us all a lot of trouble if you had." He produced a thin leather folder and flipped it open in front of Charles's eyes.

United States Customs Investigator.

Charles gaped at it, and at Tinker. The door to the office opened, and a young blond giant came in, carrying the brown paper parcel from the boot of the Mercedes. He put it on the desk, grinned at them all, and went out.

"Must be a terrible flaw in my character to make you think I'd gone bent, son," Nigel said sadly, as Tinker ripped off the brown paper.

Under the bright overhead light, the colours of the fake Raphael glowed and shimmered, and Charles could see Holly's face suffused with tenderness, looking down at the baby in her lap.

"I *told* you it wasn't the same picture . . ." he began.

Tinker whirled on him. "Picture? The hell with the picture, Charley. Where's the goddamned *frame?*"

CHAPTER 20

Colonel Jackson looked at Holly. Gone was the old man's bemused and eccentric manner, the gentle voice, the unsure step. Gone, indeed, was any trace of age. He looked small, angry, and totally terrifying.

"Where's the picture?"

"What picture?"

Jackson turned away, as if to gather himself together, and when he turned back his face was white with anger. "The picture that was left in your husband's studio the day he died. The picture your bloody father-in-law seems to have had secreted away all this time, damn him."

"I don't know what you're talking about. Reg has lots of David's pictures . . . or *did.* I suppose it was you who came in and took them all the other night?"

"If it had been me, my dear, I wouldn't have missed the only one that mattered," Jackson snapped. "Where is it?"

"But they took them all, they—"

Her head jerked back as he slapped her, hard, first on one cheek and then the other. Holly's hands were tied behind her, painfully tight around the chair. From the couch Maddie watched, a small smile of pleasure on her face. "You and that damned clerk from the consulate went out of this building carrying a brown paper package that could only have been a painting—*after* you claimed all the paintings were taken. And then you disappeared for two days. Did you sell it?"

"That wasn't a picture," Holly said. "That was one of my embroideries—we took it to Alicante so I could match some wools . . ."

He slapped her again. "And you didn't go to Alicante either, my dear, we know that much. Come along, I haven't got a great deal of time. I've been waiting two years for that picture to surface. I thought the police had it. Where is it?"

"I *told* you . . ."

He slapped her again. And again. And again.

"Let me tell you a story, son," Nigel Bland said genially from the front seat. Tinker's red Mercedes was like the inside of a drum as the rain beat down on the convertible top. Charles rode in the back with the scar-faced man and swayed from side to side as the car moved easily around the curves, sending a rooster-tail of spray up behind.

"Story concerns an old man who kept going back and forth across the border pushing a wheelbarrow full of hay. Every time he went, the border guards poked and prodded the hay, certain there was some contraband hidden underneath it. They never found anything. This went on for years. Finally, the old man lay dying. One of the guards went to visit him. 'Old man, we respect you,' he said. 'You've fooled us all this time and we don't know how. Now that it's over, won't you tell me what you've been smuggling?' And the old man looked up at him and smiled. 'Wheelbarrows,' he said." Nigel laughed. "That's what Tinker has been after, son. Wheelbarrows."

"You mean the frames? There's no duty on frames," Charles objected.

"Not the frames as such," Tinker said, over his shoulder. "What was *in* the frames."

"The pictures."

"No . . . *in* the frames. In the fibreglass itself. David Partridge carried or shipped his pictures all over the world, every one of them in those fibreglass frames he made himself, from resin honeycombed with heroin. Graebner's contacts simply intercepted the pictures after they'd gone through Customs, replaced the frames, and sent them on their way. Then they took the frames, extracted the drug, and sent it out on the street. David had gotten the idea himself, years before, apparently, but he'd only used it for marijuana. Then he got only the hard stuff and became Graebner's 'mule'—that's what we call someone who carries contraband through Customs for someone else. Sometimes they don't even know they're carrying it, but Partridge knew all right. He might have had all those scruples about his art, but not about his habit."

"David Partridge was a heroin addict?" Charles asked, amazed. "Holly never said . . ."

"She didn't know, son," Nigel said sadly. "I don't think Reg and Mary knew either. David was always a little fly-off-the-handle. When he started getting even more moody, they just put it down to the fact that his marriage had gone sour. Fact is, he'd made it go sour by becoming an addict. They aren't exactly easy to live with—especially if you don't know."

"But his work . . . how could he work?" Charles asked.

"Graebner probably kept him well supplied," Nigel said savagely. "After all, he was the ideal mule, and Graebner had to look after his livestock, didn't he? His own work suffered, yes—and I guess he knew it, which didn't help. But as long as his habit was fed, he could turn out the copies easily enough. Of course, the heroin would have killed him eventually, but I guess Graebner and the others figured they'd have found another alternative by then."

"Others?" Charles asked.

"Oh yes," said the scar-faced man, whose name turned out to be Burnett and whose job turned out to be Customs Security Liaison. Charles found it hard to equate his appearance with the role of "good guy," but he'd gradually got used to it. "Graebner was only the drug link, and a pretty weak link at that."

The Mercedes went past the broken fence and charred area where Charles's car had gone over. "Then it was these 'others' who had tried to kill Holly and me?"

"It certainly wasn't us," Tinker said. "When *that* happened, we knew we were getting close to a break. I'd been on this case a long time, but never gotten close to the people who'd financed the set-up. We hoped we'd find a clue in the stuff Holly had put in that garage, but . . ."

"*You* stripped the garage?"

"Oh yes," Burnett said. "And the penthouse, too. Sorry about the chloroform, by the way, but Tinker was afraid you'd recognize him, and we didn't want to tip our hand yet. We expected things to happen when Graebner got out of jail, you see. We'd waited for that very patiently, thinking he'd go straight to the people he'd worked with. The people who'd tried to kill him when they thought he'd talk. But he went to David's father instead."

"For a while they even thought . . ." Nigel paused.

"That Mr. Partridge was involved?" Charles asked.

"Yes." Nigel's voice was heavy. "And for a while we thought *you* might be, too."

"*Me?*" Charles was astounded. "Why?"

"You seemed awfully interested in that picture, son. We knew the man behind all this was English, and that he lived on the Costa somewhere. Could have been Alicante, could have been here, could have been anywhere. Tinker was put in touch with me because I was one they knew *wasn't* involved. But the one who *was* involved was sure to be interested in that picture . . . and you sure were interested."

Ruefully, Charles explained about the theory Holly had had about the Goyas. "I can see it was a wild-goose chase now."

"Sounds like it," Tinker agreed. "It was those last pictures that brought the ring to our notice all right, but only because one of the frames was broken in transit and some bright inspector got some of the dust on his hands and face when he opened the crate. We set up and used the accusation of 'fake' as an excuse to bring Graebner in, hoping to get a line back to his bosses. But then there was the crash and he refused to talk, so we let it drop."

"Where are the pictures, then?" Charles asked.

Tinker shrugged. "In a Customs vault in New York."

"So you were never after the picture—only the frame," Charles said, shaking his head. "It's crazy."

"What made you take the frame off, anyway?" Burnett asked.

Charles laughed. "It was too big to get into the suitcase, that's all. As I told you, it's probably still under the mattress where Holly hid it before López came." He frowned. "That's a thought. Does Esteban know about all this?"

Tinker shook his head, as they drew up in front of 400 Avenida de la Playa. "No. Remember, this has been going on—this investigation—for over two years. He only came into it from the angle of Graebner's murder. I tell you, *that* sure put what you call a spanner in the works. We still can't figure out why he was murdered, or by whom, or why he was thrown off Partridge's patio. We all felt bad about Reg being arrested, but if we'd told López about our investigation, it might have changed things. We're still after the man behind it, you know. We didn't want to scare him off."

"And you were just going to let Reg rot in jail?" Charles demanded, outraged.

"Don't get upset, son, I'd pretty well convinced them they'd have to do something," Nigel said. "Of course, when he got sick . . ." He looked reproachfully at Tinker.

"Let's get hold of this frame first," Tinker said quickly, avoiding Nigel's eye. "Then we can get in touch with this López and tell him the whole story. Maybe *he* can make sense of it."

López watched the four men going into the building and glanced at Paco Bas. "This is interesting," he said.

"Yes, sir," Bas agreed. It was not only interesting, it was absolutely and totally unexpected. Bas sighed. Nothing was simple. If it hadn't been for the fact that they'd had a man following Morland, they'd have lost track of Señorita Partridge. They'd given up on Llewellyn, and suddenly, there he was. He turned in his seat and looked back. Yes, sure enough, there was a car pulling up containing the two men who had been detailed to follow Bland and the tall American in Espina. "This is becoming quite a gathering."

López looked in the rear-view mirror, then at his watch, then up at the lighted windows of the penthouse. "We'll give them ten minutes, then we'll go in," he said.

They'd put her into a dark bedroom. They'd made her call the hospital and ask for Charles, but he wasn't there. Where was he? They'd thought she was lying again, but, of course, she'd been as surprised as they. He'd *said* he was coming to the hospital as soon as he'd parked the car. If he'd said that, then he'd meant that, it was his way. Something must have happened to him, that was the only explanation. Something terrible, perhaps. But then, if anything terrible had happened, it would have been because of Alastair and Jackson and Maddie. Tears began to well up in her eyes.

Oh, if she'd only listened to Charles from the beginning.

They could have the damn picture, *she* didn't want it. She'd told them it was at the place in Gavilán Street. Charles had the receipt . . . and now they were going to find Charles. After that . . .

She and Charles knew too much, of course.

They'd become a problem. Like Graebner.

And people like Alastair and Colonel Jackson had only one way of dealing with problems, didn't they?

They eliminated them.

"I have Mary's key," Nigel said, pulling out his key ring and selecting the right Yale from a prodigious collection.

They stepped into the dark penthouse as a crack of thunder rumbled overhead. The centre of the storm was moving away now, but there was a long night of rain and wind ahead. The penthouse was still, with the stale smell of air that hadn't circulated in days. Nigel flicked on the lights.

"You will have to come with us to Madrid to get the picture," Alastair said, dragging Holly out into the light once more. "The man in the shop won't hand it over to strangers, obviously, and your stupid friend has gone missing."

Holly looked from one to the other, her mind racing. There would be many opportunities to escape between here and Madrid, surely. And Jaime would be suspicious . . . without Charles, so he might . . .

"In case you're thinking of trying to be clever, don't," Colonel Jackson said warningly. "We'll be leaving Maddie here—and she'll be glad to take care of Reg for us, should you cause us difficulty. We would have dealt with him long ago, if that damned policeman hadn't locked him up so tight."

Holly's dislike of the conscientious López took an immediate 180-degree turn for the better. God bless your little bureaucratic heart, Don Esteban, she thought. "I hope it isn't a Goya," she spat at Alastair. "I hope it's just another fake."

"A Goya?" Alastair asked, then laughed. "Now that would be a laugh, wouldn't it? A Goya, indeed. You *are* a fool."

"It is not the picture we want," Jackson said. "It's the frame, you little imbecile. Your ex-husband was a faker, and he worked for us. But he'd been clever—my God, he thought he'd been so clever. He'd kept a little back, each time. Building up a nest egg."

"A little what?"

But Jackson didn't hear her, he was too caught up in his venom. *"He* was going to get out, wasn't he. *He* was going to 'take the cure' and do some 'real work.' The deluded fool. He had no talent, except for copying. Graebner realized what he'd been up to when he went to the studio that day and saw the Bosch in its frame, ready to be shipped to you. But before he could do anything, the police came. And then there was the crash—so convenient. It eliminated one problem, but created another."

"You mean . . . you didn't kill David? It *was* an accident?"

"On the contrary, my dear, I *meant* to do it, and I did," the colonel said viciously.

"Somebody has turned on the lights next door," Maddie said suddenly. "I can't see . . . oh."

"What is it?" the colonel asked, distracted.

"The man—the one from the consulate—he is there," Maddie said. "And the others . . . my God. They have the frame."

"What?" Both the colonel and Alastair came over to stand looking out of the rain-streaked window. Holly began to edge away towards the door, but Maddie caught site of her out of the corner of her eye and came after her, throwing her down onto the floor.

Holly screamed.

On the patio of the Partridge penthouse, the wind had taken hold of the table and umbrella and sent them over onto the tiles, where they rolled back and forth, caught in the eddies of the wind like some helpless animal. Charles, emerging first, caught the full force of the rain in his face and reeled momentarily, wiping his eyes. Nigel, Tinker, and Burnett were right behind him, and as the rain slashed at them they all stared across at the next patio.

Staring back at them were Colonel Jackson and Alastair Morland, their hair plastered down by the rain. Behind them Maddie stood in the open french window, holding Holly with her hands twisted cruelly behind her.

"Hey!" Tinker said, moving towards them.

The colonel produced a gun. "That's far enough," he said. "We'll have the frame, please."

"The hell you will," Tinker said.

"Or we kill the girl," the colonel continued. "It is all the same to us, you know."

"Jesus Christ," Tinker said. "You bastard."

"Give him the frame," Charles said, and then had to repeat it more loudly as the wind snatched the words away from his mouth.

"No," Tinker said.

"You have to, Mel," Nigel shouted. "You can't let them hurt her."

"Very sensible," Alastair called. "But then you always were the sensible type, Bland." The scorn in his voice carried through the wind.

"Throw it over," the colonel shouted.

"It's too light," Morland objected. "Those things were only fibreglass, the wind might take it."

"Bring it over then."

"If they go downstairs, they'll have a chance to phone," Morland pointed out, but the colonel shook his head.

"I didn't mean that. I meant they could bring it across . . . the way I went across, the other night. Move those pots, the platform reaches over easily."

"So *that's* how you did it," Charles said, half to himself. The colonel couldn't hear him, but he must have seen the look on Charles's face in the light from inside the penthouse. He smiled.

Morland moved the heavy geranium pots and dragged the long platform of reinforced planks over to the parapet. The colonel handed his gun to Maddie, who turned it on Holly with every evidence of enjoyment. Then Morland and the colonel hefted the long platform up to the parapet and began to push it across the gap.

"Hell of a lot easier with two," the colonel said. The gangplank—for that is what it had become—stretched easily across. It was about two feet wide.

"Now," the colonel said, wiping his rain-soaked face with his sleeve. "You, Llewellyn, you bring the frame across."

"Me?" Charles asked, in a strangled voice.

"That's right, you," the colonel said. "You've been so eager to interfere . . . and you're too stupid to try anything. *You* bring it."

"But . . ."

"There must be plenty more where this came from," Tinker called out. "Why bother?"

"There's been no more since Graebner died," the colonel said. "When he went, so did the supply line. We've been strapped ever since because that last shipment somehow never arrived. We were never paid."

"But Graebner only died . . ."

"Shut up and bring me that frame or the girl dies, too," the colonel shouted into the wind. "Come on, nice and slow, where I can see every move you make."

Tinker handed the empty frame to Charles, who took it reluctantly. His eyes met Holly's across the gap, and he smiled. She looked absolutely terrified. She kept shaking her head "no," but he could see no alternative. He'd have to go over.

He crossed to the place on the parapet where the gangplank rested and climbed up onto it, the picture frame hung around his neck.

"Take off your shoes," Tinker shouted.

Charles kicked them off and then, straightening only partially, began to edge his way across the narrow planks. Across the gap. Across the long, long drop.

The wind tugged at him, and he teetered slightly as he reached the mid-point, then fell to his knees and held on to the planks for dear life. The storm, although passing inland, was not through with Puerto Rio yet. Split by the bulk of Montgo, the wind gusted and eddied as it swirled over the plain, now blowing, now still. It wrapped itself around the tall buildings that edged the beach-front, licking them and buffeting them with glee. Sluicing between the three upright columns of 400 Avenida de la Playa, it became a random but concentrated force, uncontrollable and unpredictable.

Clinging to the planks, Charles wrenched the frame from his neck and held it out to the colonel. "I'm not coming any further," he shouted. "If you want this, come and get it."

"I'll kill the girl," the colonel threatened.

"No, you won't," Charles shouted. "What you want is right here—take it and run. We won't follow if you leave the girl alone. Come on, one of you . . . take it."

López, standing in the hall, his hand upraised to knock again, heard the terrible scream above the sound of the wind, and instantly stepped back.

"Break in the door," he ordered.

As the man fell past the first window below the parapet, Mr. Van Gelden was filling his bath and pouring in the pine-scented bath salts he loved. He froze there, jar in hand.

As the man fell past the second window, his reflection shone in the dark glass. The Murphys were away.

As the man fell past the third window, Professor Gottlieb was putting the finishing touches to his research paper on Cervantes. His pen stopped in mid-word and dug into the paper.

As the man fell past the fourth window, Mrs. Butler stiffened in the arms of the man who was making love to her, who was not Mr. Butler, and who hadn't heard a thing.

As the man fell past the fifth window, he was no more than a blur to Mrs. Greene's cat, who stopped washing a paw and stared out in amazement.

As the man continued to fall, his body twisted and turned. His staring eyes reflected the lights, his open mouth was a cavern. As he fell through the night he screamed and screamed and screamed.

Until he hit the ground.

On the patio of the penthouse Tinker, Nigel and Burnett were staring down at the gap between the towers. The planks had fallen and hit just after the body of Morland, splintering and sending pieces of wood over the terrible broken shape that sprawled on the concrete. Beside it lay the frame, also broken.

Charles, feeling the planks go under Morland's added weight, had made a wild jump forward as they dropped away underneath him. His right arm had caught the edge of the trough that ran along the top of the parapet, and his left had gone clear across it to grasp the far edge. But he could not move, and his body now hung against the wall, as the wind tore at it.

Above the noise of the storm he could hear Holly screaming, and his feet scrabbled against the smooth surface of the building for purchase.

The colonel, running back to Maddie, took his gun and started into the apartment, pushing Holly away savagely. "I'm going out of here, don't try to stop me," he shouted into the wind.

"The hell you are," Tinker muttered, moving back from the parapet and measuring the distance with careful but angry eyes.

"Help," Charles called. His flailing feet had found a hold at last, the tiny hole of a drain outlet. He'd wedged his toe into it, but his own weight and the wind pulling at him made his arms ache and he knew they couldn't take the strain much longer.

As he clung there, the rain driving down into his face, his eyes blurred by it, he wasn't quite sure of what he saw. Over his head, suddenly, like a bird of prey, flew the outstretched V of Mel Tinker's legs as he vaulted from one parapet to the other, emiting a wild, blood-curdling yell. It was the most terrible sound Charles had ever heard, and it very nearly made him let go his desperate grip.

Almost, but not quite.

The yell was followed by shouts and the sound of scuffling overhead. He heard Holly scream again, and the sharp crack of a shot split the thunder that was rolling over.

"Help!" Charles called, his voice barely audible.

"Hang on, son . . ." It was Nigel, shouting encouragement, his eyes on whatever was occurring on the far patio. Charles was afraid to ask what was happening, and kept his face pressed against the concrete, blinking the rain out of his eyes.

Tinker, just clearing the gap, had landed in the sodden earth of the flower trough and just kept going, a spurt of mud following him. He jumped down onto the tiles and skidded forward, his flailing arms eventually making contact with a stunned colonel, who'd never suspected Batman was in the vicinity.

They all went down in a sprawl, Holly rolling away as the two men fought for the gun. It went off, the bright flash just another bit of broken lightning from the storm. From where she lay, Holly could see Charles's arm stretched across the trough, the white knuckles of his hands gleaming. She could do nothing but watch as the hand started to slide up and back . . . and back . . .

Charles was going to die.

There was a hammering from within, and the sound of more shots. A moment later she saw López and a very wild-eyed Paco Bas come through the french windows. Inside, she saw Maddie held by another man.

"Help," called Charles, again. "I say . . . chaps . . ."

"Over here . . . he's slipping!" called Burnett desperately, from the other patio.

It was Paco Bas who saw the situation, and his stocky body moved surprisingly quickly. His arms went over the parapet to grasp Charles's collar, and his hair. His arms were barely long enough, but they were strong, and his ugly, glistening-wet bull's face grinned down at Charles encouragingly.

"*Momentito,*" Paco said.

CHAPTER 21

Mel Tinker helped Paco Bas haul Charles over the edge of the parapet. He came over limply, like a sack of potatoes, all elbows and knees, streaked with white from the painted concrete and with mud from the flower trough.

Squinting and wiping his face with a handkerchief Paco Bas handed him from some inner pocket of his jacket, Charles watched as Tinker went over to help Holly to her feet. He used a pocket-knife to cut her bonds.

So that's what a hero looks like, Charles thought to himself. He looked away as Tinker cut the last strand of rope and put his arms around Holly. No sense in torturing yourself, Llewellyn, Charles thought, some men have it and some don't. You've never even come close. You wouldn't know how to be a hero if . . .

"Oh, Charles, I was so afraid . . . are you all right?" Holly was clinging to him, touching him all over, taking the handkerchief to wipe his face, pushing the hair out of his eyes, kissing his ear, his nose, his mouth, and his ear, again.

Charles opened one eye to see Bas grinning at them from above. Behind him, Tinker glowered. López was hustling the colonel into the penthouse, calling for Bas as he went, satisfied to carry on with the job at hand now that he knew Charles was safe.

Holly was babbling on. "I thought you were going to die, that I'd never see you again . . ." She was on her knees next to him, her head on his chest, and apparently intended to stay there.

"Oh," Charles said, lifting his arms to encircle her in turn.

After a moment of dazed delight, he spoke again. "What about my wife and all those children?"

"You'll have to get rid of them" was the muffled reply.

He thought about that. "Oh . . . all right," he conceded. "If you insist."

"We seem to have been working at cross-purposes," López said, not very happily, looking at Tinker.

"That wasn't how it was meant to be," Mel said, his feet up on the colonel's coffee table. In the other rooms the police were searching. Charles and Holly sat side by side on the sofa, and he was not looking at them. "When I first came over here, it was strictly to follow up this drugs thing, believe me. If it hadn't been for Graebner's murder, it would have stayed that way. When I'd gathered the information I'd come for, I would have worked with you for a conviction through Interpol, obviously. But Graebner's death—that threw things."

"Why didn't you come to me *then?*" López said. It seemed to Charles a legitimate question. Perhaps Tinker thought so, too, because he flushed slightly.

"I didn't want to mess up your investigation. I really thought . . ."

"That Reg had done it?" Holly asked, grimly.

Tinker nodded. "Sorry, Holly, but yes. The evidence was pretty overwhelming. And Graebner was my only lead. I'd been waiting for him to come out of prison and make a move . . . when he was killed, I was nowhere."

"I still don't see *how* the colonel did it. Or why," Nigel said.

"I think I know *how* he did it," Charles said. "I'm just guessing, of course, but putting myself in his place, with his build and . . ." He stopped.

"Go on," López said encouragingly. "I, too, want to know how."

"I'm not sure, but . . ." Charles turned to Holly. "You know the marks on your mother-in-law's patio table?" She nodded. "Well, *I* think he murdered Graebner over here, and then was stuck with the body."

"But he was at the pictures," Holly said.

"Oh, I think he stabbed Graebner before he left," Charles said. "He went to the cinema as usual, but then slipped out of a fire exit or something—it's easily done—and came back. He wanted above all to divert attention from himself, and he had Reg living next door as a perfect alternative. After all, Reg *had* threatened Graebner's life once before. Of course, the colonel is a small man, and Graebner was big. A dead body is a terrible weight, too, big *or* small. He had to get him over onto Reg's patio and there was not time to call Morland for help.

"I think he put that platform across the gap, as he did tonight. It was a still evening, no wind. Then he tied a rope around Graebner, carried it over, and tied it around the legs of the patio table. After that, all he had to do was turn the table round and round—and winch the body over the gap. Simple schoolboy physics, very little muscular effort involved."

"But how could he have killed Graebner over *here* with Reg's sword, which was over *there?*" Tinker asked.

"He didn't. I reckon he must have used something like an ice pick or maybe a thin knife of some description. According to the post-mortem, Graebner was stabbed *twice*—at least, that's what Moreno told me."

"That is true." López nodded.

"Well, the first stab probably didn't kill him but it nearly did. I think that because when I was crawling over that gangplank tonight, I saw bloodstains on it. I expect when you piece it together, you'll find the traces there. So Graebner was still bleeding when he was winched across—and that means he was still alive. The colonel must have seen Reg playing around with that sword, so he simply went in through the french doors, got it down, stabbed Graebner *again*, wiped it—being careful not to be too careful—and put it back. That's why the actual time of death fitted. The time of the first attack was probably a fair bit earlier. Before seven o'clock, anyway."

"I noticed . . ." Paco Bas began, then blushed.

López turned. "Well?"

"In the bedroom he has an electric blanket."

López looked puzzled. "What has that got to do with anything?"

"He might have used it to keep the dying man warm, thinking to confuse the time of death?"

"It wouldn't have," Tinker objected. "The blood starts to coagulate almost immediately after death. Body temperature isn't the only guide . . ."

"No, señor, but it is one. And if the colonel realized the man was still alive . . ."

"Go and look at the mattress," López commanded.

Paco went out, and returned triumphant. "The mattress is heavily stained," he said and sat down, grinning.

López nodded, as if he had expected as much. "All of this is very well— but why throw him over the edge?"

"Because in the middle of all of this, Reg came home, turned on the lights, and then went out again," Charles said promptly. "Up to that point, I don't suppose Jackson had much in mind except getting Graebner over onto the Partridge patio. He may even have intended simply to let him bleed to death, there, as he certainly would have before morning. Reg and Mary would have had no reason to go out onto the patio when they came home that night . . . they always returned after midnight." Charles grimaced. "As a matter of fact, Jackson could have been out on the patio at the very minute Reg was in there looking for Mary's glasses. The minute the way was clear, he did what he had to do. He pushed him over to co-ordinate the time of death *exactly* with Reg's return," Charles said. "The smashed watch, remember? The colonel must have had quite a shock when he came back and found the body still lying there, undiscovered. He *had* expected somebody to have done it long before—perhaps even catching Reg and Mary in the car-park, or on their way to the bridge party. Then Reg would have had no alibi whatsoever. The colonel was supposed to be well away from the scene, at the cinema."

Holly was scratching Queenie's ears gently. "Poor Queenie . . . did you know?" The dog looked up at her, bright-eyed.

"You know your father-in-law has come through his surgery well, señorita?" López asked Holly. He looks distressed, Charles thought. He'd never seen that air of uneasiness sitting on López before, and it worried him.

"Surely you aren't going to put him back in jail, Esteban?" he asked.

"No, of course not. I knew he was completely innocent of the murder this morning—but, of course, he had already been taken to the hospital by then."

"You *knew* he was innocent?" Nigel demanded. "You'd found out about the colonel?"

López shook his head and stood up, walking away from them slightly. "I knew several things, right from the beginning. I knew, for instance, that neither of the men who arrested Graebner and David Partridge spoke English. I knew that when David Partridge was being taken away, his father had just arrived outside the studio, and he shouted at him to look upstairs at the picture on the easel. He shouted something about being 'framed,' you see. That means something now, thanks to Mr. Tinker's explanations, but at the time I thought it meant that he had been 'framed' in the sense of being—how you say—'set up'? And that, to me, meant other people. Then after the accident . . ."

"Which the colonel arranged," Holly interrupted.

López shook his head, but did not look at her. "No, señorita, the accident *was* an accident. The colonel did not even know, at that time, that Graebner had been arrested, so he could hardly have arranged anything so quickly, could he?"

"But he said *he* killed David, he said . . . he meant to do it and . . . he enjoyed it," Holly said, with a catch in her voice.

"Yes, that's true, he did. You see, after the accident, the man in the hospital was badly injured. He communicated with his lawyer, Ribes, by moving a thumb. The only part of either hand he could move, by the way. His face and his hands were smashed and burned badly. He was in agony—not just of the body, but of the soul, señorita. The bitter man in hospital and the man who came here to confront Jackson was not Horst Graebner. He was your husband . . . David Partridge."

"I *do* believe it," Reg said, his face pale against the pillows.

"I just . . . can't," Mary said, her hands twisting in her lap.

Charles and Holly watched them uncomfortably as they grappled with the new truth, and the new grief. Holly had wept hers away, but theirs lay ahead.

"He'd made a stand," Holly said. "The colonel said he had refused to work for them anymore, that he was going to go back to England and take a cure for his addiction. He knew too much, and Graebner was probably trying to talk him out of it. Then—the accident—and David's hands were destroyed. He knew he'd never work again. It . . . destroyed something else in him. You know how stubborn he could be, how he could always hold out against other people's emotions . . ."

"Mary, it's true," Reg said. "Can't you accept it? They've proved it. The man in the morgue *is* David, and the one buried in the *cementerio* was Graebner. It *happened.* He lay in that hospital bed, in torment, and probably the only thing that kept him alive was his hate for the men who'd done it to him."

"Why didn't he come to us?" Mary asked miserably. "Why didn't he tell us he was alive?"

"By the time he'd gained consciousness and realized what had happened, Graebner had long since been buried in his grave," Charles said. "Esteban said it was several weeks before Gra——before David . . . was conscious of his surroundings."

"Oh, God, the pain he must have suffered . . ." Mary wept, finally, and Reg reached out a hand to stroke her bowed head.

"He was heavily sedated," Charles said. "That meant he was at least spared the torture of withdrawal symptoms. They're very similar to the symptoms of shock from severe burns, and they didn't know he'd been an addict, of course. His arms were burned—the needle scars were destroyed."

"The addiction explains so much," Reg murmured, staring up at the ceiling, his profile gaunt against the light from the window. "*Excuses* so much . . ." No one spoke for a while, and it was silent in the room, save for Mary's soft sobbing as she mourned her lost son, again.

"What I can't understand—although I admire it—was how he found the strength finally to resist them, to turn against them and what they'd made of him," Reg went on thoughtfully. "It takes phenomenal strength to decide to break a drug addiction, and David . . ." He shook his head.

Holly glanced at Charles. "We aren't certain yet, but we think we know why," she said. "We think he found something he'd wanted to find for a long time, something that would give him the money to start over again, a way out . . ."

Reg looked at her. "You mean thirteen Goyas?" he asked wryly.

Holly shook her head. "They've checked the pictures in America—they were just bad old pictures, over-painted."

"So there weren't thirteen Goyas, after all," Mary said, looking up.

"No, there weren't thirteen Goyas," Holly murmured.

Charles spoke up. "There was only *one*. A very special one to David, I imagine. And he'd found it on his own. He over-painted it with the Bosch to get it through Customs and into England by sending it to Holly as a copy. The same system as usual. The funny thing was—when they analyzed that frame it was just fibreglass. He hadn't kept any heroin back at all. It was the colonel who assumed that. He thought it was Graebner in hospital and in jail, of course. He thought it was Graebner who'd made the appointment to come and see him that evening. He thought at last he was going to be able to re-establish the drug connection and resume operations. Of course they wouldn't have had David's copies but he was sure they could set up something else, perhaps still using the frame technique. Cheap little prints for gift shops, that sort of thing. Imagine his shock when the man who walked through his door revealed who he really was—and that he intended to expose them all. David made the mistake a lot of other people made—he assumed Colonel Jackson was a weak, feeble, little old man. It was a good masquerade, but it hid a man who was far from weak or feeble. He killed David without a second thought. When the second thoughts *did* come, they kept us all running around in circles."

"And me in jail." Reg smiled. "I gather your friend suspected I was innocent all along, but was afraid my life would be in danger if I wasn't watched."

"That's right." Charles smiled. "He felt dreadful when your ulcer perforated, but he'd been afraid to tell you the truth about your being kept in jail for fear the real villains would never make a move."

"You mean, he purposely let you and Holly get into danger?" Mary asked, amazed.

"He had a job to do, Mary, and that was the only way he could see to do it without scaring his quarry away for good. He guessed they'd get careless if they thought Reg was going to be convicted for the murder. And, of course, they did. David must have taunted the colonel, before he was killed, about the picture that would 'make him rich.' The colonel assumed it had a heroin-impregnated frame like all the others, so he set about retrieving it. Fortunately Mel Tinker was looking, too, and kept a step ahead of him, stripping the garage before he got there, and so on. The reason we were sent off the road is because they thought we'd got the picture from the garage. Maddie overdid that. For a while they assumed the picture had burned in the car. Then Alastair saw the parcel in my suitcase. They thought we were going to Alicante, but we went to Madrid, and they didn't pick us up again until we came back to Espina. By then they were so desperate they decided to come out into the open. They had nothing to lose—and that's what Esteban had been waiting for, all along."

Mary sniffed. "And I thought he seemed like such a nice man."

"Well, if I've learned anything in the last few hours, it's that appearances can be deceiving," Holly said demurely, with a glance at Charles and a secret smile.

Charles smiled back, and settled himself more comfortably against the wall, where he was leaning because there were not enough chairs in the room. Something sharp dug into his shoulderblade, and he moved again, beaming at Holly all the while.

Faintly, in the distance, a fire alarm began to ring.

CHAPTER 22

The rain pelted down on the umbrellas and shoulders of the people in the queue that wound along the pavement and up the steps of the Prado. It was the beginning of December, but for Spain, Christmas had arrived a little early this year.

The queue wound through the galleries, and the buzz of talk and the shuffling of feet echoed up to the vaulted ceilings. It was a happy sound, but the crowd, though eager, did not press forward or rush. Everyone who came to stand before the picture was given time to look, to savour, to delight in a lost one come home.

It wasn't a very big canvas, only about twenty-four inches by twenty, but it glowed with a special life. In it, in the familiar reclining pose made famous by the Naked Maja, lay another beautiful woman, wearing a loose-fitting gown of dark crimson and a small, secret smile. The smile said she knew she was beautiful, and that the artist saw she was beautiful, and was glad. All around her head, on her shoulders, on the pillows, lay the curling, tumbled strands of her flame-red hair.

Below the frame a small plaque hung.

La Maja Roja
(The Red Maja)
by
Francisco Goya
Presented to the people of Spain
by
Mr. and Mrs. Reginald Partridge
and
Mr. and Mrs. Charles Llewellyn

About the Author

Paula Gosling was born in Detroit, Michigan. After finishing university, she worked as a copywriter in advertising, a career she continued on moving to England in 1964. Her first novel, *Fair Game,* won the John Creasey Award in 1978. Since then she has published several successful crime novels, and says she is "always" working on another. Recently remarried, she is now the wife of an accountant turned businessman, and lives in Bath with her husband, two daughters, two cats, two goldfish and hay fever. She writes full-time, and finds embroidery and country walks are the best way to relax after "killing people all day long." *The Woman in Red* is her first novel for the Crime Club.